SWEET Nothings

BRITTANY TAYLOR

DEDICATION

To those who have ever crawled out of bed,
placed your feet on the ground, and forced a smile just to get
through each day.
I see you.
And I promise, it does get better.

CONTENT NOTE FROM THE AUTHOR

Hello dear reader!
Sweet Nothings is a high angst, emotional read. **Please be aware** this book contains scenes and topics which may be sensitive to some. Topics include alcohol addiction, drug addiction, scenes and descriptions of drug use, cancer, and death from cancer.
I sincerely hope you enjoy Laurel and Lennon's story.
Thank you and happy reading!
Xoxo,
Brittany

"It matters not who you love, where you love, why you love, when you love or how you love, it matters only that you love."
- John Lennon

ONE

LAUREL

Six years earlier

"It's not going to work." I stiffen my arm, unwilling to give my sister's hairbrained scheme any more thought.

"It will." Roe's long, tan legs eat the space between us as she marches across my room and rips the ID card from my grip. Giving me a pointed look, she darts her attention back to the card and narrows her eyes. She studies it as if she's mentally checking off all the reasons why using this fake ID will work. Seconds tick by before she dramatically flips her long brown hair and plops herself down on the oversized bean bag chair I stole from her before she moved from our parents' house two years ago and into her dorm. She sinks into it, crossing her legs under her. She delicately cradles the card in her small hands and stares up at me. Her pointed expression is now one of silent pleading.

I sigh. "The girl in the picture doesn't even look like me, Roe."

"Yes, she does," she disagrees. There's an edge to her voice as if she's on the brink of resorting to flat out begging me to go with her.

Frustrated, I unravel my legs from my bed and cross the room to stand in front of her. She looks up at me with unwavering confidence; the only kind I've ever seen woven into her expression. Firm set jaw. Placid, perfect, full lips. Her brown eyes are both menacing and kind, at the same time. Kindness hidden behind her tough exterior; Roe doesn't surrender easily when she has her sights set on a goal.

But I haven't given up my fight yet. Staying in my room and snuggling in the comfort of my own bed while watching crime documentaries sounds infinitely more exciting than the illegal adventure my sister is convincing me to partake in.

I stab the card with my finger, preparing to go through my list of reasons why I positively know this won't work. "Half her hair is blue."

She waves me off, breaking her plain stare. The corners of her mouth curl deviously. "Blue hair is usually temporary," she argues. "It could have faded."

"Her hair is blonde at the roots. My entire head is as dark a shade of brown as it can get."

"You could have dyed it."

"Okay, now you're really starting to sound like a lawyer." I groan, ripping the card from her hands the same way she took it from me. I lift it to my face and shake my head. Uncertainty wobbles in my belly, and my chest flutters. It feels as if a thousand electric shocks are shooting underneath my skin.

"Come on," Roe whines.

Now she's resorting to begging.

"It's your nineteenth birthday, Laurel. And my twenty-first. You're my baby sister and my best friend. We can't celebrate separately. We never have and never will."

She's right. We haven't. We've always been together every single year.

But something about this birthday is different. The air in my room feels stale. The thrill of going out and celebrating seems lackluster.

"You need to get out," Roe continues. "Meet new people."

I roll my eyes. "I'll meet new people when the semester starts in a month. If you haven't forgotten, I'm going to Harvard, too. We'll practically be living together again."

My sister Monroe is exactly two years older than me to the day. Despite our two-year age difference, we look nearly identical: long, dark chestnut hair, big, equally as dark brown eyes. But the way we look is where our similarities end. Monroe is far more sociable than I am. She's louder and has about one hundred more friends than I do. Hence why she's currently sitting in front of me, pleading with me to go out with her. She's always begging me to tag along. I used to deny her flat out when she begged, but the older I've gotten, the more I tend to cave.

I'm trying my hardest to not let her win this time.

"We can go another night," I tell her, dropping the card on my desk.

With a huff, she sits up and swipes the card back. She grabs my purse and tugs my wallet free, swapping it for my actual ID card. The one that says I'm currently nineteen.

"I've been using this card for the past year," she admits. Satisfied the card is tucked away safely in my purse, she crosses the room again and wraps both her hands around mine. "Please."

I nervously chew on the inside of my cheek. "I'm still not sure this is a good idea."

"I'm telling you." She blinks with a knowing grin. "This is the place to be tonight. The Underground is where everyone from Harvard goes on nights like this. I've even seen a few Boston College guys there. Maybe you can meet one. There's this one guy I've been talking to, and I could use you as my side-kick. I need you there."

The idea of meeting someone tonight causes my stomach to somersault. It's been six months since I ended my relationship with my ex. I thought he was everything I wanted, but he wasn't.

I felt no fire. No butterflies. Nothing.

I was left feeling unfilled. So, I ended it.

Now, though, I'm thrilled for what the future has in store for me over the next few months. Starting with Harvard Law School.

"How do you know this will work?" I ask my sister. I love her and want to celebrate this night with her, but I can't shake the uneasiness I've been feeling.

"Because it's worked for me every other time," she practically sings. Her eyes flicker with excitement. She knows I'm cracking. "Because we're Monroe and Laurel Branford."

My sister has a point. Born into a family such as ours comes with privilege. Even though our parents aren't considered as well-known in Boston as our extended family, our name still carries weight. The Branfords are one of the wealthiest and respected families in the city. It's a name I feel incredibly lucky to bear.

I hate using my name to my advantage or for exclusive privileges, but the moment I lift my hands to fix the diamond encrusted tiara lined with bright pink feathers sitting on top of my sister's head, the last bit of fight I have in me dissolves.

"Fine." I groan. "I'll go with you. But if this doesn't work and we get arrested, you're calling Dad to bail us out."

It worked. Roe's fake ID actually worked!

The doorman barely glanced at the card I held gripped between my fingers before waving us through the double black doors of the club. Maybe it's because Roe is so well known here that no one bothers to question her. I let the air leak out of my lungs slowly, willing my pulse to slow and my muscles to relax.

Once through the doorway, Roe immediately reaches behind her and grabs my hand, pulling me through the sea of people in front of us. White flashing lights dance across the entire club, and seas of people move back and forth, some dancing, some just trying to make their way through.

Roe heads straight to the bar, saying we need to at least start with two shots to "get our blood warm."

I don't bother asking her what type of alcohol is in them. Sour followed by sweet, I down the two shots as quickly as I can before Roe orders us another round plus a martini.

I'm sipping on my second martini when a man appears behind Roe, sliding his arms around her waist and pulling her to his chest. She looks up at him with a grin and a slightly unfocused gaze.

He must be the Boston College guy she was telling me about. His sandy hair dances across his forehead as he bends down, whispering in my sister's ear.

She giggles and curls her shoulders inward, then looks up. "This is my sister, Laurel. Wish her a happy birthday, too."

"Happy birthday, Laurel!" the man yells over the music.

"Thank you!" I yell back. Heat blooms across my face. I'm unsure whether it's from his sentiment or from the alcohol. Either way, I'm suddenly self-conscious of everything around me. I quickly run my fingers through my loose waves, tucking them behind my ears, then tug on the hem of my skintight, black leather cocktail dress. I straighten my birthday tiara and give my sister a reassuring smile.

"We're going to go dance!" she yells over the music. "Do you want to come with us?"

"No." I shake my head. "I'm good. You go ahead."

"Are you sure?" Her perfect eyebrows knit.

"Well, if you don't want to hang out at the bar by yourself, you're more than welcome to sit at my table," her date chimes in, moving beside Roe, but keeping his arm wrapped around her. He leans forward so I can hear him better. "I came with a few friends and classmates. They're sitting in the booth over there in the corner." He jerks his head back. "We have a private server. Feel free to order anything you want."

I swing my eyes up in the direction of the table Roe's date mentioned long enough to gauge who is over there. I count a total of six incredibly gorgeous people: Two pairs are obvious couples and the other two are waiting as the waitress fills their shot glasses to the brim. They sling the shots back and slam them back down onto the glass table. After one of the men finishes his shot, he wipes his mouth with the back of his hand and nudges his friend with his elbow. The friend's face is blocked by the woman straddling his lap and running her mouth down the side of his face, but I get a better look when he turns to look at his friend.

Clean cut, yet somehow still rough around the edges, with thick, dark as night hair, and stubble lining his chiseled jaw. Brooding and mysterious, his eyes glint in the light, along with the shiny, oversized watch on his wrist, and the long silver chain tucked beneath his collared shirt. He screams money. Admittedly, he's beautiful. Almost too beautiful. He has nearly every single trait we Branfords recognize. The instinct to identify those in our circle is built in our DNA.

"Laurel?" Roe's voice pulls my attention back. Her eyes have softened. "What do you want to do?"

"I'll figure it out." I blink. "I'm good here for now."

"Okay." She frowns. It only lasts two seconds before she's grinning again. "Don't forget to mingle and meet people. Find a hot guy or... something. That's why I brought you here."

I laugh, knowing it isn't the only reason. Monroe dragged me here as her wingman to give her the confidence she clearly doesn't need.

After my sister and her date disappear into the crowd, I lift my drink to my mouth and survey the crowd around me over the rim of my glass. The place is packed.

I lose track of how long I stand at the bar. Finally, chest warm and my stomach bubbling with anxiety, I down the rest of my drink, slam it on the bar top behind me, and aimlessly move. I don't know where I'm going. I just move. I only know I don't want to stand here watching strangers dancing.

I concentrate on my breathing until I find myself standing out front of the club, the bright neon sign blinking behind me. The security guard checking IDs at the door glances in my direction curiously before resuming his work.

My anxiety ramps up again. I can't explain it. I'm not like Monroe. I'm not bold. I'm not popular. I'm not outgoing. It's not as if I'm not used to places such as this—extravagant restaurants and bars filled with people who make more money than others make in their entire lifetimes, several times over. I'm one of them.

Yet I'm not.

I fish my phone from my purse and call an Uber. I consider calling our family driver but remember he has the night off. When my ride is confirmed, I quickly type a text to Roe to tell her I'm feeling sick and I've ordered a ride home. I know she won't buy it, but I don't care. She probably won't even check her phone until I'm already back home, snuggled in bed.

I've finished typing out my text when an alert pops up on my phone telling me my ride is here. A black sedan.

I look up just as it pulls alongside the curb.

"Thank God," I mutter with a sigh of relief, stuffing my phone in my purse.

After opening the back door, I slide along the smooth black seat, with the scent of clean leather filling my nose.

Reaching behind me, I tug the door, but it won't budge. Looking up, I catch sight of a hand gripped onto the top of it, keeping me from closing it.

Suddenly, the man bends, lowering his face in my view. Two dark-as-midnight eyes stare at me. A long silver necklace dangles from his neck, surrounded by a black button-down shirt beneath a black suit jacket. He runs his fingers through his near-black hair. Everything about him is dark.

Dark and brooding. The men my mother has always told me to avoid.

He's the man I saw sitting at Roe's date's table earlier. The one with the woman practically dry humping him.

"What do you think you're doing?" he asks, smelling like cigarettes, whiskey, and mint.

"What do you mean?" I ask, stunned.

"You're in my car," he states, unamused. His cobalt blue eyes flick to the driver.

I catch the driver watching me through the rearview mirror. Holding a breath, I look around as if I'll find a clue to help me figure out what the hell is going on.

I lean back to see if I can find the rideshare company logo on either the front or back windshield, but my head swims, and I grab the seat like I'm on a carnival ride. Uh-oh. The drinks have finally kicked in.

"Oh, I thought this was the rideshare I ordered." I frown and tilt my head to the side and scoot forward. "Sorry," I mutter.

My cheeks are burning, and I can't tell if it's from the alcohol or the utter embarrassment brewing inside me. *Kill me now*.

"It's fine." The man stops me. "I can give you a ride."

I peer up at him, confused. He's a stranger, and the first rule you learn as a child is to never take rides from strangers.

"It's okay, I already have one. I just got confused." I shake my head, close my eyes, then reopen them, but the man is still staring down at me through his open door.

"I saw you talking with Collin earlier," he says, his body blocking my ability to leave. He brings an already lit cigarette to his mouth, draws in a long, deep inhale, then tips his head up to blow the smoke into the night.

"Collin?" I ask.

"Yeah." His soft lips press together. There's a sadness in his eyes I hadn't noticed until now. Maybe it's just the weird lighting from the neon club sign shining down on him. "Collin's my frat brother."

I nod, the realization dawning on me. "He's dating my sister."

"Sister, huh?"

I don't speak another word. I can't.

The fact this man noticed me in a jam-packed club, surrounded by hundreds of other people? He saw *me*, and from all the way across the room, too.

I can't stop looking into his eyes. It's as if I recognize them from somewhere, but I know deep down I don't. Maybe it's the pain I see hidden behind his cobalt blues. The corners of his mouth are turned down in what seems to be a permanent frown.

"Slide over," he orders, dropping his cigarette and stubbing it out with the toe of his shiny black dress shoe. I scoot deeper into the car, not realizing I'm doing it until my back hits the opposite door. "Ray can drive you home."

"I don't know you," I say, but the slur in my words makes me cringe. "How do I know you're not a serial killer or something?"

He shrugs with a blank expression, but I can see the alcohol swimming in his eyes. He's as drunk if not more than I am. "You don't." He leans forward and whispers, "But even if I was, I wouldn't kill you. At least not now. Too many witnesses."

I swallow the lump forming in my throat. I can't explain it, but I tell Ray my address, and he pulls away from the club.

We drive through two sets of traffic lights before I risk a glance at the man beside me and notice his expression has changed. His blue eyes are still sad, but they look glassier than earlier. It's as if he's going to burst into tears at any moment. He rests his elbow on the door and massages his chin with his fingertips.

"Rough day?" I ask, hoping to lighten the mood.

For the first time, the corner of his mouth turns up slightly, though it quickly fades. "Something like that."

"Same."

"It's your birthday." It comes out more as a statement than a question.

"It is." My hand flies to the tiara on my head. I'd almost forgotten I was wearing it.

"Was it your party you left early?"

"Not exactly." I shake my head, biting back the urge to word vomit on the man nice enough to give me a ride. I keep silent about it being my sister's birthday as well. While she's my best friend, I've always existed in her shadow, never been taken seriously.

"Why were you out tonight?" I ask.

He pauses, considering his answer carefully as if he's dissecting it before voicing it out loud. "To escape. To forget."

I don't ask him to elaborate. I let his confession hang heavily in the air between us. Maybe it's because I understand him. I can relate. Leaving the club was my way of escaping, too.

The passing streetlights outside make me dizzy. My eyes flutter shut and then they snap open when I feel a hand glide across my cheek.

"A feather from your tiara was in your hair." A tiny, pale purple feather is pinched between his long fingers.

"Thank you," I whisper. "That was sweet." My cheeks bloom with heat.

"Um, okay." His dark eyebrows knit. "What was sweet, exactly?"

"What you did. Thank you." I blink, unsure why I'm being so honest with a stranger. Flushed and panicked, I swallow the words, hoping we can clear the awkwardness wrapping its arms around us. "It's nothing. Don't worry about it."

"Sweet nothings," he says quietly. He shakes his head once and looks down, and I swear I see the faintest tilt in the corner of his mouth.

"Sweet nothings?" I ask him.

"Never mind." There's an edge to his voice. It's distant, but there's an edge.

"Sweet nothings," I repeat, trying to decipher it as if it were some sort of code phrase. "What are sweet nothings?"

He pauses and rubs his finger across his stubbled chin. "It's when..." He allows his voice to trail off. His eyes search my face. "Never mind. It isn't important."

I have no idea what he's talking about.

I bet it's what he was whispering into the ear of the woman riding his lap back at the club. I bet it's what he tells every woman he meets: sweet nothings.

"Thank you for giving me a ride home." I clear my throat. "I don't think I said it yet."

My eyes unconsciously drop to his mouth. The overwhelming urge to kiss him comes over me. I want to wipe the sadness from his lips. I want to take away the glassiness in his eyes. I've been drinking, but I think I would be attracted to him even if I hadn't been.

I know I'm not as bold or as confident as my sister, but I'm still me. I want to kick off this new year trailing my own path instead of following Roe's. I want to be daring and confident like her, but in my own way.

I open my mouth to speak, but the words don't leave my throat before the man's mouth lands on mine. I welcome it, sinking into it with every breath. I close my eyes and breathe him in. His mouth on mine is as beautiful as the first time I saw him. I drink his kiss in as if it's the first kiss I've ever had. It isn't. Not by a long shot. My first kiss was when I was eight. The first time I had sex was when I was sixteen.

But this is different. It's a fevered yet measured kiss. His mouth tastes exactly how it smells: whiskey, cigarettes, and mint. His hands land on my hips, tugging on me. I lift my leg and straddle him. I don't know how far we are from my apartment, but I don't care. My body is humming with his touch. I'm already wet between my thighs. His cock is hard as stone beneath his expensive suit, begging to be set free. He must press one of the buttons on his door because the sound of the partition between us and his driver fills the air, giving us privacy.

He doesn't break his mouth away from mine. Effortlessly, he slides his hand between us, unzipping his pants. I urge him to keep going, wrapping both hands around his face. The stubble lining his jaw cuts into my palms. I bite down on his lip when the back of his hand grazes against my wet center. His knuckles roll across my clit, causing a moan to climb up my throat.

When he finally frees his cock, he pulls a condom from his pocket and slips it on. Grabbing onto my hips with his firm fingers, he guides me over him. I lower myself, feeling every inch of himself bury deep inside me. My walls clench around him, begging him to keep going. I grab onto the collar of his crisp, black shirt, pulling him to me.

Coaxing my lips apart with his tongue, he slides it along mine, tasting me. My legs burn as I lift myself up and down. My heart is racing. Maybe it's the alcohol or maybe it's because I haven't had sex in six months, but I already feel myself approaching the end. I'm going to come all over him before the car has stopped.

This is meaningless. Tomorrow, we'll both wake up and remember this night, knowing we'll likely never see one another again.

Men with our social standing usually don't stick around long, at least the ones I've experienced: my dad, my uncle, our rival families in this city. All have a reputation of putting money before love—a little-known fact only those in our circle know. Everyone else in this city is too busy with their own lives to pay attention to the secrets of the insanely wealthy.

A pawn. A game. Collateral Damage.

I'm no stranger to being used.

Roe used me to get to this party tonight. The man I'm in the car with is using me for an escape. But I don't blame him. I'm using him as an escape, too.

My body vibrates and my chest explodes when he pulls away long enough to whisper against my mouth.

"Happy birthday, sweet nothings."

TWO

LAUREL

Present Day

"Tell me again why we're here."

"Someone died, Laurel." Roe sighs beside me.

I bite back the groan roaring up my throat and sling back the rest of the champagne. The bubbles pop and fizz their way down, taking my groan along with it.

"I'm aware someone died, Roe." I deadpan. "But no one gave a shit about James Harding. Most of all, our family."

A server wearing all black passes by us. I quickly drop my empty glass on the tray and grab a fresh glass of champagne, immediately taking a drink from it.

"You're drinking as if you've never had a drink in your life." She giggles under her breath.

"Not going to lie, it's the only thing that's making this funeral tolerable." I smooth my hand down the front of my stark black dress. I'm just another person dressed in black filling the large marble dining hall. Large French doors are propped open, displaying the acres of land stretching all the way out to the water's edge in the distance. The sun is bright, and there isn't a cloud in the sky. If it weren't for every single person dressed in black, I'd think this was just another rich cock sucker party disguised as a fundraiser. Unfortunately, we're familiar with functions such as those.

"Honestly," she sighs. "I don't want to be here either. I'm just not as obvious about it as you are."

I give her a sidelong glance, nudging her shoulder with mine. We're standing at the edge of the crowd, people watching. It's one of our favorite pastimes. Or it could be that it was the only way we used to survive functions like these growing up by being invisible yet obvious at the same time.

"No one gives a shit this man died."

Roe's eyes continue to roam the crowd. "I'm not sure that's entirely true. Someone in this room must have genuinely cared for him. If they didn't, it would be pretty fucking tragic."

The overwhelming need to leave blooms in my stomach. I keep my attention on the crowd, screwing my mouth to the side, attempting not to seem too obvious or speak too loudly. "We could sneak out through the back," I whisper. "Make it look as if we're exploring the grounds."

"You're insufferable." She shakes her head, tucking her long brown hair behind her ears. Her nails are painted a thick, rich black. Mine are a bright pale pink.

I half expect her to laugh or smile, but she doesn't. Her eyes seem far away even as they scan through the people passing by.

The funeral ended less than an hour ago. After James Harding was buried under six feet of cold, hard dirt, where he rightfully belongs, we all headed toward the Hardings' summer house situated along the coast.

Until today, I'd never been to any of the Hardings' homes. Rumor has it they have at least twenty with ten of them in the Boston city limits alone. A little over the top if you ask me, but then again, our family isn't used to *this* kind of money.

We have money, but not Harding money.

I look at my sister. Her skin is pale and her lips are painted a faint pink. She's softer than her usual appearance, especially for events such as these.

"What's wrong?" I ask her, my stomach turning. I'm not sure if it's the unease in her expression or from the lack of food in my stomach.

"Nothing." She doesn't blink. "Just going over this sketch in my head I've been working on for the museum. It's due next week and it looks like shit. I'm anxious about it, that's all."

"I doubt it looks like shit."

When Roe started Harvard eight years ago, she was on track to follow in our family's footsteps. Graduate from Harvard Law and become a partner in our uncle's firm. But in her third year, she changed her mind. Out of the blue, she switched her major to art, claiming to follow her true passion.

Our uncle was shocked. I, however, was not. Roe always blazed her own trail.

I stuck to my plan and enrolled with Harvard Law. Predictable. Having just graduated, I've been interning with our uncle at the Branford Law Firm, located three floors below James Harding and his coveted business, Harding Holdings. Our family's unofficial rival, competing for the city's attention.

I've never been adventurous or a risk taker. The last time I allowed myself to break out my comfort zone, it bit me in the ass.

"I doubt anyone will notice we're gone." I can't drop the idea of escaping this funeral. The prospect of seeing *him* again has my stomach wobbling with nausea as rough as the time our father took us out on our yacht the summer I was ten. Being around the Hardings, knowing our family's distaste for them, has made it difficult. And being around one of them in particular has become practically near impossible.

"Yes, they will," Roe says, unamused, pulling me from my thoughts.

"They'll probably notice you being gone. Not me."

"Come on, Laurel." There's an edge to her voice that wasn't there before. "Don't start that shit."

"I'm not starting anything. I'm just saying everyone always noticed you over me... or Mom."

"Not true," she says, her voice growing smaller. "At least not the part about me. Everyone always noticed Mom over anyone else."

My throat swells, and pressure builds behind my eyes. Losing her three years ago was the worst pain imaginable. Facing that I was going to spend the rest of my life never seeing her smile again, or the way red highlights popped in the strands of her chestnut brown hair when she stood under the sun has been a difficult pill to swallow. Losing her and our father in a sudden mountain climbing accident was the first tear in the fabric of our family. Now there's a large gaping hole that is past the point of repair. I'm convinced the grief will never fade.

"Okay," Roe persists. "Well, you can't stay standing over here with me all day. Maybe we can find you a date or something. Someone to talk to." She rises on her toes and cranes her neck. She's hunting, searching for anyone who catches her eye.

"Gross." I scowl. "Are you seriously trying to set me up at a funeral?"

She lifts one shoulder, rocking back on her heels. "I mean, it doesn't hurt to keep an eye out."

"I don't need anyone." I sigh heavily. "I don't think this setting is appropriate for finding a date. It's weird. Besides, there's no one here I'm interested in."

"I'm just saying it wouldn't hurt if you found someone you were into for longer than six months. Just when I think you've found the right man, you break it off with him. I can't keep up..." She trails off.

I jerk back, the sting of the direction in conversation hitting me harder than expected. "Ouch."

"I'm sorry." She pinches the bridge of her nose and rests her hand on my arm. Her eyes flutter open and she looks at me sympathetically. "That was a real bitchy thing to say."

"You're right. That was pretty bitchy."

Roe smirks, and the corners of my mouth lift, but only a little.

The problem is, she isn't completely wrong. My track record has been one crash and burn after another.

"I know it's been hard to move on since your marriage ended," Roe says sympathetically.

I close my eyes and breathe. When I open them, I look at her. "Please." I wave her off. "I would hardly call what David and I had a marriage."

"You made vows, and you lived together as husband and wife for three months."

I roll my eyes, bringing my glass to my mouth to take a large swig. "Our marriage was annulled, so it's almost as if it never happened. Plus, he admitted to using me to get to our family law firm, Roe. He didn't even attempt to deny it."

She frowns, lowering her gaze to her own glass and tapping her nail against it. "I shouldn't have brought it up."

"It's fine." With a reassuring smile, I run my hand up and down her arm.

I'm lying. The sting of what David pulled has faded, but the memory is still fresh. I'm no stranger to being used.

Relationships haven't always come easily for me. It's hard to trust others when they've used and chewed you up for their own benefit. I shouldn't have been surprised. I still shouldn't be. Our marriage was short lived, and in hindsight, we were merely playing roles. I should have seen the red flags David was constantly waving when it came to his constant barrage of questions about my family's law firm and how he could quickly move up in the ranks. But my heart simply hasn't gone completely numb yet. There's still a tiny fragment of the beating muscle in my chest that burns at the thought of all the times I've been chewed up and spit out for other's benefit.

"It's not." She shrugs. "But I still don't think you should close yourself off to those in front of you."

"I'm not, and no one is in front of me."

"Whatever you say." She smirks, turning her attention back to the room. "Maybe you should marry one of the Harding brothers, then. They're in the money hungry corporate world, just like you. Although, I hear the middle one is off limits. In my opinion, the oldest looks more your type. His mouth looks like it could do some damage. The good kind, of course, if you know what I mean."

I attempt to ignore the unrelenting fluttering going on in my stomach. Heat spreads across my chest remembering how it felt to have his tongue taste my skin in the back seat of his car. Fortunately, or unfortunately, I'm all too aware of the damage Lennon's tongue can do. Fucking ridiculous considering it's been *six years*.

I turn away from Roe, fearing my face might give her an unwarranted confession of the night I first met Lennon. Pushing aside thoughts of his delicious tongue, I replay my conversation with Roe.

Why is she urging me to marry a Harding? I've spent the past several years dedicated to my career and interning at Branford and Branford. I don't care if my sister thinks life would be better if I were with someone else. Even if I were to entertain Roe's suggestion, I wouldn't stake my hopes on finding my soulmate at a funeral. Somehow, I find it worse than picking someone up at a bar.

"If I marry again, I'm marrying for love," I confess to my sister.

My eyes dance across the room, still searching for the best possible escape route without being detected. I consider leaving Roe behind since she seems to be perfectly content seeing this funeral through to the end.

I think I've found it but stop when I see the tall, wide man heading in our direction.

"What are you two doing over here?" Frederick asks. My uncle takes a sip of his glass of whiskey before popping one of the salmon puffs into his mouth another server was passing around.

"Just talking," Roe says.

"You two are always talking." He frowns. "Steven couldn't make it?"

Roe twists the ring on her finger and takes a quick drink from her glass. "No. He had a big deal to close in New York."

"Understandable."

"We made a few rounds and greeted some people from the country club we recognized," Roe adds.

"Good." Frederick nods. He adjusts his black tie, shifting his attention to me. "I know you aren't the biggest fans of the Hardings."

"Are you kidding?" I ask him, struggling to maintain my composure. "Neither are you. In fact, our entire family despises them. No one likes them. And I'm fairly certain they feel the same way. They've done more damage to this city than good. Everyone knows it, they're just too afraid to say it out loud."

"Laurel," Frederick scolds, hissing between his teeth. He quickly glances around as if he's worried everyone in attendance at the funeral can overhear our conversation.

I can't help it. Something about today has me on edge.

I can't get the familiar blue eyes out of my head. The way his dark hair rested against his forehead. The silver chain wrapped around his neck.

I grind my teeth and count to ten. The inevitable is coming. It dances in my bones, humming through my veins. "Sorry," I apologize. I'm not exactly sorry for what I said—it's the truth— but it's the only word I can bring myself to offer my uncle.

"The Hardings have been great business contacts for years," Fredrick points out.

"Is it worth it, though?" I ask. "They hate us. I don't understand why we're bothering. I don't understand why we're here when our families are at odds. They've stolen clients and cases from us. We tried to forge a business relationship with them last year, and James practically spat in our face."

"We aren't at odds with them." His dark, bushy eyebrows knit as he squares his shoulders. "Their admonishment for this family lies squarely on the back of your brother. He's paying the price for the choices he made and for putting our business relations in jeopardy. It's his fault we are in this position, but I won't stand for it. I'm determined to get our family back in the Hardings' good graces."

I chew on the inside of my cheek until it stings. My chest twists and aches. "Are you truly that desperate?"

My harsh question hits my uncle harder than I intend.

I don't like talking about my brother.

"Honestly, Laurel." My uncle shakes his head, frowning. "Aside from their aggressive business tactics and obvious flagrant disregard for flaunting their money, the Hardings aren't the monsters you're making them out to be."

I snort. "Right."

Roe snaps her head in my direction, her eyes glaring. "Where does your contempt come from? I get it. They're bad, but I think you're being a little over the top. You could at least practice *some* self-restraint. We're at a funeral, for God's sake."

I attempt to hide behind my nearly empty glass. My cheeks flame red. The twisting sensation in my stomach grows. I seriously need to get a grip.

No one knows the reason for my contempt of the Hardings, not even my sister. It runs deeper than their disgusting business tactics and lack of moral compass.

But my hatred for Lennon Harding is one I keep buried deep in my chest.

"Regardless of how or why you feel this way about them," Frederick starts, stuffing his hands inside his black slacks. "We can't afford to lose our relationship with this family. Or others in this room. We aren't here for a funeral."

Of course we aren't.

"Why? Is everything okay?" Roe asks him.

I want to leave this conversation, but I can't. My feet are glued to the floor, catching sight of the man entering the room, followed by his two younger brothers.

"We're fine," Frederick answers Roe, unconvincingly. "But I won't lie in saying our accounts are dwindling. Since Kellan went to prison two years ago for his embezzlement charges, and what he did to cover his tracks by dipping into your trusts, our family name and reputation have been tarnished. Despite what our shareholders and public relations team predicted considering our businesses are completely different, our rebound into this community has been slow at best. Something needs to happen fast if we're going to fix this."

"That bad?" Roe scrunches her nose.

"Unfortunately, yes." Frederick reluctantly nods. His cheeks flush with pink. "I'm afraid our family is living on borrowed money at this point."

"Oh..." Roe's voice trails off. She attempts to hide her anger, but the ticking muscle in her jaw gives her away. My chest squeezes. Our older brother Kellan was arrested and charged with stealing money from his law partners at another firm and inflating his assets, forever tarnishing our reputation.

A liar to his core.

A traitor to his family.

I want to punch my uncle in his large, round belly for bringing him up. Fury and rage simmer under my skin when remembering how my brother not only stole money from our family's company, but how he also stole the inheritance our parents left behind for us. Named as executor, he had control of mine and Roe's trusts until we turned twenty-five. When Roe turned twenty-five and was ready to buy a house with the money our parents left behind, she was shocked to find the account empty. Mine as well.

After he went to prison for his crimes, I used to sit and rack my brain, trying to figure out how or why he made the choices he made. Part of me thinks it was the grief of losing our parents. The other part thinks he was just a selfish asshole, but I don't think we'll ever know the full truth. Roe and I haven't spoken to him since the day of his sentencing.

I eye my uncle, wondering what our tarnished reputation means for my position as junior partner at his firm. From the worried expression in his wrinkled forehead, I'm afraid our family's once coveted castle is beginning to crumble.

Roe nervously bites on her bottom lip. There is a distant look in her eye that wasn't there before.

The room slowly grows quieter. What were once loud voices, straining to talk over the other, are now hushed in whispers. One by one, everyone's attention is directed to the front of the dining hall.

All three Harding brothers move to the front of the room. Each is dressed in a crisp, black suit. The youngest brother, Micah, stands at the end. His hands are shoved into his pockets, and his brown-near-black hair is slicked back. Jude, the middle brother, stands between Lennon and Micah. With a grinding jaw and a vacant stare in his eyes, I can see he feels the same way I do. He doesn't want to be here. He has the same look in his eye as if he's only staying out of obligation.

Then there's Lennon.

Smug. Stern. Sharp chiseled jaw. Piercing blue eyes. His suit speaks perfectly to the kind of person he is: mysterious, vacant. Where his brother's at least have a pop of white with their pressed collared shirts, Lennon's is midnight black.

While he shares the same eyes as his brothers, he's different in every other way. He's darker and difficult to read, as if he keeps his secrets buried deep down where he believes no one can see them. Under all the pretenses and displays he puts on for others, I'm convinced he must have a heart. Right? Although, truth be told I've never seen it.

The reality is, I've tried, and failed miserably, to put my distaste for Lennon Harding aside. At least as much as I could stomach. Last year, his father attempted to rope me into their circle and gain my attention so he could get in on our family's money. I could see in James's smug expression that he thought I could be bought.

I should have known better, but I was still an eager law student, determined to create as many business relationships as possible. Naïve is what I truly was. That was the night I learned the truth about the Harding family and the power James had over all of them. Once he tried to hand me over to his son Jude, I realized the truth of why I was there.

I was nothing but a pawn that night. A game. Collateral

damage. A piece of meat tossed into the lion's den. They were ravenous, and I was served on a silver platter for them to feast.

Nothing I'm not already familiar with.

But what stung worse that night than being used as an object, sitting in that booth with James's arm draped across my shoulders, was the look in his eldest son's eyes.

Empty. Unaware. Unrecognizable.

Lennon Harding looked at me like I was a stranger.

I laughed and smiled my way through the endless refills of champagne and arrogant conversation about how James Harding controlled nearly every top corporation in the city. Immoral business tactics and questionable investments or what they called 'donations'.

James Harding was a predator simply seeking his next prey. That night, he was hoping I was his. But all I could do was watch Lennon while wearing the mask of a woman who pretended she belonged. After all, it's what my uncle requested I do, hoping to strengthen the business relationship between the Hardings and the Branfords.

The crack in my already fractured heart splinters once more when Lennon scans the crowd in attendance at his father's funeral. His alcohol-soaked eyes catch me for a split moment before resuming his survey of the crowd. Nothing. Not a flicker of recognition. I may as well be invisible.

He lifts his full glass to his mouth and drinks half in one gulp.

I watch him carefully, focusing on the pressure of my fingers pinching the stem of my own champagne glass.

"Excuse me." Lennon raises his hand in the air. He slowly lowers it as the chatter filling the room quietens completely. "My brothers and I would like to extend a deep, heartfelt thank you for coming today." He presses his smooth, full lips together and glances down the line at his brothers. They both nod in agreement.

"As many of you know," Lennon continues, clearing his throat before he swallows deeply. "Our father was anything but shy about the kind of man he was: dedicated, well known, proud, hardworking. I remember when I was a kid no older than three or four, and I was the only Harding brother to exist yet." His mouth curls into a reminiscent smile before fading. A low rumble of laughter filters through the crowd. "My father used to sit me in his office chair, spin me around until I was facing the whole of Boston. He'd wave his arm and tell me the city was mine and anyone else's who was unafraid to leave their mark on it. Well, twenty-five years later, he sure as fuck left his mark on this city. And you being here today is living proof. He was admired by many in this city. His death was sudden and unexpected. He will be missed dearly."

"How exactly did he die?" Roe whispers to Frederick.

He leans back slightly, and half turns his head, keeping his focus on Lennon. "Heart attack."

Roe raises her eyebrows and slowly pulls back.

Lennon lifts his glass in the air and scratches at his jaw. He looks around the crowd again. "To James Harding!" he yells.

"To James," the crowd mimics in unison. Everyone lifts their glasses to their mouths, most drinking it all in one gulp. I lift mine and drink what's left down to the last drop. My cheeks are warm, and my heart is beating faster. When I lower my glass, the two eyes staring directly at me nearly make me choke on my champagne.

The heat in my face radiates. It swells, and fragments of a night I've attempted to forget roll back in my mind like waves crashing onto the shores of Cape Cod.

Forever passes when Lennon finally tears his eyes away from mine. He turns, whispers in Jude's ear, then leaves the room. He doesn't speak another word to anyone else before disappearing around the corner.

"Respectable and loving speech. James would be proud if he'd heard it," Frederick says, turning around. "In fact, I think he'd be proud of his sons and where they're headed in life."

I bite the side of my tongue. Lennon's speech was anything but respectable and loving. I've felt pain and loss before. Losing both my parents years ago. Lennon isn't torn apart by the loss of his father. His face may look saddened, but his words said otherwise.

"You've spent time with them," Frederick says to me. "What do you think about maybe holding a business meeting and seeing if they could swing some clients our way? Maybe you could get close to Lennon and see where we stand. Harding Holdings could steer our dwindling assets in the right direction if they would put in a good name with their connections, and it would be nice if you could get to know him a little more. Think of it as getting in some good and much needed PR."

"I already tried that last year," I mutter. "Didn't work."

"Wouldn't hurt to try again. Could have a better chance with Lennon than you did his father. A deal with the Harding family would give our business the boost and cushion we desperately need."

I don't answer Frederick; the silent pleading in his eyes is too much. Instead, I stare at him with a blank expression. His eyebrows are arched across his aging forehead.

Roe blinks, waiting for my answer. My chest weaves into knots, the expectant pressure building inside. I want to explode. I want to yell at my uncle for, once again, using me as a pawn to further his agenda. I want to scream at him and my sister for always turning to me for answers.

Silence falls between the three of us. I can't think about work. Not when I have my family staring at me expectantly as if

I'm somehow the magic key to solving our ever-growing financial problems. The thought of willingly walking up to Lennon and pretending we've never shared more than business pleasantries with one another, or that he's basically a carbon copy of his father, sounds like an insurmountable feat—one I don't want to partake in again.

"I have to use the restroom," I tell them both. I leave and push through the groups of people congregated around us. When I'm sure I'm no longer in their sight, I make a hard left. My heels click across the marble. Sweeping past the cocktail and snack table, I swipe an open bottle of champagne, wrapping my fingers around the neck, and carrying it with me like a life raft.

Emerging from the open French doors, the clicking of my heels stops when they meet soft grass so lush and green, it's perfect. Entirely too perfect. There are rows of tall green trees. Lines of purple flowers dot the yard in clusters. A setting sun has the orange glow sparkling across the water. If I didn't know I was standing on the coast of Massachusetts, I'd think I were somewhere else.

Worried Roe may be following me, I take a swig of champagne and move. After sneaking behind a far row of trees, I follow a cobblestone path. The clicking begins again. I tread carefully. The last thing I need to do is roll my ankle from venturing across uneven stone while tipsy. I follow the path until I come to an opening in the grove. Stone benches sit in front of an old stone brick wall. I'm lifting the bottle to my mouth, once again, when I abruptly stop.

Lennon is leaning against the brick wall. Pinched between two fingers, he holds his cigarette. He inhales a long drag, tilts his head back and blows it harshly between his perfect lips.

I stand frozen in place. My heart races. Unexpectedly seeing Lennon out here isn't the only reason. It's the woman on her knees in front of him. Her black dress is tight around her small frame. The bright red bottom of her stilettos are on full display. Her long, curled, blonde hair sways against her bare back as she jerks her head back and forth. She grips Lennon's cock with one hand, moaning as she slides his length inside her open mouth. Her body shudders when Lennon reaches down with his free hand and grips the back of her head, shoving his cock farther down her throat. She pauses briefly before giving in, letting him take control.

I tighten my grip on the bottle and lift it to my mouth to take a giant swig, hoping it will mask the nausea swimming in my stomach stop. Then my breath is stolen completely when he drops his head back down, and his eyes shoot in my direction. He stares at me with those familiar deep blues. They narrow and study me, heartless and empty. I don't make a move. Every ounce of energy he forces out slams into me like a sledge-hammer to the chest.

Thirty long, agonizing seconds must pass with nothing but the deep, stomach-churning sound of moaning against Lennon's dick. The corner of his mouth curls. A line creases in the corner, deepening the meaning behind his stare. Crude, daring, and unfeeling. This is the genuine Lennon Harding. His father's twin.

"If you came out here looking for me," he grunts, the sneer on his too-perfect mouth deepening. "You'll have to wait your turn."

My hammering heart screeches to a halt. Staring at Lennon with this much anger and disgust burns. My eyes and my soul. A soul that's been marked far too many times already.

I hate him.

Forcing myself to breathe, I finally gather the strength and spin on my heels.

Tears sting the corner of my eyes as I stomp my way back to the funeral.

I wish my parents were still here, I wish my brother wasn't a fucking asshole, and I wish I knew why Roe suddenly looks distant and tired all the time. Most of all, I wish I could forget Lennon fucking Harding and his cold, black heart.

THREE

Lennon

The hate I have for my father is as deep as the love I have for my mother.

It's a shame she died before him. Infinite doesn't begin to describe how much better of a human being she was than him.

I remember the second I was told my mother took her last breath. A tight ball of emotion solidified in my chest as if it were forcing all the emotions to pour out of me without hesitation. It was the first time I cried since I was fifteen, when my father forced me to go to one of the strip clubs he frequented. The image of him snorting a line of cocaine off one of the dancer's bare backs will forever be stained in my memory.

I didn't cry when my father died. I didn't shed a single tear when I found him passed out on his balcony surrounded by shattered glass, spilled whiskey, and a bag of cocaine in his hand.

He died the way I'd always expected: alone. I should have felt sad. The panic and grief should have set in, but as I watched him be wheeled out of his penthouse in a black body bag, I felt nothing.

I'd lost empathy for him long before that day.

The thoughts in my head are harsh and visceral, but that's what you get when you're James Harding's eldest son. Raised to be ruthless and unfeeling. I'm convinced it was in his blood from the moment he was born. And his father before him, and so on, and so on. Each of us Hardings come from a long line of money hungry, corporate pricks.

The Hardings have had a long history of keeping up the thin veil of what's hidden underneath. Scandal and greed. My father went to great lengths and used whatever means he felt necessary to not only line our pockets, but stuff them as well.

Ten thousand black roses. Ten thousand people dressed in black. Ten thousand bodies pretending to care they even remotely loved my father. The sympathy in their eyes when they hugged me and my brothers, sharing their deep condolences for our loss. The way Jude's neck bobbed up and down every time he forced himself to utter the words 'thank you.' I was convinced he was going to vomit all over the Italian marble we were standing on more than once. I don't blame him. Out of the three of us Harding brothers, our father fucked Jude up more than Micah or me.

While still working on wrapping my head around the damage my father has done to our family, I haven't been able to bring myself to a place of forgiveness. Not even remotely.

But despite all the ways I disagreed with him, we only shared one love.

Our family company.

And continuing to keep up with the Harding image was crucial to our status in the city. I didn't agree with the way my father handled himself, but I understood to a degree.

The image of our family to the eyes of the city and the world mattered.

It still matters.

Which is why I'm making it my number one mission to run

the firm in the legacy he built. In fact, I plan on running it better than he ever did or could.

"Coming from the person who picked on me for edibles, you might need to look in a mirror every now and then." Jude moves to stand beside me. "Maybe consider switching to something a little less harsh."

"I'll quit smoking." I argue. "Will that be enough?"

He spins around and rests with his back against the wall, his hand shoved into his pockets. He doesn't answer my question. His light brown hair is slicked back and cut short at the sides, reminding me of how he used to be. Jude backed out of any involvement in the company a while ago. The longer he's been away from our world, the more he's changed, and for the better.

I laugh and shake my head, pouring myself another whiskey. I'm already bordering on being too drunk for public, but I don't give a shit. Days like today call for this level of drinking.

"Come on." I shake my head and gesture toward Jude with my now-full glass. "One more for good measure. You know Dad would have approved."

His smile immediately turns to a frown. I feel like a dick for being the cause.

"Whatever." He sighs heavily, pushing himself off the wall. I don't miss the way his eyes roll as he steps away. "I just hope we can get this shit show over with quickly so I can go home as fast as humanly possible. I don't even know why I'm here."

"Because you're still his son." I deadpan.

If I weren't already a dick for my comment a second ago, I definitely am one now. I've just added more gasoline onto the fire that is my brother's resentment to our father. I don't know what it is. Maybe it's the funeral or the day in general. Something has me on edge.

"A fact that will never change," Jude mutters. "For the record, I only came to the funeral to show support for you and

Micah. I get I no longer have a place in the family company, but you're still my brothers."

"Let's just see what happens." I give him a reassuring smirk.

"Sure," he says unconvincingly, then he leaves me in front of the beverage cart without another word.

I stare at the gold painting hung above it, beside where Jude was just standing. I can't explain it, but it angers me. The way the light reflects off the gold brush strokes. The way I couldn't even tell you where it came from or how long it's been nailed to this fucking wall. Every inch of it ignites a fire beneath my skin.

I lift my glass, down its contents, and I'm quick to refill it.

My younger brother Micah walks into the study and heads straight for the beverage cart I'm standing in front of.

"Leave enough for me?" he asks with a light smile.

The youth in his expression doesn't waver. He's twenty-three but acts as if he's still sneaking liquor out of our father's secret stash at the office at the ripe old age of eleven. He's always been the little brother who tagged along with his two older ones.

"Of course," I tell him.

His smile deepens when I pour him a glass. He takes a gingerly sip and points to me. "I didn't think we were supposed to have this meeting until next week. Isn't that usually how these things go?"

"Perry flagged me down after our toast out in the great hall." I look away from the gold painting. "He said talking over the will couldn't wait until then."

"Oh." He nods, sucking a sharp breath in through his teeth. I can tell he's nervous.

Micah is mine and Jude's half-brother, but we've never thought of him any differently than if he were our full blood brother.

Conceived from one of his countless affairs, our father couldn't risk the reputation he might have created had he not claimed Micah when his mother told everyone she was pregnant by the famous James Harding.

Treating Micah like a business transaction, Dad considered the pros and cons, deciding the pros of having another son outweighed the cons of denying he had another and the media spinning a story of scandal surrounding our family name.

Classic James Harding.

Micah leaves me and sits beside Jude in one of the large leather chairs situated in the room. Surrounded by old law books and dark leather and espresso-stained furniture, my stomach turns. This isn't how I remember this room, and with the way Jude refuses to look away from Micah, I know he's thinking about it, too.

Thankfully, the ping of a text coming from my pocket pulls me away from my thoughts before they stray too far.

I unlock my phone to a message from Madison.

> Madison: If you're ready for round two, I'll be in the courtyard. Come find me...

A picture of her hand, slipped between her slick folds, pops up underneath her first text. Her fingertips are pressed against her clit. She's resting against a flourish of bright pink and red flowers as she's fingering herself. Not at all too different from where I was with her only twenty minutes ago.

I tighten my grip on my phone and fight the urge to leave the room and play Madison's game, but this meeting with my father's lawyer is too important.

My phone screen fades to black the second I hear the sharp clicking of heels meeting the smooth marble floor. My father's assistant, Sienna, strides into the room, followed by our family lawyer, Perry O'Connell.

Sienna moves to stand near the largest window overlooking the back gardens jutting up against the bay—most likely where

Madison is waiting for me. Sienna sniffs and swipes the tips of her fingers under each of her eyes as if she's erasing her tears. As if we won't notice she's been sobbing since the second she found out about my father's untimely demise.

After wiping her tears, she sips on her glass of champagne in silence. Tangled up in her grief, she's drank every glass of champagne offered to her since the reception started.

As horrible as it is to say, I look at her with pity. I know the affair my father and her had over the years meant more to her than it did him. All his affairs were meaningless. Two years ago, I walked into his office for a meeting as she was crawling out on all fours under his desk. Pink cheeked and tousled hair, she shuffled out of the office without daring to chance meeting my eye. My father leaned back in his chair and smiled as if his eldest son hadn't just caught him with his assistant's mouth around his cock.

Still, today, I can see the shame and embarrassment in her eyes. My pity for her has grown, knowing my father used her like he did everyone else in his life.

"Thank you for coming, everyone," Perry says behind me.

I spin around to face the room, turning my back on the gold painting.

Perry O'Connell, my father's long-time attorney, sits on the large, leather sofa situated in the middle of the study. The one none of us wanted to claim when we entered the room.

Jude and Micah are seated in chairs opposite the sofa. I walk over and stand between them, clutching onto my glass as if it's giving me the will to stay and listen to what Perry has to say.

Sienna remains near the window.

Perry half turns, looking at her over his shoulder. "Thank you for coming," he tells her. "I know it's strange for you to be here when this is a family matter, but you're mentioned in the will."

Sienna's eyebrows shoot up. Shock settles in her eyes as they dart between my brothers and me. None of us answer her silent question, all of us shocked to hear she's in the will as well.

"Now," Perry addresses the three of us, "I'm sorry we had to meet on a heavy day such as this one."

Jude scoffs, and I snap my head to the left, pinning him with a hard stare.

He shrugs and a small smile spreads across his mouth.

Resting in Perry's lap is a large, leather-bound folder. He cracks it open, the material stiff as though it's never been opened before.

My eyes fall to the first page.

In large bold letters at the top, I read:

THE LAST WILL AND TESTAMENT OF JAMES DEAN HARDING

"Before we get too deep into this, I'm going to begin with Sienna," Perry starts.

Sienna moves through the room and stands behind me. She keeps her distance, but she's close enough to join us. Her body tenses while she holds her breath.

Perry flips three pages, then looks up. He slides a piece of paper from the pocket of the leather-bound book and holds it out for Sienna. "This is in James's words. I've been instructed to read it as it is written." His eyes shift nervously between Sienna and me before looking down at his lap. "To my assistant, Sienna Thompson. Your employment at Harding Holdings is to be terminated the moment this statement is read to you. I've instructed my lawyer to give you a severance pay for your years of dedicated service to my company. Since I am gone, your services are no longer needed."

Silence descends upon the room. Well, aside from Micah muttering, "What the fuck?" under his breath.

Jude blows out a heavy breath. I watch Sienna's shaking

hand grab the check from Perry's hand. A single tear spills over her eye. Then another one. She immediately looks at me. Immense sadness and pain fills her gaze. More than it has all day.

This is it. This is the moment where my father finally breaks her. After what feels like several agonizing minutes, but is probably only seconds, Sienna inhales a sharp gasp. She quickly covers her mouth and wraps her arm around her stomach as she spins, then without another word, races out of the room, her cries filtering through her covered mouth on her way out.

We all remain silent until we can no longer hear the clicking of her heels.

"What the fuck was that?" Jude asks, stunned. He runs his fingers through his hair and leans forward, resting his elbows on his knees.

"I'm sorry," Perry apologizes. "I knew the reading of your father's will wasn't going to be easy. He insisted I address Sienna before continuing with the rest. Honestly, I think it was for the best I let her go now. Saved her from having to sit here through the whole thing before finding out she was let go."

I narrow my eyes in disbelief. That's exactly the kind of logic my father would use in life. Treat people like shit then convince yourself you did it for their benefit.

"I'm not sure what I envisioned for this meeting," I say, "but I can't say I'm surprised."

"Agreed." Jude sighs, sitting back in his chair.

"Okay, next order of business." Perry breathes out, flipping another few pages. "Micah. You're next."

Micah straightens his back, sitting taller. He turns to me and Jude, giving us a small, nervous grin in anticipation.

At this rate, we're all biting the tip of our tongues, waiting for the unexpected.

"To my youngest son, Micah Lucas Harding. I leave you all

four of my properties overseas. The houses in London, Edin-burgh, Paris, and Barcelona."

Perry hands Micah a single document. He takes it and keeps his head down as he reads over the fine print.

"This paper goes over all the basics," Perry explains, point-ing. "You'll need to come down to my office, or I can meet you at yours to sign all the paperwork necessary to get the properties into your name."

"Wow." He nods, taking a resolving breath. "I don't even know what to say."

"Um..." Jude's eyebrows arch. "Congratulations, brother."

Micah nods as he looks down at the paper in his shaking hands. The heavy thoughts are glaringly obvious. "Thanks, I guess. I don't know why, but it feels wrong to be excited about this."

"You should be excited." I reach out and massage his shoul-der. "Don't feel guilty."

He gives me a relieved smile. "I appreciate it."

"For my middle son, Jude Ryan Harding." Perry flips to the next page, then quickly looks up. He hesitates and clears his throat before reading the single line on the paper. "I leave him nothing but this message: the choice you made years ago to put yourself and your own interests above your own family has brought you here to this moment. You played with the fire long enough, you were bound to get burned."

My lips part the second I attempt to inhale. Air squeezes through my lungs as I look down at my younger brother. He doesn't move. His eyes are trained forward, staring at Perry.

"Jude?" I ask, nervously adjusting my tie.

"What, Lennon?" Jude asks, snapping his head to the right. His eyes are glazed over, but there isn't a hint of sadness or anger.

"Are you okay?" I place my hand on his shoulder.

"Of course." He sighs, life returning to his face. "If that asshole would have left me anything, I planned on donating it anyway. This just proves to me that I made the right decision. Every time."

"I'm sorry." I look at him sympathetically. "If I could do anything..." I hate what our father did to him. Since finding out the truth, it's been difficult to not keep business and family separate. But this career I've built is bigger than my father and the shit he pulled when he was alive. I hate the pain my brother has suffered through, but the only life I've ever known is this one.

"Don't be sorry," Jude reassures me, running his hands along his knees. "In hindsight, I think I expected this. I'm surprised I'm mentioned in his will at all."

I open my mouth to let my brother know I still love him. I want to tell him I've only ever wanted to erase the memory of our father in this city but keep the legacy he built. But Perry interrupts before I can tell him I aim to do whatever I can to make it better for the Harding name.

"Now onto Lennon." Perry addresses the room.

I nervously shove my hand in my pocket and curl my fingers into a tight fist.

Perry flips to the next page. From where I'm standing, there are clearly more words typed on the page than either of my brothers'.

"To my eldest son, Lennon James Harding. For your unwavering loyalty, I leave one hundred percent of the shares in Harding Holdings, LLC. I give you the entirety of the company, along with all its employees and clients. I gift you the three penthouses in Boston, the house in Cape Cod, along with all my vehicles and belongings." Perry glances up. "He's listed each of these properties and assets on the next few pages."

"Wow." I nod, running my hand down the side of my face in disbelief. "That's quite . . ."

"There's more," Perry interrupts.

"More?" Micah laughs, draping his arm over the back of his chair, relaxing his back against it. "How could there possibly be more?"

"There's a condition."

"A condition." I should have expected this. My throat runs dry. Any condition from my father won't be a simple one.

"A small formality." Perry scrunches his nose and blinks in a way that makes me think it's anything but *small*.

"What formality?" I ask slowly.

"Your father says you receive all of this under the condition you get married."

"You're fucking joking," Micah blurts out. He's sporting a smile but it's more in disbelief than humor.

Jude clears his throat as if he was expecting this right along with him not receiving anything from our father.

James has always had the ability to dangle the prize in front of you, enticing you with its luster, and roping you in, but it always came at a cost. Always.

"You're not honestly going to get married just so you get all this?" Jude asks, twirling his finger in the air.

I open my mouth, but no words come out. I'm frozen in place. Oddly enough, my mother's face comes to mind. The kindness in her eyes and how the color faded in them with every passing day until the day she died.

"Are you kidding?" Micah interjects, directing his astonishment at Jude. "He'd be losing the entire company if he doesn't."

"What happens if Lennon doesn't marry?" Jude asks Perry.

"Your father was very clear in his instructions." He answers Jude's question but keeps his attention on me. "If you don't marry within thirty days of today and remain married for at least one year, everything will be sold, and the firm will dissolve."

"Shit." Micah hisses. "Thirty days to get married? Thirty days is insane. Not to mention the need to *stay* married for an entire *year*."

"Yes," Perry adds. "Once Lennon marries, he will own one hundred percent of all the assets your father listed and will be able to run the company freely. But if at any point he divorces before the first year, the condition becomes null and void."

Jude leans back in his seat and runs his hand down the side of his face.

The heaviness of silence descending upon the room allows the reality of my situation to hit me full force.

Fuck James Harding.

I admit knowing my father was an asshole when he was alive. A drug induced, money hungry, rich prick. But the longer I stand here, thinking of the lows my father has gone to even after his death, brings my disgust for him to a whole new level. Somehow, I hate him more as a dead man buried in the frozen, Boston dirt than when he was standing in front of me alive and breathing.

My chest aches, twisting into knots, and my stomach flips at the thought of marriage. It's not that I've completely written off the idea of being tied to someone for life, but I've honestly never given it much thought. My father wasn't exactly the greatest role model when it came to my mother or anyone else he was involved with.

I swallow the lump in my throat.

"What are the details?" I manage to ask. "Since it's coming from my father, I'm assuming there are more details written in the fine print."

"Len," Jude warns. "I'm surprised you're even entertaining this foolish condition."

I inhale a deep breath and turn my head in my brother's

direction. He's looking at me with nothing but care and concern, which I appreciate, but it isn't needed.

"I'm not exactly in a position to put my pride above doing what's best for this family, Jude."

"Bullshit," he spits angrily. "That's exactly what this is all about. Your pride."

"I'm not getting into this with you right now. You know me better than anyone, and you know I don't have a choice."

He pauses, swallowing his argument. "All I'm saying is, you deserve to marry someone you love. You deserve more than a contractual marriage."

"I get that, but this is what I *need* to do." I don't give him another opportunity to convince me not to go through with this. "What are the details?" I ask Perry again.

"Well..." He sighs. "Along with the thirty-day deadline, your father also stipulated you must marry someone from a specific family." He pauses, looking me straight in the eye. "The Branford family."

"You mean, Branford... as in Paul and Frederick Branford's law firm?" Micah asks.

"Yes." Perry nods. "But Paul Branford, Frederick's brother, passed away several years ago when he was on a camping trip with his wife in northern New Hampshire. Kellan Branford, their son, is currently serving a prison sentence for embezzlement charges and falsifying tax records."

"Great," I mutter.

"Kellan may be in prison, but Monroe and Laurel are considered to be fairly successful, despite the mark he's put on their reputation," Perry explains. "In fact, I saw them at the funeral today with their uncle."

"I wondered why they were here," Micah chimes in. "Dad never had anything good to say about their family." He looks up at me. "I wonder why he would have you marry into a family he hated."

I frown, unsure of his motivations, and unable to get my mind off Laurel.

I keep my mouth shut about the fact I already noticed her with her family at the funeral. I couldn't help watching her as she walked back to her car after the burial. Her black dress hugged every curve, and her eyes constantly moved, begging to be anywhere but where she was.

Then I saw her standing near the back of the crowd before my speech at the reception.

And again, in the courtyard when I had Madison's mouth wrapped around my cock.

I swallow the thoughts of Laurel as Perry slides the top paper out from his folder and hands it to me. I quickly read over it.

Everything Perry is saying is true.

The handing over of the company and all of our family's belongings only happen under the event I marry a Branford within thirty days.

Having nearly taken on every major legal case, both civil and criminal, in the Boston city area for the last thirty years, the Branfords have built their own reputation here.

I think back to last year when he'd tried to pawn Laurel, the niece to the head of the Branford law firm, onto me and my brother Jude the night we'd met at Eclipse for one of our weekly dinners.

Her dark, raven-colored hair. Those large, bright indigo eyes. Laurel sat across from me in her tight-fitting dress and her red-painted lips. It took all the strength I had not to stare. She thought I hadn't recognized her. Remembered her. I could see it in the way the corners of her mouth tilted down into a ghost of a frown.

But I did remember her. It's impossible to forget a face like hers.

The two names at the bottom of the condition of marrying catch my eye.

"Both Monroe and Laurel are listed here," I point out, attempting to keep my voice even toned.

"They are." Perry winces. "Although it appears you are given a choice, it isn't quite that simple. One of them is currently married."

My beating heart drops into my stomach like an anchor into the sea.

"Monroe has been married for a few years now," he explains. "Her sister Laurel, however, is single as far as I'm aware."

The truth in Perry's explanation hits me like a barreling train to the chest. My father may have given me the choice to marry whichever Branford sister of my choosing, but ultimately, I'm left with no other option.

Laurel is *the* only option.

The woman with raven hair and indigo eyes.

I look back at the gold painting hanging above the bar cart. The anger I felt staring at it earlier has subsided. Perhaps it's the alcohol. Perhaps it's reality setting in.

Thirty days until the company is mine.

Thirty days to convince Laurel Branford to marry me.

This is either the easiest business deal I've ever made or the most foolish one.

FOUR

LAUREL

I should have been a professional poker player.

I've spent the better part of two hours attempting to keep a straight face for a potential client. A case my uncle insists we need to take on, promising we will receive a large sum if we secure it.

"What do you think my chances are?" the man asks around a mouthful of the sandwich he's just bitten into. He doesn't wait for me to answer before taking another bite.

I fight the strong urge to gag at the sound of his chewing.

"Well..." I sigh, tapping my finger on the table. "Not good. I'm not sure you even have a case, Mr. Wright."

"What do you mean?" He's shoving some of his unchewed food into the corner of his cheek. His giant, meat-stuffed sandwich falls from his fingertips. "My wife is cheating on me, Ms. Branford. *With our gardener.*"

"I'm aware." I nod, biting the tip of my tongue. "But you admitted to also having an affair with the gardener. At the same time."

Mr. Wright lifts his napkin and wipes his mouth with more

force than necessary. Crumbs from his sandwich fly out, landing in front of my own plate that I haven't touched for over an hour.

"Listen," he sneers. "I didn't make a call to your uncle expecting him to set me up on a meeting with his incompetent niece to talk me out of suing my wife for her infidelity. I was under the impression you were going to help me. In fact, I would be doing you a favor if you took on my case. The way my name announced as one of your clients would thrust you, Laurel Branford, into the spotlight would do wonders for your career. You're a new lawyer who *needs* someone like me."

My nostrils flare as the frustration bubbles in my chest.

"I don't think my uncle was aware of all the details, Mr. Wright. You told me you had an affair with the gardener. Then two weeks later, you caught your wife with him in the exact same spot you were with him. Do you not see how it's a little hypocritical?"

"No." His eye twitches. "I don't. I'm almost certain she's going to leave me for him and take nearly all of our money with her."

"Has she given you any indication she will leave you?"

He blinks as he sucks his teeth. "Well, no, but she did buy a brand-new Porsche without asking me first."

I sigh and pinch the bridge of my nose. I look at Mr. Wright and realize the frustration I feel isn't for him and his diluted belief he can sue his wife for simply having an affair with the same person.

I wonder if my uncle truly didn't know the details of the case Mr. Wright is trying to put forth, or if he's so desperate to keep up our image, he doesn't care how ridiculous the case may seem.

I click my button on my phone, seeing a missed call from Roe and a text from my uncle. Looking up at Mr. Wright, I tilt my head to the side and force my mouth into a pout. "I'm so sorry to skip out on the rest of this meeting, but I have to go."

Mr. Wright's face turns a bright shade of red. He points a stiff finger in my direction. "You're making a big mistake here, Ms. Branford."

My chair scrapes across the tile, and I snatch my purse from the empty seat to my side. "Something tells me I'm not." I lean forward and place my hands on the back of the chair, lowering my voice so others in the café don't hear. "But I'll leave you with a bit of advice: next time you catch your wife with the same person you were fucking only weeks before, may I suggest you ask them if you could join in? May make things a little less complicated and confusing for the next time you catch them fucking in your backyard."

Mr. Wright's jaw drops, and his face turns an impossibly deeper shade of red. If it were possible, I'm positive steam would be shooting out of his ears at this point.

But I don't care.

I leave him and his half-eaten sandwich at the café as fast as my heels will carry me. Once I make it to the street, I begin walking the three blocks back to my office.

The sounds of the city are a welcome relief from the insufferable meeting I've just endured, but they don't calm the thoughts racing in my head.

I slide my phone out of my purse and call Roe. I haven't spoken to her since James Harding's funeral three days ago. After I caught Lennon in the courtyard, I didn't bother going back inside to join her and Frederick. I was too drunk, and the image of Lennon getting his cock sucked outside of his family mansion was burned in my memory. It swirled and danced with the same memories I have of him on my nineteenth birthday. The one he doesn't remember.

I snuck out of the funeral and hitched a ride from my

uncle's driver before my sister or Frederick would notice me missing.

I shove my annoyance for Lennon Harding aside and tap the call button. It rings three times before going to my sister's voicemail.

"Roe," I groan, dragging out her name as I jog across the crosswalk. "I really wish you would pick up. You won't believe the client our uncle set me up with. I'm not going to lie, the lawsuit he was attempting to bring onto his wife could have been something written out of a novel." I pause and breathe a heavy sigh. I bite down on my bottom lip. "I'm sorry I haven't talked to you since the funeral. I don't know. Between turning down this client and the conversation Frederick had with us then, I just don't know what the hell I'm even doing anymore. I know our family isn't exactly in the best position right now, but I don't think that warrants me taking on any client who waltzes through our door. We need legitimate cases to reestablish our family name. You know what I mean? Anyway, I just wanted to tell you I'm sorry. I know I've rambled on too long for a voice-mail, and you probably won't even listen this far into it, if even at all since you despise voicemails. I love you. Call me later."

I quickly hang up, knowing Roe will never listen to my message. She'd rather just call me back than sit there and sift through the twenty other messages she probably has sitting on her phone just to get to mine. I don't blame her. I hate voice-mails too.

FIVE

LAUREL

"Are you out of your mind?" Frederick slaps a folder against his desk and falls back into his chair with a huff.

I sit in the seat opposite him and cross my arms over my chest. "He didn't have a case."

"That wasn't for you to decide," Fred argues. He stands from his chair and firmly places his hand on his hip. He starts pacing the five-foot space behind his desk. "I didn't send you over there to turn him down or talk him out of a lawsuit."

"What exactly did you send me over there for, then?" I ask skeptically, pinning him with daggers. "The man is having an affair with his gardener, and so is his wife. It's not as if she's stolen money from him and has run off with it. They were both screwing the same man. She hasn't done anything he hasn't already."

"Our firm needed this." He frowns, disappointed. He repeats it the same way he's said it the past one thousand times. He stabs his finger on the desk. "You could have found a way to make a case."

"Frederick." I sigh, sitting forward in my chair. I rest my hands on the edge of my desk. "You know that isn't how it always works. I'm a damn good lawyer, and you know that, too."

"I do." His eyes sadden as he turns to me. "You're like your father in that way."

I ignore his comment. I don't want to be like my father.

"I promise I will find another case I know we can win."

"I hope so." My uncle sits back down behind his desk, rocking against his seat. Sadness and guilt weigh heavy in his expression. He looks me straight in the eye. "If you weren't my niece, I would have been forced to let you go at this point. I don't want it to come to that but..."

The sincerity in his statement weighs on my shoulders. I swallow, knowing the struggle he's facing with keeping the firm afloat is in direct relation to what my brother did to the Branford name. The crimes he committed have had a lasting effect on our family and me in particular. Like my uncle, I've tried to keep our heads above water, hoping to rebuild what's been broken. And although my uncle may be desperate enough to consider taking on clients like Mr. Wright, I'm not ready to give in so easily.

"I understand." I nod. "I'll find another case to take up—one that is worthy of being represented by our name. There's no use in forcing cases when they will only further damage our reputation, Fred."

"Fine." He waves me off, clearly done with this conversation as well.

Frustration forms a tight knot in my chest. All my uncle ever sees is dollar signs, not caring the path he takes to make his money. Legitimately. Although my uncle's morals aren't as askew as my brother's, I can't help but sniff the same undertones of greed surrounding him.

I slide out of my chair and leave his office. I'm ready to call this shit show of a day to an end, but if I'm going to prove my decision of refusing to pick up Mr. Wright's case was the right one, I need to start putting feelers out for a new potential case.

On the way to my office, I check my phone to see if Roe called me back. She didn't, but I at least have a text from her.

> Roe: Sorry, I was having lunch with Steven. I'll call you later tonight.

I type out a quick reply to my sister and push through the door to my office. The second I make it through the door and shut it behind me, I slide out of my heels and my blazer.

But when I look up, I gasp and fall back against the door. I raise my hand to my chest and stare at the person sitting behind my desk.

"Is this a habit of yours?" he asks, slowly wagging his finger up and down. "Getting undressed in your office?"

"What are you doing here?" I concentrate on my hand, counting the breaths I'm taking. Lennon Harding has never step foot in my office. Ever.

He's sitting in my chair, relaxed, with a smug expression. His deep blue eyes roam up and down my body as he runs his thumb across his lower lip. He smirks in delight before pushing away from my desk, rolling in my chair. He stands, adjusting his tie and buttoning his jacket as he crosses my office toward me. His eyes move up and down my body again. The corner of his mouth slowly curls, and his dark eyes flicker. "How far does this go? Is it your skirt next, or is it the blouse?"

He stops close enough to touch me. My cheeks burn. I lower my hand and take a deep breath, inhaling Lennon's scent. I try not to make it too obvious the way my body reacts to it.

"You're ridiculous." I lower my hand and push off the door, walking around Lennon.

He's quick to follow me, sitting down in the seat opposite

my desk. I sit down in my own desk chair, thankful to have a three-foot-wide piece of furniture now between us.

Lennon's black suit hugs every inch of him. He doesn't look different than any other time I've seen him. Dark suit with tattoos peeking out of the sleeves of his undershirt. His dark hair resting just above his brow.

I raise an eyebrow and lean back. "Is this a habit of yours? Breaking into people's offices when they aren't in them?"

He laughs, his smile reaching his dangerous blue eyes. "It's hardly breaking in when the door is left wide open."

I shake my head in disbelief. "Having the Harding name doesn't give you permission to go wherever you please, Lennon."

His smile fades, and the light in his eyes disappears. He clears his throat. "I was under the impression Branfords thought the same."

He tilts his head to the side, narrowing his sinfully gorgeous eyes. If I weren't already sitting, I'd know the way he's looking at me would make me go shamefully weak in the knees.

I chew on the inside of my cheek and sigh. "What do you want? I've had an awful day already. Don't you have your father's business to take over and run now?"

He pops an eyebrow. "That bad of a day, huh?"

"Yes." I don't tell him about my meeting earlier with Mr. Wright or the discussion I just had with my uncle. "I'm sure you get bad days every now and then, too, but then again, that would mean you have feelings." I pause, giving him the darkest glare I can summon.

He's quiet as he rests his elbow on his chair. His eyes move to the window behind me overlooking the city.

"I saw you at the funeral." His eyes swing back to mine.

I swallow. It's difficult not to look at him without the image of the woman kneeling in front of him, sucking on his cock. But it's also difficult looking into his eyes now, remembering the vacancy in his eyes that day. Losing a parent is a feeling I'm all too familiar with. I wouldn't wish it even on my worst enemy. Even Lennon.

"What do you mean?" I swallow again. My skin tingles as I hold my breath. Does this mean he remembers our night together?

"You're a Branford." He states, dryly. "Branford's always seem to insert themselves in places they think will benefit them."

"Oh," I shoot him an icy glare and clear my throat, brushing off his calloused comment. And the disappointment working its way under my skin. "I was sorry to hear about your father."

"I wasn't."

I nervously swipe my tongue across my lips, unsure how to answer him. Maybe he doesn't feel the same grief I did.

"Oh, well." I wring my fingers in my lap.

"It's no secret my father was an asshole, Laurel. You certainly know that more than others."

"I do," I admit, thinking back to the night at the restaurant, Eclipse. James had brought me there, hoping to get me into one of his sons' beds so he could sneak his way into making a deal with our law firm. Despite the trap he'd put me in, he lost that night. He didn't make a deal, and I hadn't fucked either of his sons. That night, at least.

"Well," I grip onto the edge of my desk and stand. My feet pad across the floor as I round the desk, holding the door open for Lennon. "I have an appointment with a client in less than thirty minutes. So, if you'll excuse me."

Lennon stands and crosses my office. He places his hand on mine, keeping eye contact with me as he closes the door. I hold my breath, and my skin grows hot.

"I haven't gotten to my reason for being here." The door clicks shut.

I find myself standing in the same position I was in when I first stepped in here. My back is against the door and Lennon is in front of me, impossibly close.

Suddenly, I'm more nervous than I've ever been. The oxygen gets caught somewhere between my mouth and my lungs, never making it all the way down.

"Marry me."

The two words float between us like a hot air balloon. They swell, pressing against our chests.

Now the oxygen is completely stolen from my lungs, choking me.

At first, I don't think I've heard him correctly, but the lack of movement or follow up from Lennon tells me he's serious.

"Excuse me?" I gasp.

He lifts his arm and rests his hand on the door above my head, his scent surrounding me again.

"My father." His voice lowers. "My father placed a condition on me inheriting the company."

"And that condition is to get married?"

"Yes."

"Fine." I raise my chin and rest my head against the door to look up at him towering over me. "The woman you were with at the funeral seems like she would be a perfect choice for your wife."

He shakes his head slowly, the corner of his mouth curling. "It isn't that simple."

"Marrying someone isn't simple."

"You're right. But this condition makes it more complicated than usual. You're the only one I can marry."

A laugh escapes my mouth. Lennon doesn't flinch.

"Me?" I ask in disbelief. "Why me?"

"My father never felt he had to give reasons for his decisions, Laurel. It's part of the reason he got our family to where it is now." His eyes search my face. "He gave us thirty days to get married. I've already wasted three."

"He gave us less than a month to get married?"

"Yes," he says firmly. "And we have to stay married for at least one year or else our marriage doesn't count, and I lose the company."

"I'm not marrying you."

My shock transforms to anger. Lennon's proposal is reminiscent of my marriage to David. Despite the feelings I have when I'm around Lennon, it still doesn't change the fact I would only be his wife out of mere convenience. I would only be used as a means to an end. The same as what happened with David.

"I don't think you understand how badly I need this," he says. "I need to take on this company. If I don't, no one else will, and our entire empire will fall. We will lose it all."

"What do you mean, you'll lose it all?" My anger is twisting and tightening in my chest. "Don't you have two other brothers who can help? You can't tell me you don't have some sort of loophole you can find to get out of this."

"It's not that simple, Laurel. Don't be so naïve. There is no loophole, and no one else can run this company. You know my brother Jude no longer works for our firm, and Micah isn't ready."

My eyebrows shoot up. "Micah isn't ready?" I don't hold back my cynical laughter. It climbs up my throat with minimal effort. "And what, you think you are? You can't force someone to marry you, Lennon."

I know my tongue is laced with resentment, but I can't help it. The realization Lennon is proposing to me in the only way he's capable of makes my bad day somehow turn even worse.

A business transaction. No feeling. No emotion hidden behind those cursed, beautiful eyes.

There's still no recollection of the night we met buried behind them. No sudden epiphany. No memory of the night I straddled his lap while he whispered sweet nothings into my ear.

His eyes are as vacant as his heart.

My body betrays my mind. Because as much as Lennon has shown me who he is over the past few years, I saw a different side to him the night we met. There was a softness to all the edges he's kept sharpened since.

I'm drawn to Lennon despite his coldness, but my mind won't allow me to entertain his proposal.

"Tell me what it will take for you to agree." He squares his jaw, unwilling to back down. "Is it money? I've heard your family doesn't have the same notoriety it once had. Sounds like they could use a marriage like ours."

"Yeah." Tears sting the back of my eyes. "My family might need this, but I don't."

I blink and inhale a deep breath, stepping to the side to get out from under Lennon's body, but his free hand is quick to wrap around my wrist, stopping me before I have the chance to turn away. "How much?"

My chest fills with immense shock. "You can't *buy* me, Lennon. I deserve a marriage that holds more value than money."

I hide the echo of the pain from my marriage with David. A marriage that only held monetary value and nothing else.

"Trust me, Laurel." He growls. "When you're my wife, I'd make sure our marriage meant more than money."

My breath catches and my heart pounds. I don't exactly understand what he means. Much like the night we met when he talked about sweet nothings. Cryptic and mysterious. That's all Lennon will ever be.

I swallow his promise of what a life would look like if he

were to make me his. "I'm not certain you can do anything that isn't self-serving."

Lennon's hardened eyes soften only slightly. At first, I think I might get a glimpse of the Lennon I met all those years ago, or at least a moment of recognition, but it fades before I'm even certain I saw it.

He loosens his grip as if my words are an arrow shooting straight to his inflated ego. Slowly and deliberately, he drags the tip of his finger along the length of my arm. I shiver, and my breath catches. His eyes follow his touch. He stops at the base of my throat as if to count my pulse.

The memory of his touch six years ago comes back full force. A trail of heat blazes up my arm to where his hand is resting on my throat. I imagine a ring wrapped around his fourth finger. One that would show everyone he was mine.

Considering the type of man Lennon is and the world he comes from, it's a difficult concept to imagine. Especially in a world where the ring would be tied to me.

"I'm not trying to buy you. I..." He closes his mouth, and his nostrils flare. His eyes meet mine, cold as fucking steel. "Forget it."

With bitterness simmering in my veins, I manage to speak around my racing heart. "A pleasure as always, Mr. Harding."

With a hardened stare and a fixed jaw, he pushes away from the door. His stiff, rigid shoulders don't so much as flinch when I open the door and hold it open for him once again.

It isn't until he brushes past me and he's left my office do I finally allow oxygen to fill my lungs again.

Then reality hits.

Lennon Harding just asked me to be his wife and I said no.

SIX

Lennon

I don't know what I was expecting.

It's not that I had imagined Laurel immediately saying yes and jumping at the chance to marry me, but I didn't expect her rejection to cut as deep as it did.

I'm sitting in my office, but all I can think about is the woman I asked to be my wife working three floors below.

"Explain it to me again," Micah mutters, tapping his finger on the screen of his phone. He hasn't looked up once since he sat down fifteen minutes ago. "What exactly did you say to her?"

"I asked her to marry me, and she said no." I massage my forehead with my fingertips and read over the contract Micah brought in with him, looking up long enough to gauge my brother's reaction.

He stops tapping and finally looks up. "Did you ask her to marry you, or did you tell her to?"

"What's the difference?" I ask, dropping the paper.

"It matters. You honestly didn't believe she would say yes that easily, did you?"

"I was honest with her and told her the conditions which

were placed on me to secure the company. She's a business-woman; I thought she'd understand. Or at least consider it."

I'm only giving my little brother half-truths. Laurel is more than a businesswoman, and on more than one occasion I've seen her lead with her heart rather than her mind. She's smart, but the kindness in her gorgeous eyes is difficult to ignore.

Women like her don't simply marry for money or notoriety. She deserves more than a transactional marriage.

I look at my brother, hoping he'll offer me words of wisdom, but he doesn't.

"What am I supposed to do?" I ask him, hoping I can dig some advice out of him. It's not as if he's an expert when it comes to marriage. As the youngest out of the three of us, and the one who travels the most, I've never seen him with a woman for longer than a few weeks.

"I don't know." He shrugs. "Not that I'm saying it was never a possibility, but the idea of you being married is a foreign concept. I never thought we'd be in the situation we're in now."

"Neither did I." I sigh.

"I'm sorry, brother. I can't imagine what it's like to have to convince a stranger to marry you. Let alone to *be* married to one."

I hide the truth behind a chuckle. "Yeah."

"Do you know much about her?"

I curl my fingers into a fist under my desk. "Not really." I lie. "I know she's a headstrong lawyer. Her record is great, but her working for her uncle isn't doing her any favors. I also did a little research into her brother. It seems he's going to be in prison for quite some time and he's facing some heavy charges."

"What about her parents?"

"They died three years ago in an accident." I shrug. "I didn't read the article, only the headline." I swallow, wishing I had a drink in my hand to drown the feeling coming over me.

"Huh." Micah rubs his chin in thought. "Seems our family has a lot in common with the Branfords, then."

"It appears so." I toss the paper into Micah's lap and cave, standing to pour myself a drink. "I'm useless here until I get this situation figured out."

"There was nothing in Dad's will that didn't say you couldn't help me with our offshore accounts.".

He's right. Micah deals mostly with our international clients. It's probably why our father left all the properties overseas to him. It makes it easier for him to acquire more clients when he has more of a presence over there.

"I'm not going to be of much help, even if the will didn't prevent me from advising you." I sigh, downing half my drink.

Micah stands and slides the contract back into his leatherbound folder. "I have a flight to catch, anyway. I need to get this out to London before we lose out of the deal altogether." He gives me a sympathetic smile. "I'll text you when I get there."

I give him a smile in return, and once the door shuts behind him, I refill my drink and sit back behind my desk to click the button on my desk phone.

"Yes, Mr. Harding?" my assistant Olivia's voice comes through the small intercom.

"Do you have any messages for me?" I ask her, imagining what Laurel might be doing in her office, half undressed.

"Um. No, sir. Were you expecting a call? I can make a note of it so I can let you know as soon as I hear from them."

"No," I'm quick to answer. "It's fine, but I'd like it if you could clear my schedule for the rest of the day." I let go of the button and realize there wasn't much of a schedule for Olivia to clear. I can't get a single contract signed or client agreement until I solve the issue of being married.

Our entire company is at a standstill. I wonder if my father ever considered the repercussions of putting such a heavy stipulation on my inheritance.

The silence in my office becomes too much to bear and the memory of being in Laurel's office yesterday bleeds into my thoughts.

Her skin was smooth and warm. An unfamiliar feeling snuck its way into my chest, jump starting my heart as if it were on the brink of collapsing. The jolt didn't last long, disappearing as fast as it grew to life.

I slide back in my chair, my eyes falling to my desk. The past several years have been spent grinding and proving my worth to my father. I spent countless days and weeks, pushing aside the pain of losing my mother. My world spun on its axis that day, spiraling out of control, and I wanted nothing more than to forget what it was like to feel. Caring no longer mattered when I found myself trapped in a world where she no longer existed.

Until I met *her*.

While taking a sip from my drink, I crack open my desk drawer. Wisps of air brush along the delicate purple feather resting beside a black velvet box. I rub my thumb over the box, attempting to bury my thoughts once again.

The way Laurel's skin prickled as I whispered into the hollow of her ear.

The hope in my mother's voice as she told me what she wished for me.

I slam the drawer shut and down the rest of my drink before I give the memories a chance to swallow me whole.

SEVEN

LAUREL

Marry me.

The memory of Lennon's voice hasn't faded since he said those words to me two days ago.

Depositions and court filings- you name it -I've poured over nearly every legal document in my office in the hopes of getting my mind off Lennon. His touch. The way his voice sounded when he said the words *'when you're my wife,'* and the way it made my thighs instinctively clench.

Even his scent still lingers in my office. I haven't been able to get rid of it. I've even gone so far as lighting a few candles and buying a few plug-in air fresheners. Either they haven't worked, or I subconsciously bought ones that smelled exactly like him.

Although I haven't been able to rid my office or mind of his presence, I'm thankful for the certain relief the weekend will bring. It took all I had not to think of Lennon working three floors above me. Since learning Lennon remembered our night about as well as someone suffering from amnesia, it's been diffi-cult knowing he's only a short elevator ride away. Not that I planned on seeing him after his outrageous proposal, but I'd be lying if I didn't imagine what life as Lennon Harding's wife would look like. Even if his reasons are purely for corporate gains versus his actual feelings toward me.

The sun peeks through the windows, and the scent of banana muffins fills every corner of my small, one-bedroom apartment. The brick interior and piles of books on every bookshelf are a stark contrast to the corporate life I lead. Between the apartment and the muffins, I think of my mother. We may have come from a rich family, but my mother never let that stop her from baking.

Muffins, cookies, breads.

You name it, my mother baked it. Luckily for me, she taught me as best she could, and ever since, I've found it's a great stress reliever.

I'm sliding my tray of banana muffins out of the oven when the lock on my front door twists and clicks. Roe struggles with her key before finally yanking it out. Her hair is tied in a tight ponytail. The end swishes across her back as she dramatically closes the door behind her.

"Just in time!" I yell over my shoulder, turning back to my creation. "Muffins just came out."

"You really need to get that lock adjusted. My key always gets stuck," she says, dropping her keys on the counter.

I crack a smile and turn off the oven. "I should have left it unlocked since I knew you were coming over."

It feels like it's been ages since I've seen or spoken to my sister. Despite her text message the other day, she didn't bother to call me back until last night. With quick hands, I pop two muffins out of the pan and place them on a plate. After grabbing a knife and the tub of butter from the refrigerator, I spin around to face Roe. She's sitting on the opposite side of the counter with her arms resting on the top. The space under her eyes is slightly darker than the last time I saw her. I think. It's been a while so I can't be certain.

"You're either stressed or you're seeing someone."

I hold my knife mid-slice. Steam billows through the crack I've created in the bread. The heat wanders up to what I'm sure is a suspicious expression on my face—one my sister most likely can read.

"What makes you say that?" I laugh.

"Because..." She holds up three fingers and points at each of them. "You only ever bake when you're stressed, sleeping with someone new and you don't know where you stand with them afterward, or you're dating someone."

I roll my eyes. "Not true."

"It is." She cracks a smile. "So, which one is it?"

I dig out a clump of butter and spread it across the muffin, watching it disappear. Shaking my head, I hand Roe her muffin, then cut into mine.

Once I'm finished with mine, I put the butter back into the refrigerator and look at Roe. The story of Lennon's surprise proposal sits on the tip of my tongue. I played over this moment, imagining the look on her face when I tell her the richest, most eligible bachelor in Boston has asked me to be his wife. I also imagined the expression on her face when I tell her I turned him down.

Because for me, I know a marriage with Lennon would develop as more than transactional on my part, and the possibility of never being more to him solidified my decision in saying no.

It isn't until this moment, as I'm biting into my butter-soaked banana muffin, do I realize my fake marriage to David has done more damage than I thought.

Baking truly is therapeutic.

"It's neither." I swallow my bite. "Everything is fine. I was simply in the mood to bake."

"Does this have to do with the other day at work, after that meeting you told me about? The one with Mr. Wright?"

Goosebumps prickle down the back of my neck. I comb over mine and Roe's texts, wondering if I somehow accidently let it slip about Lennon's proposal.

His hand on my wrist. His deep voice begging me to be his wife.

Marry.

Me.

I inhale a shaky breath and open my mouth to begin my denial, but she stops me.

"Frederick is going through a lot right now with the firm." She places her elbow on the counter and cradles her chin with her hand. "I'm sure he didn't mean it when he said he might have to let you go."

Relief washes over me.

"You may be right." With all the uncertainty of Frederick's law firm, I have considered why I haven't left yet. It's almost as if I see it coming down the line. I'm standing on the tracks, watching as the train comes barreling toward me, blasting its horn a thousand times in warning. But still, I stay.

I stay because of my family name. I stay despite the way my uncle undermines my ability to be a good lawyer more times than he's placed his faith in me. Maybe I'm staying in the hopes I can somehow turn the eyes of the city back onto us with admiration instead of pity.

While swiping my mouth with my napkin, my eyes fall to Roe's untouched plate.

"What's going on with you?" I ask her, tilting my head to the side. "Are you and Steven okay?"

She blinks and her eyebrows rise. "Of course. What made you ask?"

I shrug. "I just haven't seen him in a while."

"Oh." She frowns, picking at her muffin. "Right. He's just been busy traveling, looking for new works and exhibits to buy for the museum." Her eyes remain focused on her muffin.

I dip my head lower to pull her attention back. "What's up, Roe?"

When she swings her gaze up to mine, my heart cracks and splinters. With two large, glassy eyes, tears line her lashes, spilling over the second she blinks.

She hiccups as she inhales a splintering breath.

My heart drops. When we were eight, I sat with her as she cried after her best friend told her she didn't want to play with her at recess anymore. When we were sixteen, she'd climbed into my bed in the middle of the night, sobbing, telling me she'd just given her virginity to her boyfriend, and immediately after, before they both re-dressed, he broke up with her.

But the pain in Roe's eyes then is a different depth than the one I see now.

"I need to tell you something." She sniffs. Her chin quivers, and I hold my breath.

"Okay," I whisper.

"I, um..." Her voice trembles. "I have cancer."

When the main character in nearly every novel I've read hears devastating news or tragedy strikes, they always describe it in great detail. Unsteady and knocked off balance; the world crumbles at their feet. Their vision grows blurry, and the ringing in their ears is so loud, it feels as if they've been submerged under water.

But none of it is true.

The world falls silent. Painstakingly silent.

I don't hear my shallow, ragged breaths. I don't hear Roe's uncontrollable sobs climbing from her chest.

There's only silence. Seconds pass before I'm able to hear again.

"What?" I manage to ask. "What do you mean you have cancer?"

"I went to the doctor a few weeks ago." She's sniffing as she wipes her nose with the back of her hand. "My back had been hurting and I couldn't think of anything that might have caused it. After they took a scan and ran some tests, they found cancerous cells in my cervix."

"Isn't that treatable?"

"Normally, it is. But the cells have spread, and they found a tumor attached to my lung on the scan."

Next thing I know I'm wrapping my arms around my sister and pulling her to me. She rests her chin on my shoulder, then shifts her head to bury her face into it. Her tears soak into my shirt, but I don't care. I hold my sister, thinking of all the moments in the past few weeks when I've noticed a shift in her appearance. In her mood. I hold her and think of all the times we've been there for each other.

After a few minutes, she loosens her arms around me, pulling away.

"So, what's the treatment plan? I'm assuming they have one, right?" I've gone into planning mode. My tears haven't exactly dried, but the initial shock has faded enough for me to start asking questions.

"I'm supposed to start the first round of chemo next week, then after eight weeks they want to do surgery to remove the tumor on my lung. Combined with the size and where it's sitting, it's too dangerous to remove it without shrinking it first."

I nod and digest what she's telling me. It's hard to concentrate on her every word when my heart is still breaking with her news.

"Okay," I tell her, lifting my hand to tuck a few loose strands of hair behind her ear. I slide onto the barstool next to her. "I'll be there for you. Whatever you need."

"Thank you." Her bottom lip begins to wobble again and another tear spills from her eye. "But I won't be able to do the treatment."

"What do you mean? Of *course* you're doing the treatment."

"Well, since I started working freelance, only selling my pieces one at a time, I have no insurance of my own. I only have Steven's medical insurance. And after my diagnosis, I found out they will only cover twenty percent of the chemotherapy and none of the surgery."

"What the fuck?" My skin burns with anger.

"Yeah," she chuckles. "Turns out our medical insurance isn't that great."

"I'll give you what I can." I don't hesitate, trying to remember the amount of money I currently have sitting in my bank account. "It isn't much, but it has to be worth something."

With my uncle keeping me as junior lawyer at the firm, and with our brother tarnishing our family name, my income hasn't exactly been up to par for a Harvard Law graduate.

"Treatments are thousands and thousands, Laurel. Not to mention the surgery alone will be insane. If Steven and I hadn't used all of our savings to buy the house and pay off the tuition for my master's degree, we'd be able to afford it. Between my empty trust fund and our depleted savings, there's simply nothing left." My sister swipes at her cheeks. "I can't ask you to pay for it, Laurel."

"You're not asking me. I'm offering."

"No. I won't allow you to go broke because of me."

"It's not as if you're asking me to buy you an expensive purse or pay for you to go on some ridiculous trip," I cry. "I can't sit by and do nothing. We'll figure out a way. What did Steven say? Surely he or his family can help."

"His family never agreed to our marriage. We haven't

spoken to them in years." She looks right at me. "We can't ask them."

"Okay." I slap my hands on my lap and run my hands along my thighs. "We'll talk to Frederick. Maybe he can—"

"No," she cuts me off. "I'm not asking him for money. The law firm is losing money by the week. Plus, I don't want anyone else to know. At least not yet."

"You have cancer, Roe." My vocal admission makes me want to vomit. Somehow saying it out loud makes it even more real, as if that makes a difference. The cancer is still inside her, threatening to consume her.

"I'm aware," she clips back with watery eyes. "That's why it's my decision on who gets to know and when."

I'm falling apart. Maybe what they write in novels is true.

The pain swirls and transforms in her eyes. With the way our brother effortlessly ruined our family's reputation, it's difficult for Roe to trust. Same could be said for me.

"Of course." I swallow the rock in my throat.

"Please. The last thing we need is for a rumor to spread about how one of the Branford daughters is sick and they can't afford treatments. After the publicity covering Kellan's case, and Mom and Dad's death years ago, this will only make it worse. I refuse to be the victim in a family already suffering from greed and grief." She wraps her hands around mine and squeezes them. I feel absolutely helpless. I want to take her pain away. I want to wake up and realize this is all a very, very bad dream. But it isn't.

Her hands wrapped around mine are real, and the drying tears on her cheeks are cold, hard evidence.

Resentment and rage bubble to the surface. I don't often think about Kellan. After his sentencing, I made a promise to myself to never think about him or talk to him again. The sting of what he did only worsened our parents' deaths. He'd taken the legacy our father had built and completely destroyed it.

"I know it isn't fair to ask you," Roe continues. "But you and Steven are the only ones who need to know. At least for now."

"But what about the money?"

"I told you." She gives me a weak, reassuring smile. "I'll figure it out. Don't worry."

"But what happens if you don't?" I'm not entirely sure I want to know her answer. Or maybe I already know it. I just don't want to hear it spoken out loud into existence.

"I don't know." She shrugs and runs her thumb across the back of my hand. "The probability of me surviving the chemo and surgery is low, Laurel. It might not even work."

"Don't say that!" I cry, pulling her close. I cradle her head in my hands and hold her against my chest. Her small arms wrap tightly around me. I've never seen Roe this vulnerable. This scared.

I hold my sister until her tears have dried and her shoulders have stopped shaking. Insistent on going home, Roe eventually leaves my apartment an hour later. She never did eat her muffin. I toss it in the trash and slide the plate in the dishwasher. The echo of our conversation vibrates against the walls, and I find myself crawling into bed before the sun has completely gone down.

It takes me longer than usual to fall asleep.

I lie curled under the safety of my sheets, but when I close my eyes, all I see is Roe. I see all the times she was there for me growing up. I see her teaching me how to write my name. I see her placing flowers in my hair for prom. I even see her positioning my matching birthday crown on my head the night of my nineteenth birthday.

But amidst all the memories rolling through my mind like a movie reel, worry and reality nestle in between each clip. My stomach wobbles with the uncertainty of the future, and thinking about the future makes me think of my mother, then thinking about my mother makes it a struggle to breathe.

Unable to stop my thoughts, I scramble out of bed looking for a solution and check my bank accounts. Every single one. There's enough to help Roe with her surgery, but it would take all the money I have. Fiery anger burns in my chest, my hate for my brother Kellan growing. It's been two years since he was convicted, but the pain and agony he caused our family hasn't waned. The damage he left behind hasn't faded. If only Kellan hadn't stolen my inheritance, Roe would have all the money she would need.

When my eyes feel like they're about to pop out of my head, I slap my laptop shut and climb back into bed. I lay on my back and stare at the ceiling, replaying the movie of today in my mind. But when my brain finally decides to shut off, and the movie comes to its climactic end, my eyes grow heavy. And before my mind completely fades to black, one more thought creeps in.

No matter what, I'll find a way to help Roe. Because I'll do anything for those I love.

EIGHT

LAUREL

I haven't been able to sleep.

My skin is sticky, and the sheets cling to my body as if I climbed into bed after walking down the street on a misty Boston summer morning. The air in my apartment is thick and heavy. I throw my blanket aside, slip out of bed, and walk like a zombie across my bedroom. After opening both windows, my face is met with a cool breeze. I close my eyes and savor the sense of peace it temporarily gives me.

When I'm satisfied, I trudge back over to my bed and crawl back under the sheets, leaving the windows open. My skin is no longer damp, with goosebumps from the cool, dry air now pouring into my room and sending a shiver down my spine.

I don't know how long I slept, but the quiet, dark street in front of my building tells me it was probably only a few short hours.

My mind wanders to Roe. Her visit earlier comes crashing back like a wave rolling onto the shore, rough and untamed. I've never seen Roe suffer from more than a stuffy nose or a sore throat. But this is a sickness that isn't as insignificant as the common cold. Cancer eats away at muscle, bone, tissue, and soul until either one concedes. And that's *with* treatment.

Roe might not get it unless we find a way.

I swipe my current read from my nightstand, hoping it will take my mind off the helplessness and pain I'm feeling.

Cracking it open, I read the first line.

I read it again.

Then I read it again.

And again.

I snap the book shut with a huff and toss it beside me on the bed.

Reading isn't helping.

Groaning, I reach for my phone. I don't have any messages from my sister. I think about texting her, but she's a ridiculously light sleeper. Even the faintest noise wakes her. I never understood how she was one of those people who wake at a tiny ping of an incoming text.

I'm mindlessly scrolling through social media when a tiny bubble pops up in the top corner of my screen. I gasp, immediately recognizing the large gold letter 'H' as the user's profile image.

With a shaky finger, I tap the bubble and read the message.

Lennon Harding: Having a hard time sleeping?

How could he have possibly known that?

I prop myself up on my elbows and peek through the open windows of my bedroom. Lennon can't possibly know where I live. Having only been classified as business acquaintances at best over the past year, I doubt he's taken the time to figure out where I live.

The street is just as quiet and empty as it's been since I've been awake.

I shake my head and feel myself cracking a small smile. It doesn't last long but it's enough for me to notice.

> Me: How did you know? Unless you're standing outside my building, peeking through my window like a creeper.

> Lennon: I'm not outside your window... unless you want me to be. ;)

My heart hammers in my chest.

> Me: Doesn't answer my question.

I chew on my thumbnail, anticipating Lennon's response. I may be ignoring his last message in my reply, but I read over it again, aware of his meaning.

A small bubble pops up underneath my message. Three dots roll repeatedly as he types until it comes through.

> Lennon: I couldn't sleep either.

> Me: I tried reading a book, but it wasn't helping, so I found myself absentmindedly scrolling. Maybe you could try reading a book.

> Lennon: I don't even think I own a book.

> Me: You've got to be joking. Everyone owns at least one book.

> Lennon: Have you reconsidered my proposal, Mrs. Harding?

I jerk back as a gasp escapes my parted lips. Apparently, it's his turn to divert the conversation. I'm quick with my response, ignoring the giddiness I feel inside at reading *Mrs. Harding*. It does things to my insides I don't have the energy to admit.

> Me: No, and the answer is still a no.

My thighs tense and my stomach flips. I haven't been able to get the other day in my office out of my head. Our conversation pauses for entirely too long considering the rate of our responses up until now.

Now he's called me Mrs. Harding, too. I wasn't expecting the physical response that would occur when reading a name that isn't even mine, but one that *could* be.

The bubbles return followed by the tiny, short vibration in my hand.

> Lennon: I'm not joking about the book, but even if I had one, I doubt it would help.

His response surprises me. Lennon is relentless in his business pursuits, much like his father, so I'm caught off guard by his lack of argument. Maybe sleep deprivation is to blame.

I stop chewing on my thumbnail and inhale a deep breath before typing out my next message. Curiosity gets the better of me. I must be going out of my mind.

> Me: Do you want to tell me why you couldn't sleep?

The bubble with three dots appears and disappears several times before a message finally comes through.

> Lennon: Only if you tell me why you couldn't sleep either.

I roll to my side and allow my fingers to hover over the screen. The realization that I'm messaging Lennon Harding in the middle of the night finally sinks in. On top of having a conversation with him, he's the one who initiated it. A spark flickers in my chest at the idea I'm seeing a side to Lennon few have ever seen. *Three a.m., can't sleep Lennon.*

I can't tell him the true reason why I haven't been able to shut my mind off. I promised Roe.

Me: You go first.

Lennon: I found my father the day he died. He was laid back on his balcony in a puddle of whiskey with a bag of cocaine clutched in his hand. After calling the police, I stared at him and felt nothing. I wasn't sad. I wasn't angry. At his funeral, I didn't shed a single tear. One after one, people we've known our entire lives came up to me to offer their condolences, and again, I felt nothing.

Lennon's confession hits me hard. I hold my breath and consider how to respond. One minute he's teasing me about standing outside my window, the next he's confessing his lack of empathy for his father's death.

I imagine what he must be doing now, lying in bed with the blue glow of his phone on his face the same way as mine. Shirtless and covered in tattoos. I've never seen all of them. Even the night we met, though he didn't have nearly as many then. I only know this because I remember watching my hands as they glided over his bare chest and neck through the small opening of his collared shirt. Now his tattoos easily peek out of those five figure suits he wears.

But along with imagining him in his bed, I also imagine the pain in his eyes. The same pain I caught a glimpse of as I straddled his lap before he effortlessly slid his cock inside me.

> Me: I haven't spoken to my brother since the day of his sentencing. When the jailers cuffed him, before they ushered him out of the courtroom, he looked back at me and mouthed how he was sorry and how he would make things right again. For him and for our family. I didn't answer him. Instead, I silently hoped he wouldn't. I wanted him to pay for what he did.

> Me: I think grief wears many different masks, Lennon. Some of us are just better at wearing it than others.

Without even realizing, I've told Lennon a truth I've never spoken out loud. I've never even told Roe. She wasn't there the day of the sentencing, refusing to face him.

Assuming Lennon already knows the story about Kellan's arrest, I wait as he reads my response.

The bubble with three dots doesn't pop up for several minutes, and I think I've made a mistake. I tell my hammering heart to relax, but it doesn't. It's as if every word typed out between us has sunk in. Maybe I went too far. Maybe Lennon wasn't looking for a deep heart to heart conversation in the middle of the night. Considering his heart is cold and black, I curse myself for my momentary lapse in judgment.

> Lennon: Your turn.

I'm not surprised by his lack of acknowledgement to my confession.

Lennon will always be a Harding.

> Me: My turn?

> Lennon: To tell me why you couldn't sleep.

> Me: Oh, right. It's just been a bad day. A very, very bad day.

> Lennon: This is the second time this week I've caught you on a bad day.

> Me: Doesn't the average person experience bad days every now and then? I hardly think I'm an exception.

The familiar sarcasm and cynicism I have when talking to Lennon has returned.

I huff and drop my phone beside me, then stare at the ceiling. I've allowed him to access the part of myself I've tried to suppress—the resentment for his lack of memory on my nineteenth birthday. Was I truly that forgettable? Even in a drunken stupor, I never guessed we'd be where we are today without him remembering.

Placing my hand on my chest, I count the beats beneath my skin and bone. I'm foolishly hoping it will ground me, and even though I hate myself for showing a side of myself I'm not all too fond of, I realize Lennon elicits other feelings buried deep inside me as well. Even without him here, the mere thought of him peering through my window in the middle of the night has my heart racing and my thighs twitching with desire. I need to get a grip.

Other than the Mrs. Harding comment, he hasn't even remotely said anything sexy or alluring. I can't even hear his voice. But if I did, I'm sure my reactions would be far worse. The man could be reading over a twenty-page contract, and I'd be soaking wet.

I'm lost in an imaginary world where I see Lennon's dark eyes staring up at me from between said thighs when my phone pings.

> Lennon: Did you know the confetti they release in Times Square on New Year's every year is literally made of people's wishes?

> Me: Um... no, I didn't.

Biting on my bottom lip, I re-read his message, double checking to make sure it was Lennon who sent it. It's out of place and completely off topic. It doesn't make sense.

Although it's odd, I find the corner of my mouth curling into a smile. The idea of a million strangers throwing their wishes out into the universe in the hopes they would come true in the new year is a sweet thought.

> Me: I guess it's a little bittersweet knowing the trash I've watched tossed out into the air every year on television has a little bit of meaning. What makes you bring that up?

I wait several minutes, but there's nothing.

No bubble. No three little dots. No response.

My eyes grow heavy, and although I've spent the last few minutes replaying my entire conversation with Lennon, disappointment burrows in my chest.

Talking with and seeing a different side to him played for a perfect distraction, because even though it was short lived, he opened the door and presented an escape from reality.

When sleep is on the brink of consuming me, my phone pings, and with a hammering heart, I read his message through heavy, unfocused eyes.

> Lennon: Good night, Ms. Branford x

I frown. Unsure why I'm filled with disappointment.

Exhaustion. Reality. Helplessness. Regret.

The truth.

My sister is dying, and she can't even afford the chance to lessen the odds.

Reluctantly and foolishly, I've let Lennon Harding back in.

Before my eyesight fades to black, I consider my options, remembering I would do anything for those that I love.

Even if it makes me a hypocrite.

NINE

Lennon

I've never been the sort of man who liked counting his days. My mother used to count down the days until spring, sometimes even the hours. I remember seeing her stand in front of the large window above her small garden overlooking the bay.

Seeing nothing but naked trees and not a single budding flower, she'd cross her arms and stare at it all with a smile. Then, while rubbing her hands over her arms to ward off the late winter chill that New England can never seem to shake, she'd quote her favorite Beatles song to me with an unwavering smile. "Here comes the sun, Lennon." Her grin would reach her blue-gray eyes. "Spring is coming. Twelve more days. I can feel it."

My mother may have liked to count down the days to her favorite season, but I've never taken on her tradition. Not until recently, anyway.

There are only nineteen days until my deadline to marry Laurel Branford. I should be focused on the nineteen days, but all I've been able to think about is how it's been three days since I've spoken to her at all.

Well, more like *messaged* her.

After another routine nightmare, I'd woken up in the

middle of the night to complete and utter darkness, drenched in my own sweat. The city below my high-rise apartment did nothing to bring light to the cave I'd found myself in. Darkness has consumed me long before now. I'd been absentmindedly scrolling through social media—a pastime I never indulge in—when I'd come across her gorgeous face; perfectly painted red lips and indigo eyes that shined just as bright as in person. No filter.

Laurel Branford is pure, natural fucking beauty.

It's been three and a half days since I messaged with her that night, and it takes everything in me not to press the floor level button in the elevator to her office right now. With a stiff finger, I press on my level and shove my hands into the pockets of my suit, hoping it will stave off my craving to pull the elevator to an abrupt stop when we reach her floor.

"Tomorrow morning, you have a conference call with Erik Larsson—one of your newly secured clients in Sweden. Micah emailed over the contract for his investment to start the expansion of his hotels in Boston, Cambridge, and Braintree." My assistant Olivia hands me a leather-bound portfolio. I flip it open and scan the document as she continues. "Erik understands your situation..."

I shoot her a glare.

She clears her throat.

I've tried my best to keep my father's ridiculous condition from being leaked to the media, as well as our existing clients. The last thing I need is for the media to run another scandal or story about how my father has been able to manipulate and control his family from beyond the grave.

Olivia's face immediately flushes with panic. "I'm sorry, Mr. Harding. I didn't mean to hit a nerve." She nervously licks her lips. "I just didn't want you thinking he was expecting more than a consultation tomorrow. He understands nothing will be set in stone. From what Micah said, he told Erik you were still grieving the death of your father and wouldn't be getting back to operating your full business until the beginning of next month."

"Of course he did," I mutter. Leave it to Micah to come up with a lame excuse that actually makes our business appear weak and incapable.

Worry sets in as I look up and count the levels as the elevator continues to climb to the top. We're approaching Laurel's floor.

Fuck. What is wrong with me?

Gripping the leather portfolio, I hold my breath as we pass Laurel's level. I don't breathe again until the elevator stops for my office and the doors slide open. Olivia and I step out onto the marble floor. I walk ahead of her until she reaches her desk situated outside the large oak doors to my office. She sits in her chair, booting up her computer.

"Message my brother and ask him if he ever considered discussing this excuse with me before he ran with it, or if he took it upon himself to make an executive decision without my approval," I call over my shoulder.

"Yes, Mr. Harding."

I push through the door and slam it shut behind me.

I've taken only two steps into my office when my breath is stolen from my lungs.

Seated in my oversized leather chair, with her legs crossed and a sinful smirk playing out across her red painted lips, is Laurel Branford.

"Now," she says wistfully, leaning forward on her elbows and pointing toward me. "Is this a habit of yours? Slamming the door after you enter your office, barking orders as if you own the place?"

My mouth spreads into a wide grin. The vision of her in my private space does indescribable things to my insides.

Eyeing her, I scratch at my chin, then I curl my fingers into a fist. Anything to distract me, forcing my cock to calm down.

A chuckle rumbles from my throat as I walk toward my desk. I drop Erik Larsson's contract on the top of it and bend down, leaning far enough forward to be level with Laurel, compelling my eyes not to fall to the swell of her breasts peeking out between the open collar of her white blouse.

"I seem to be rubbing off on you more than I expected, Ms. Branford." I growl. "I've underestimated you."

Her smirk has faded as she leans back in my chair. She stands, moving around the desk so we're on the same side.

Her black mini skirt hugs the full curves of her hips with every step she takes. My eyes fall to her bare feet.

I find myself grinning again. I can't remember the last time I smiled this many times in such a short time span.

"I figured if I were to go toe to toe with the infamous Lennon Harding, I may as well have ripped a page from his own book." She shrugs.

She's standing incredibly close to me. Close enough for me to touch. Close enough for me to reach out and feather my fingers across the length of her body.

Of all the sides to Laurel I've seen, this one is my new favorite.

"I wasn't aware we had a meeting scheduled," I tell her.

"We didn't... but since you left your office door open, I figured it wasn't necessary."

I swipe my thumb across my mouth, hiding my smirk. She truly did take a lesson from my playbook.

"My office is open to you always, Ms. Branford," I say, lowering my voice.

A small gasp escapes her perfect lips. Her scent surrounds me, making it impossible to concentrate on anything else other than her. I don't care she broke into my office without me here, and I sure as fuck don't care that she's interrupted and thrown off my entire schedule. "To what do I owe the pleasure of this unscheduled meeting?"

I won't deny the way my stomach lurches at the idea that she might be here because she's reconsidered marrying me. Aside from my proposal, I doubt Laurel would want anything to do with me otherwise. After she found out the truth about my father's true intentions for her, Laurel has kept her distance from me, our business, and the Harding name. At least publicly, anyway.

Without breaking eye contact, she reaches down and picks up a black folder, slaps it against my chest and tilts her head, staring into my soul with her indigo eyes. I place my hand over hers.

"I've reconsidered your proposal, Lennon," she says, her eyes falling to our connected hands. She clears her throat and slides hers out from under mine. Her gaze lifts back up to my face. "I'll marry you."

The feeling stirring inside me isn't one I was expecting. I expected to be thrilled and relieved she's accepted my father's outrageous request, but I can't ignore the echoing ache inside my chest. I told Laurel that if she were married to me, she deserved a marriage that was more than transactional, and I meant it.

She deserves more.

But I can sense her hesitance. Her uncertainty. Even when she lifts her chin and plants her hands on her hips. She thinks this is purely transactional.

"What made you change your mind? I thought you said you deserved a marriage that was more than transactional."

She blinks and swipes her tongue across her lips. I fight the urge to press my mouth to hers just to know what she tastes like.

There's an unmistakable sadness in her watery eyes. She

sniffs, playing it off as if her thoughts are beginning to stray. Something about the way her body shifts makes me want to wrap myself around her just so she isn't feeling whatever it is she's feeling.

She stabs my chest with her finger, snapping me out of my thoughts. "This is a list of conditions I have in order for me to marry you."

I pop an eyebrow and open the folder. "Conditions?"

"Yes." She nods once. "Your father put conditions on your inheritance. I think it's only fair I place a few conditions of my own."

"I wouldn't expect anything less from a lawyer," I tell her, sliding the paper out from the folder. I drop it on my desk and focus my attention to her list.

It isn't very long, typed with her family firm's letterhead at the top.

"Are these conditions negotiable?" I ask before I begin reading.

She frowns and shrugs. "Possibly. I assume these could be a starting point for negotiations. I don't want to marry you without understanding what our lives will look like once we say our vows."

I let out a small laugh and read her conditions.

Terms and Conditions to marry Lennon Harding:

1. I, Laurel Branford, will continue to work as a lawyer where I see fit. Under no condition can my husband, Lennon Harding, compel me or force me to resign or dictate which firm I work for.
2. I, Laurel Branford, get to keep my apartment, along with my property and possessions inside it.

3. I, Laurel Branford, get to have a say in all wedding plans and how it will be executed.
4. I, Laurel Branford, get to stay in contact and keep all my relationships with family and friends.

Below her list of conditions is the letter x with a line for my signature and today's date.

I look at her with raised eyebrows. "This is a fairly short list, Laurel."

And an interesting one.

She crosses her arms over her chest. "It may be short, but they're important issues to me. I just want to be clear. You know, so there wasn't any confusion on where we stand. I don't want to sacrifice the important parts of myself just by agreeing to marry you."

Her stern expression softens.

I drop her conditions on my desk and take a step closer, bringing the toes of my shoes to the tips of her bare feet. "I don't have a problem with your conditions."

Surprised, she jerks back, and her brow creases. "You don't?"

"Nope." I lift my hand and feather my finger down her cheek. I've lost all resolve. I need to touch her, and it seems she's surprised I'm not acting like the monster she clearly believes me to be. The one she's seen me be in front of society.

Little does she know she was there for me on the worst night of my life. For her, I'm never the monster.

Focusing on my path, I watch my finger as it follows the curve of her jaw and across her chin. I drag my finger across her lip. She stays still, never taking her eyes from mine.

I drop my hand.

"But I have a few conditions of my own."

"Okay," she breathes, her cheeks flushed pink.

"You can keep your apartment and everything you own inside it, but you'll be living with me at my place here in Boston."

Her eyebrows knit. "So, we'll still be staying in the city? I figured you'd want us to be in one of your other houses. Like the one where your father's funeral was held."

Caught off guard, I bite the tip of my tongue and fight the image of seeing Laurel anywhere outside of my apartment.

"No," I simply say. "My apartment in the city is where I spend most of my time. It only makes sense we live there."

The corner of her mouth lifts into a small smile, and I know she's satisfied with my answer. I can sense she wants to press me for more information, but thankfully, she doesn't. "Agreed, then."

"Good." I nod.

"What's the next condition?"

"You have access to my accounts, my drivers, and all the perks that come with bearing the Harding name."

Her eyes light with humor. "The Harding name holds that much power, does it?"

I lean closer and drag my nose along the length of her jaw. The longer we stand here, the harder it is for me to keep my resolve. It's as if all this pent-up frustration over the last few days, being forced to wait out Laurel's silence, has finally burst.

A wall has been broken down, and I can't explain how or why.

I breathe her in. My head grows dizzy from the perfume peppered along her neck and embedded in her hair. I tuck the loose strands behind her ear. Her chest stills beneath me. Her skin prickles with goosebumps as I bring my mouth to the hollow of her ear.

"I told you, Mrs. Harding," I growl. "When you're my wife, our marriage will mean more than money."

Several seconds pass before she pulls away. I look into her eyes as if I'll figure out what it was that caused her to change her mind and agree to marry me. There's a faraway look in them again. Is she running from something? Or someone?

Does she feel for me what I've always felt for her?

She still believes I don't remember our night together. At least, that's how she acts. She may not have said it to me yet, but I can see it in the way she looks at me as if she's waiting for the moment I'll prove her and everyone else right. I'll prove that I'm the cold, black-hearted asshole they all believe me to be. I'll prove I'm just like my father.

"I'm not so sure," she whispers. "All of those conditions have to do with money, Lennon. Let's not pretend this is something more than what it is."

Her words are like a sharp dagger to my chest. She only sees me for who she believes I am. As does everyone else.

Maybe that's my own doing. I've spent most of my life looking up to my father. Even when he would force me to go on his so called 'business trips'. Sure, the first part was always spent with a client, going over contracts and signing multi-million-dollar deals, but then we'd spend the next twenty-one hours in a strip club, and I'd watch as my father snorted lines of coke and drank himself into oblivion. Often, my father's driver would end up taking me back to the hotel just before I found him passed out on the floor with a stripper digging through his pockets for cash.

Living a life such as that and being the eldest son of a billionaire doesn't afford you the privilege of determining your own image. Society does that for you.

I was known as James Harding's clone, made to follow in his footsteps in every way.

Maybe that's why my father placed this condition on me. He wanted me to be just like him, hoping I'd marry for money, not for love. Love is an inconvenience. A poor business decision. One that forces you to be selfless; a trait my father was incapable of possessing.

I look into Laurel's eyes and think about my mother. I've been thinking about her a lot lately. More so than normal.

"Then, what is this, Laurel? What kind of marriage is this if we're only going into it for the money?"

"It's one of lies," she says too quickly. "One of masquerades and convenience."

"I never said it wasn't those things," I argue. "And I never said it was."

"No, you haven't... but I also know you. I think it's best we keep this business-focused."

I tilt my head to the side and study her. Laurel is fire and ice, hard and soft, both headstrong and vulnerable. She's a complex creature I can't seem to escape, and one I don't *want* to.

"Any other conditions?" she asks, her voice timid now.

"One more."

"Let's hear it, then."

"In public, we will portray ourselves as a real married couple in every way. Charity events, business meetings, family dinners. Because as I said before, our marriage will hold more value than money."

Even if this marriage was one arranged and orchestrated by my father, I made a promise, and I don't intend on breaking it.

One of her perfectly sculpted eyebrows twitches. I've noticed how her chest hasn't lifted with a breath until she whispers, "Agreed."

"Nineteen days." I smile, keeping the toes of my shoes touching hers as I twist and grab a pen from my desk. I sign my name on the line below her conditions and hand them to her. "Nineteen days until you're my wife."

"Nineteen days," she repeats. "Wow, that's coming up fast."

A small smile tugs at the corners of her mouth. It's a light one, not as convincing as the one I saw her wearing earlier, but it's enough to make my heart pound right out of my chest.

"We'd better get to planning a wedding then, Ms. Branford." I lift my hand to her face once again. I trail my finger along her cheek, tucking her hair behind her ear again before dragging my finger back down to her mouth. "By the way, that's the last time I'm ever calling you by that name. Starting now, you're Mrs. Harding."

She lightly laughs. "Lennon, I don't think it works that way. My name doesn't change until we meet at that altar, and we say, 'I do'."

"Maybe to everyone else." I growl. "But not to me."

Dropping my hand, I back away from her for the first time since we began our negotiations. I move around my desk and reclaim my chair.

I open Erik Larsson's file and look up long enough to see Laurel's chest finally expand as she takes a breath. She bends down and slides her feet back into her shoes.

Once she's finished, she stands in front of my desk and places her hands on the large oak surface. She bends down, revealing the perfect swell of her breasts beneath her thin blouse.

Her soft eyes fall to my hands, then on a shaky breath, she swings them back up to me. "I'll email you a wedding checklist tomorrow morning."

"No." I'm quick to dismiss her. "Meet me in my conference room at nine a.m. sharp."

Fuck an email. I'm itching to see her again already and she hasn't even left yet.

What is happening to me?

She straightens her back, narrowing her gaze as she looks

down at me. She crosses her arms over her chest. "Sort of bossy, don't you think? You don't own the company —or me—yet."

I pause, the familiar spark igniting under my chest. "I like this side of you, Laurel."

She gives me a challenging expression, then her shoulders relax as she unravels her arms. "Fine. We'll meet in your conference room. If we're wanting people to take this marriage seriously, we're going to need a wedding that convinces them that it is."

I grin. "Whatever you need, Mrs. Harding."

Nineteen days.

Nineteen days until we're married and the company is officially mine.

Let the countdown begin.

TEN

LAUREL

Every time he called me Mrs. Harding, I was certain I was going to combust. My skin grew hot, and I immediately became wet between my legs, my clit begging to be touched. After my impromptu meeting, I wanted to go home and change my panties, but I was already late for another meeting with a client I've been consulting for the past several months. Our case is scheduled to go to court in the next few months and I need to be as prepared as possible.

Luckily, I keep a spare pair in my desk for emergencies.

Once I've changed, and when I finish with my client, I email over the latest paperwork to Frederick and message Roe asking if I can come see her this weekend. She tells me Steven is out of town again to bid on another artist's work and she could use the company.

My heart has been heavy since she told me she was sick. I've spent the past several days researching everything I possibly could on what type of cancer she has, the survival rates, and the treatment plans. Hours of pouring over research and joining cancer support groups made my head spin and my stomach nauseous. I forwarded over all the information I found to Steven but haven't heard back from him yet. I figure if we're going to get Roe through this, it's best we work as a team to support her the best we can.

I want to tell Roe I've come up with a solution to gather up the money so she can get the surgery and the chemo treatments she'll need after. But I want to tell her when I have an invitation in hand—proof this is for real. Relief settled over me knowing Lennon still wanted to marry me, even though I turned him down when he first asked. I don't plan on touching his money for Roe's treatment. In fact, I plan to use his income as a safety net in case Roe's treatments take more than what I have in the bank.

Thankfully, the salary I make working for Frederick affords me a little wiggle room, allowing me to set aside a savings account for emergencies. And Roe's sickness is an emergency.

By the time I make it home, eat dinner, bake about a dozen more cookies than I could possibly eat, I take a shower and climb into bed, thinking about Lennon.

I'm going to be married to Lennon Harding in nineteen days. Scratch that. Eighteen days. This day is practically over.

Although the echoing pain of my marriage with David years ago will forever be engrained in my memory, something about the idea of marrying Lennon feels different.

Being around him stirs feelings inside me I never felt with David: a pounding heart, weak knees. His eyes look into mine as if I'm an algebra equation he can't solve, causing my skin to flash with heat. All physical reactions I haven't been able to control.

There's a connection to him I didn't realize I had until today, and although Lennon is using our marriage to win owner-ship of his company, I don't feel used in the same way David used me. Maybe it's because, in part, I'm using my marriage with Lennon to gain something as well.

At peace with my decision, I let sleep overtake me and try to get Lennon's voice out of my head.

Mrs. Harding.

Unlike yesterday, this time when I show up to Harding Holdings, I'm greeted by Lennon's assistant.

She's standing in the middle of the lobby, waiting for me as the elevator doors slide open. A tablet is clutched between her delicate hands as she holds it to her chest.

"Good morning, Mrs. Harding," she practically sings, holding her hand out to me. "I'm Mr. Harding's assistant, Olivia."

"Um, good morning, Olivia. It's nice to meet you." I shake her hand and smile. "But you can call me Laurel. My name isn't Harding yet."

"Oh." She blinks. "Mr. Harding informed me this morning that I was to address you by name. He insisted I call you Mrs. Harding."

Of course he did.

"No," I tell her, tightening my grip on the black leather bag I'm carrying. "Lennon may have wanted you to call me that, but I insist. You can just call me Laurel."

"Sounds good... Laurel." She breathes a sigh of relief, then gives me a smile that reaches her soft blue eyes.

She's younger than I expected her to be. Maybe slightly

older than me, but not by much. Her long blonde hair cascades way past her shoulders. A large diamond ring is wrapped around the fourth finger on her left hand.

Mine will look like that in eighteen days.

Olivia holds her arm out, gesturing down the hallway. "The conference room is back this way."

I follow Olivia down the same hallway that leads to Lennon's office but makes an abrupt turn down a different hallway. On this side of Harding Holdings, everything changes from pure white walls and floors adorned with the signature gold Harding emblem to brown wooden accents, and floor to ceiling glass walls. From the side of the floor, I can see the entire Boston skyline. Far out in the distance, I see Fenway Park and the Boston Harbor. It's the same view from my office, only a few levels higher. Three floors to be exact.

I see Lennon before I've even made it to the room. His dark blue eyes lock onto me the moment I'm within view. They follow me down the length of the glass wall. I may as well burst into flames right now.

My breath rushes out of my lungs in one gasp. His black suit clings to his muscles as he sits back in his seat, twisting a gold pen between his long fingers. His peppered jaw ticks in concentration. This is all so official and business-like. None of what Lennon and I are doing is traditional as far as engagements go. I remind myself that this is the only world he knows.

Olivia's hand wraps around the long, silver handle of the conference room door, tugging it open. She holds it out for me, and I step in.

"Mrs. Harding is here to see you, Mr. Harding," she tells Lennon.

I snap my head in her direction and shoot her a glare—one that tells her she was supposed to call me by my first name. The satisfaction on Lennon's face can already be felt in the room.

He grins, not breaking his darkening gaze away from me. "Thank you, Olivia."

Olivia mouths a quick, "*I'm sorry,*" before she shuffles out of the room in a hurry.

Her loyalty must know no bounds.

I take a seat at the opposite end of the large table. It stretches from one end of the room to the other. There are at least ten chairs on either side between Lennon and me.

I don't know why I choose the opposite end from him. I think part of me is forcing myself to keep a respectable distance from him to keep myself in check. I figure I won't be able to smell him with twenty feet of distance between us. Our past few encounters have pulled reactions out of me that became stronger than the last, which is probably part of the reason why I asked Olivia to stop calling me by Lennon's last name. I'm no stranger to the pull he has on me. I experienced it the night we met.

He's like a light switch. One flicker of the gaze in his eyes, one touch, or one shift in the tone of his voice has me melting into a puddle.

I press my legs together and lean to the side, pulling my notepad and pen out of my black leather bag. I've already made a list of several important aspects of a wedding I figured we would need to go over. I straighten my notepad and weave my fingers together, placing my hands over my notepad.

"Good morning, *Mr. Harding.*" I smile, hoping he can sense the cynicism dripping from my tongue.

"Likewise." He taps his pen on the table.

"I hear you're already having your assistant call me by your last name." I nod my head to the side, indicating the hallway Olivia ran off to before she got more of my cold stare.

"Olivia's a great assistant. She's very efficient when it comes to executing the tasks I've given her."

My stomach coils. I don't know how deep his statement goes or how far Lennon has taken his relationship with her outside of the work environment. She's possibly the woman I saw kneeling in front of him, happily giving him a blow job the day of the funeral.

I nervously swipe my tongue across my lips and adjust myself in my seat as Lennon stands. His tall frame commands the room, as he always does.

He grabs his folder and pen, carrying it to my end of the table, where he drops in the vacant spot beside me. His scent immediately surrounds me. Dammit. He smells the same as yesterday and the day he was in my office.

"Enough small talk." He sighs, leaning back in his chair. He rests his head on the back of his seat and points with his pen in my direction. "Tell me your ideas and we'll make them happen."

"Okay." I flip to the first page in my notebook. "I have all the basics down: dress, flowers, cake, venue, rings—"

"What do you want?"

"What do you mean?" I ask him, confused.

"You wrote all the basic elements to a wedding, but is that the kind of wedding you envision?" He stretches out his legs, crossing them at the ankle under the table. He angles his body in my direction, his leather shoe touching the bottom of my heel. Him going out of his way to touch me has my stomach igniting with flames again. My legs twitch, and all I can concentrate on is the bottom of my foot.

I clear my throat. "Considering our circumstances for marrying, I doubt it matters what type of wedding I want."

"No." He frowns, resting his elbow on the arm of his chair. His dark blue eyes study me. "I won't have a wedding you aren't going to be happy with."

"You're marrying me out of obligation. It's in your father's *will*."

The light in his eyes disappears. "I'm aware."

"Does it really matter then?" I ask, inhaling an unsteady breath. "We're only going to be married for a year. Why waste the time and money when it won't last?"

The conditions James put on Lennon's marriage to me is a tough pill to swallow. The idea of putting effort into a marriage, especially in the ways he outlined last night in his conditions, has me worried. I'm worried I'm setting myself up for heartbreak without realizing it.

Because I already know how easy it is to fall for Lennon.

I want to take his signs of willingness to compromise with me on wedding details and his teasing over the past week as signs I've somehow managed to thaw his frozen heart. They're hard to ignore. But with Lennon, I take everything he says and does with a grain of salt. The fact he's marrying me to gain control over his family's company always pulls me back down to earth. It's a fact I simply won't ignore just because he's given me a small glimpse into another side of himself.

"It's not your responsibility to make me happy," I confess, filling the silence.

"I think you must be confused," Lennon says, lowering his voice. "You're going to be my wife, Laurel. Your happiness is one hundred percent my responsibility."

I nearly choke on Lennon's words. He utters his confession with confidence and without hesitation.

"Now..." He waves his hand over the table. "Tell me the wedding you truly want."

I bite down on my bottom lip and imagine the wedding I've always dreamed of. David and I were married at one of the courthouses in the city. After spending a day on my uncle's yacht in the harbor, we'd taken a walk through downtown when he'd pulled us to an abrupt stop outside the courthouse. Dressed in sandals and a short summer dress, with my still wet bikini hidden underneath, he rushed with his question, and I rushed with my answer. A quick ceremony followed by a signature, and thirty minutes later, we were married. In that moment, I thought David was being romantic and spontaneous. Turns out he was simply taking advantage of me and my foolish love for him.

I stare at my future husband and picture exactly the kind of wedding I've always dreamed of.

"Although I come from a wealthy family, I've never wanted a large ceremony. Maybe about ten of our closest friends and family." I shrug, biting back the tears threatening to come. "Ever since my parents died, I haven't been able to picture a large wedding without them. I don't see the sense in having a huge affair if my father won't be there to walk me down the aisle. Of course, I'd be wearing the dress I was convinced was made for me because it must have been for it to make me feel as beautiful as I would that day. Instead of a large ten-tiered cake, we'd have a small two-tiered blueberry cake, with a honey-lavender butter-cream. The same flavor my mom used to bake for me every birthday." I lift my eyes from my generic list and look back up at Lennon. "I imagine getting married surrounded by flowers. Flowers and the ocean."

"Hmm." Lennon straightens his back. "That's better." His familiar, firm expression has now softened.

The emotion of talking about my parents' absence and the lack of my father's ability to walk me down the aisle weigh heavily on my chest. It feels as if I've held my breath for far too long. My lungs wheeze and contract, starved for oxygen, the pressure aching from the inside out.

Lennon reaches across and shuts my notebook, then presses the button on the small, black machine sitting at the end of the table. It beeps before Olivia's voice comes through.

"Yes, Mr. Harding?"

"Olivia, please return to the conference room. Make sure to bring your tablet with you."

"Yes, sir."

Lennon removes his finger from the intercom.

I open my mouth to ask him if he has any ideas for our wedding but am stopped when I see a flash of blonde hair rush down the hallway. Olivia's heels shuffle across the marble floor. She screeches to a halt and swings the door open

She stands beside Lennon, just behind him, not sitting down. I bite back a smile at her eagerness. I'm liking Olivia so far.

Tapping on her tablet, she hovers her stylus over the screen, ready to take notes.

My gaze falls back to Lennon who is staring directly at me.

"Olivia, call every bakery in Boston to see which one will be able to make a two-tiered blueberry cake with a honey-lavender buttercream. We're also going to need ten invitations printed off for our wedding date, eighteen days from now. Have a local printer design them with both mine and Laurel's name along with the date and address of the summer house on the cape."

Olivia's hand stops abruptly, and her eyes lift to the back of Lennon's head.

Summer house on the cape? I wonder if that's the same house where James's funeral was held. Unless the Hardings have more than one house along Cape Cod. I wouldn't be surprised if they did.

Olivia blinks a few times before resuming her scribbling.

"What design should I have the printer use?" she asks.

"Flowers. Lots of flowers. Be sure they email over a proof to Mrs. Harding for approval. Look for a photographer that has an opening for the day of the wedding, but make sure it's one who knows their shit. Since money isn't a problem, I expect it to be a fucking good one." He locks eyes with mine. "Also, call every bridal shop in the city and tell them they should be expecting my fiancée in to try on as many dresses she wants until she finds the one she thinks was made for her." He lifts one dark eyebrow, the corner of his delicious mouth curling into a satisfied grin. "Does that about cover it?"

I hesitate, unsure of what to say. I'm speechless.

He has me melting for him again. This time he hasn't touched me with a single finger. The only connection we have is the tip of his shoe still pressed against the bottom of my stiletto.

Heat blooms across my chest, up to my neck. I can feel tears welling behind my eyes. I don't want to cry in front of Lennon, but the fact he's giving me my dream wedding has feelings stirring inside me I haven't allowed myself to face. I'm getting my dream wedding, and my parents won't be there to see it. Not even my brother Kellan. Not that I would want him there anyway, even if he weren't locked in a prison cell.

Lennon taps his toe against the bottom of my shoe.

Is he playing footsies with me?

With my heat-flushed cheeks, my eyes fall to his hands and his long, strong fingers that once touched me in places I only find myself touching these days. But I know my touch or even my boyfriends since haven't come close to what I've experienced by the hands laid in front of me. A black rose tattoo peeks out from the bottom of his black sleeve, its stem prickled with thorns wraps and weaves down his wrist, connecting to a blooming rose on the back of his hand.

"Rings." I clear my throat. "We didn't discuss the rings."

"Right." He nods. A smile cracks along his mouth. "You leave that part to me."

We sit in silence and stare at one another. I can't explain the million thoughts running through my mind. Lennon is anything but predictable. Here I was, thinking I was waltzing into this conference room, assuming it would be like any other business meeting I've attended. But somehow I feel like Lennon has managed to rip open my chest in the sweetest way, pick apart my soul, and sew it back together again, even going so far as to place a gentle kiss on the healing wound to make it all better.

Wearing a satisfied grin, he dismisses Olivia. She rushes off to get to work on the tasks Lennon's given her just as quickly as she arrived.

When I turn my attention back to my fiancé, he's sliding a credit card in my direction.

"No." I hold my hands up. "I don't want it." It feels wrong to take his credit card.

He laughs. "You'll need it for all the shopping you're about to do."

I sigh. "I can't take your credit card, Lennon. Doesn't feel right."

He grabs my hand and turns it over. Slapping the card in my open palm, he folds my fingers closed over it. "You're going to be wife, Laurel. You can," he whispers.

I roll my eyes and sweep my tongue across my lips. His eyes fall to my mouth, but I can't stop thinking about his hands holding mine. His skin is warm, the sensation sliding all the way up my arm like silk.

I slowly and reluctantly pull my hand away, dropping the card into my black bag.

My heart hammers inside my chest as he drags the toe of his shoe down the center of my stiletto. He stops on the backside of my heel, using his shoe to pry it off my foot. With a muted clunk, it lands on the floor.

"What are you doing?" I ask, working my voice around my pounding heart.

"I like our business meetings better when you're like this." His eyes darken.

"What, shoeless?"

"No. Comfortable."

I can't help but smile.

And I don't know what's worse. The fact I'm marrying Lennon under the pretense that I won't completely fall for him, or if it's getting married to him, knowing I already have.

ELEVEN

Lennon

It's happened again.

My hands are clammy, and my muscles seize under my bed sheets. I wake in a cold sweat as heat pumps through my veins. I force myself to calm my shallow breathing, focusing on counting each breath. The blood in my veins feels like it's been injected with a straight shot of adrenaline.

Concentrated breathing usually helps, but it never erases the same nightmare from my brain. Sitting up, I drive the heels of my hands into my eyes and want to scream. I fucking hate this bullshit. It's been six years, and somehow, I still haven't moved on.

I roll out of bed and head straight for the shower to let the scorching hot water run down the length of my back, washing away the memory of my nightmare. For the first few years after her death, I saw a therapist after finding myself waking up in a panic more nights out of the weekend than not.

She'd given me medicine to help me sleep longer and harder, but it didn't work. After a year of trying, I stopped altogether. Then she'd wanted to try some hypnotic therapy, and after the first session, I decided it simply wasn't for me. I was too freaked out to do it more than once. So, instead of solving the problem or searching for another solution, I've been suffering from the same nightmare for the past six years. Without fail. Some weeks are worse than others. Sometimes the dream only appears once. If I'm lucky.

It's become a part of me; a sliver from my life I choose to ignore. At least, of course, until I wake up again, feeling as if I've been pushed off the edge of a cliff and plummeted to my death.

My tense muscles relax under the hot water, and I'm thankful for the relief it brings. I try everything I can to get my mind off my dream. I think about the wedding and how in five days, Harding Holdings will finally be in my control. With a daunting task and client list ahead of me, I think of all the money I'm going to be raking in once I'm able to close all the deals I have lined up. Erik Larsson's being one of them. The closer we reach the thirty-day deadline, the more I understand my father's reasoning. At first, I thought he was foolish for putting the company in jeopardy, considering how thirsty for power and hungry for money he was. But even though I haven't been able to close any deals and deposit money into our accounts, we haven't even made a dent in our capital. Harding Holdings has been built to sustain itself for quite some time.

After my shower, I head for my large walk-in closet, opting to wear my usual black button down and black suit. I'm closing a cufflink when my phone vibrates on top of my dresser.

My heart pounds in my chest when I see Laurel's name flash across the screen. Only five days until we're married and she's mine.

I've tried to tone down the way I react when I do or say anything that involves her, but I can't. Maybe it's nerves or maybe it's the weight of what we're about to do finally hitting me. But I won't deny the way she effortlessly pulls a reaction out of me.

I sit on the edge of my bed, sliding my feet into my shoes as I open her text.

> Mrs. Harding: Invitations are done. I told Olivia I wanted to hand deliver mine, so she left them with my front desk at work. She's sending yours out in the mail today.

Below her text is a picture of one of the invitations. Dark crimson red, purple, and black watercolor painted flowers border the small rectangular card. Printed in gold lettering is mine and Laurel's names, the date and time of the wedding, and the address of my mother's summer house. When Laurel told me she dreamed of getting married surrounded by flowers and the ocean, it was the first place that came to mind.

Normally, going to that house would be difficult, but this is different. I know my brothers will be shocked when they receive their invitations as well. I haven't spoken to them since Laurel agreed to marry me. Not because I've been avoiding them. Although if I did happen to catch sight of them, I probably would, mostly to avoid the million questions I'm certain they will have about how I convinced Laurel to go through with the wedding. A question that remains unanswered. But for the most part, I'd avoid them because I'm worried they'll see how different I am with her. For years, they've watched me keep woman after woman at arm's length. Superficial relationships. Women who are only interested in a good fuck or a juicy rumor.

I may be in the business of money and luxuries among other things. A serious relationship not being one of them.

I smile reading Laurel's text. I find myself doing that a lot more lately. It's especially odd after having woken up from my nightmare again, the adrenaline still slithering down the length of my spine and latching onto the back of my mind, refusing to let go.

I inhale a deep breath and remove the heartbreak and sadness in my mother's eyes from my mind, replacing it with the vision of Laurel the other day in my conference room. The sound of her heel falling to the floor and the gasp I heard pass through her lips. My cock started to swell at the sound, as well as from the way her body radiated heat. I imagined my fingers re-exploring her body just to watch how she reacts. Would her back arch as my thumbs grazed over her peaked nipples? Would her legs spread farther for me if I bent her over the table and slid my hand slowly along her inner thighs? Would her eyes turn hungry as her pretty little mouth begs for my cock to be inside her?

My heart is starving for the answers. I've never felt this way for any of the women I've been with.

I've been working to keep Laurel at a distance and my feelings in check. There have been a few times where I've caught myself being vulnerable with her. The first time I caught myself was when we were messaging in the middle of the night after not being able to sleep. It's not that I want to give Laurel a terrible perception of me. Although, I know she has already made one, especially since I haven't talked about the night we met. And I've pushed her away at every turn up until my father's will reading.

Wow, I can be an asshole.

But I made a promise, and I don't intend on breaking it.

Promises are sacred. Promises are spoken oaths forged in invisible steel. Promises are absolute, and a promise made on your mother's deathbed is one that is unequivocally absolute.

I type out a response.

> Me: Black flowers? A little dark for wedding invitations, don't you think?

Grinning to myself, I make a quick espresso before heading

down to meet my driver, Ray. Teasing Laurel has become my new addiction. Soon, I won't be able to control myself and I'll give in.

I'm sliding into the back seat when my phone vibrates in my hand with her response.

> Mrs. Harding: I figured it was appropriate. They match the color of your heart. lol

I try to focus on the 'lol' at the end but something in Laurel's text hits me in a place I don't expect it to.

Does she think our marriage is equivalent to a funeral? Is she dreading marrying me?

I know this situation isn't ideal, but I swear I can feel something between us. Surely, I'm not the worst person she'd be tying the knot with, right?

Hope wraps around my worries, reassuring me she wouldn't have agreed to this if she thought that way, regardless of knowing her reasoning or not.

After shutting my screen off, I stare out the window and all the buildings passing me by.

I swallow around the thickness in my throat.

Fuck, this woman owns me and she isn't even officially mine.

But even when she is and I slip the ring on her finger, she still won't be because this is all transactional. A marriage of convenience. An arranged marriage. Whatever you want to fucking call it.

But again, I made a promise, and anything other than a real marriage simply won't do.

I digest Laurel's dig and continue this game we've played for the past few weeks.

> Me: Touché. Well, I hope you're ready to marry me and this black heart in just a few short days. Have a great day, Mrs. Black Heart.

Ray pulls the car along the curb outside my building when Laurel texts back. I find myself smiling when her message is a simple black heart emoji.

Yep, this woman owns me and this little black heart of mine.

TWELVE

LAUREL

"Why did you ask me to meet you here?" Roe scrunches her nose and reads the bright, white sign hanging above the door behind me.

I try not to focus on the way her skin has paled since the last time I saw her in my apartment. Unlike then, her hair cascades across her shoulders, her loose curls framing her thin face. Without thought, my gaze falls to her chest where her chemo port is now connected, the silhouette of the small square visible under her black T-shirt.

Roe's dark eyebrows are knitted as she lowers her gaze from the sign to me, but her eyebrows move from confusion, arching into realization.

"Laurel..." She says my name so quietly, it can barely be heard over the heavy flow of traffic behind her. Her eyes dance back and forth between me and the sign. "This is a bridal shop, Laurel."

"Yep." I nod, with a closed mouth grin. I cross my arms and move to stand beside her, joining her in looking at the sign. "You're going to help me pick my wedding dress."

"What?" This time her voice is loud enough to be heard

over Boston traffic. She turns and latches onto my arm. Squeezing her fingers tightly, she forces me to face her. "What do you mean *your wedding dress*? You're getting married?"

"Yes." I nod and shrug my shoulders. I'm suddenly nervous telling Roe about the wedding. "I'm getting married... in five days."

"Five days?" she booms, her eyes practically bugging out of her sullen face.

"Yes." I bite down on my bottom lip, shrinking further. I'm worried she's going to be angry with me. I tell myself she can't possibly when the reason I agreed to marry is to ensure my savings are available for her treatments should she need it. Excitement bubbles in my chest as I pull the white, shimmering envelope from my purse and hold it out to Roe.

Her eyes widen as she takes it from me. "I don't under-stand," she says, ripping it open. She isn't gentle, not wasting any time to learn the details of my sudden impending nuptials.

"The invitation explains it all." I scratch the back of my head. My sister's opinion has always meant the most to me. Even if we might be competitive, and even when I feel her opin-ions aren't warranted, I still value them. I've worked out how to tell Roe I'm marrying Lennon by the end of the week. Ulti-mately, I've decided to wing it. Sometimes the best strategy is to go into these types of situations without a strategy.

Roe doesn't break her attention away from the invitation when she slides it out of the envelope. She turns it over and runs her fingers over the embossed black, purple, and red flowered border. What feels like hours but is probably only seconds pass by as she reads the black and gold lettered script printed in the middle.

Laurel Eleanor Branford
&
Lennon James Harding
REQUEST THE PLEASURE OF YOUR COMPANY
ON THEIR WEDDING DAY
SATURDAY, 19TH JULY
CEREMONY TO BEGIN AT 5PM IN THE AFTERNOON
RECEPTION TO FOLLOW
2147 BAYBERRY LANE
CAPE COD, MASSACHUSETTS

. . .

"OH, MY GOD," she breathes as she slowly and finally looks up from the invitation. "You're marrying Lennon Harding? *The* Lennon Harding?"

I nod, the words getting stuck somewhere between my heart and my throat. I open my mouth, but all I can do is hold my breath, anticipating my sister's reaction. My chest moves. I'm breathing but words fail me.

"Let me see the ring," she squeals, grabbing for my hand. She flips it over, her face falling when she sees it's empty.

I cover my hand and take in a shaky, nervous breath. "I don't have it yet. Lennon said he's taking care of it."

"Okay." She frowns, disappointed.

"It's not a big deal." I casually wave her off.

"When did you start dating Lennon?" She's looking past me as if she's mentally searching for a time when I would have mentioned dating Lennon. She catches on quickly, finding the answer. "Why didn't you tell me? How could you keep this from me?"

Hurt and sadness flash across her face. I want to wrap my arms around her, but I don't. She deserves an explanation—one I'm hoping will make sense and not make it sound like I'm making a huge mistake.

"Um." My ability to speak returns. "We haven't really been dating. We've only been engaged for a couple of weeks."

"Wait." She places her hand on her forehead, still looking down at the invitation. "You've been engaged for a couple of weeks, and you didn't bother telling me? This is huge, Laurel." Her watery gaze shoots straight for my heart. "Especially since I was telling you to go for him at the funeral. Is that why you were so against it? Because you didn't want me to know?"

"No." I shake my head, wrapping my hand around hers. "Not at all. I didn't know he was going to propose then, and we weren't dating yet, either."

"Hold on." She laughs but there's no humor behind it. "You weren't dating then? Laurel, the funeral was less than a month ago. Are you insane?"

"I know it was." I can't explain it, but the need to defend mine and Lennon's engagement kicks in. I'm aware Roe doesn't know all the details or know that, although my marriage to Lennon is strictly business, marrying him won't be the worst mistake I'll ever make. No, my marriage to David is still strongly holding first place in that race.

"Do you even really know him? I mean, besides the wonderful things you had to say about him and his family at his father's funeral."

She's resorted to sarcasm. I ignore her comment, my non-strategy strategy finally kicking in. I'm diving headfirst into the truth.

"More than you think," I confess. The floodgates have opened. "I first met him on our nineteenth birthday."

"Nineteenth birthday?" Her eyebrows knit.

"He was a friend of the guy you were dating from Boston College. Lennon was sitting with their group that night," I explain. I can tell she's trying to remember which guy it was she was dating at the time. "After you and your date went out on the dance floor, I left. I was waiting for my ride outside the club when I accidently got into the wrong car. Lennon's car. After an embarrassing exchange, he offered to give me a ride home."

"Oh," she mutters with distant eyes. "I had no idea."

"We had sex that night," I blurt out. "In his car."

Her jaw drops. "Laurel Eleanor!" She slaps me on the arm. A familiar ghost of a smile appears on her mouth. It's been a long time since I've seen her crack one. One that isn't forced, at least.

"Yeah, well... we didn't meet up again until I met the Hardings for dinner over a year ago."

"I remember." She nods, looking at me with pity for that night. I'd filled her in on every detail, leaving out the part where I'd felt awful for Lennon not having recognized me. "How was it seeing him since that night, though? That must have been awkward for the both of you. Or maybe not, considering you're marrying him now."

I lift a shoulder. "It was definitely awkward, but not because it was the first time we'd seen each other since that night. It was awkward because I expected him to look like a deer in headlights, you know what I mean? Like, shocked we'd run into each other after all this time. But he didn't. He'd looked at me as if he'd never met me. Introduced himself and his date to me. Then I was forced to push through the entire night wearing fake smiles and making polite conversation." Pressure builds behind my eyes, and I can feel tears springing behind them. I don't want to cry. I want to keep today light and fun, not focusing on the fact my soon-to-be husband couldn't remember me.

"That's terrible," Roe says, moving our joined hands so she's now holding my hand instead. She squeezes it. "If you were so upset with him not remembering you, how is it that you're now engaged? Help me fill in the dots here, Laurel."

Refusing to shed a single tear, I inhale a shaky breath. "A few days after the funeral, he came to my office and asked me to marry him. His father apparently left the company and everything to him, but only under the condition he get married within thirty days."

"So, he chose you?"

"Not exactly." I sigh. "He had to marry a Branford. Either me or you, but considering you're already married... well, that left only me..." I let my voice trail off, allowing the information to sink in. I give Roe a few seconds to process, eyeing her emerald cut diamond ring wrapped around her fourth finger.

"Why us?" she asks the question I don't think any of us know the answer to. Not even Lennon.

I shake my head. "I don't know. I don't think anyone does. I turned him down that day though."

"You told him no?" She chuckles.

"Yes. I was angry with him, too. I couldn't get past the fact he didn't remember me and then had the audacity to ask me to marry him."

"What changed your mind?"

"You." I allow my confession to dissolve in the air between us.

She gasps. "Me?" Roe allows a tear to slip from her eye as she shakes her head. "How did I change your mind when I didn't even know until now?"

"You need the money, Roe. You need the money for your treatments. Lennon told me he will take care of me and that I won't have to pay for anything anymore. But I made sure I'm not sacrificing myself in the process. With Lennon's support, I can give you what I have. All my savings. You were worried I was going to lose all the money I have but this way, I won't."

"I can't believe this." Warm, fresh tears slide down Roe's porcelain cheeks. I can't tell if she's brokenhearted, angry, or relieved. But when her eyes find mine, they're none of those options. Instead, all I see is pain and fear. "I can't let you marry him for me, Laurel. It isn't right."

"You're my sister." I pull her in for a hug and bury my chin into her small frame, allowing her warmth to wrap around me. "You honestly didn't believe I'd just sit by and watch you not be able to get all the treatments available to you, did you? You need this money, and this is a win for everyone. Lennon gets the company. You get your treatment." I loosen my grip Roe, holding her at arm's length, secretly keeping the part about how I'm not exactly dreading marrying him to myself.

"And what about you?" Roe's chin trembles.

I let out a small laugh. "I get to be Mrs. Harding for a year, I guess."

Roe laughs with me. It feels good. Relief washes over me. She isn't angry or bitter. Maybe she's too tired, considering she starts her chemo treatments this week. Or maybe she understands where I'm coming from.

"Have you told Frederick?"

"Not yet." I shake my head. "You're the only one who knows. But even when I tell Fred, I don't think I'm going to tell him my marriage to Lennon will be a contractual one."

"Understandable." She nods.

I sniff and eye the white bridal sign above the door, my mind wandering to thoughts about what married life with Lennon will look like.

"There's more, isn't there?" She eyes me suspiciously.

"What do you mean?" I wipe my hands across my cheeks, drying the tears I gave up fighting.

"You care for him. I can see it in the way your eyes lit up when you handed me the invitation. I can see it in the way you smile when you say his name."

"No, I don't. I don't react in any sort of way." My cheeks flame with my lie.

I react with Lennon. Very, very much so.

Roe sees through my lies. "Laurel, this wedding and marriage might go a little smoother if you stopped lying to yourself. If you didn't have feelings for him, you wouldn't have been so hurt when you realized he didn't remember you. You also wouldn't be this okay with marrying him. After your marriage to

David, I know you don't take this lightly. You made that very clear at James's funeral."

I shake my head. I don't want to talk about my feelings for Lennon. Or Roe's cancer. I want to shop for a wedding dress. "Even if I did have feelings for him, he doesn't feel that way about me. Lennon is a businessman, and that's all this is to him: business."

"Well, I guess we'll see who's right at the wedding." She breathes a heavy, cleansing breath and smiles, grabbing my hand and squeezing it. "Thank you, Laurel. I may not agree with the way you're going about this, but if this isn't love, then I don't know what is. I can't tell you what this means to me."

With the truth of mine and Lennon's relationship now in the open with Roe, I feel a weight lift from my shoulders. The pain and fear that comes with Roe's diagnosis hasn't disappeared, but at least there are no secrets between us. And when we step into the bridal store, another wave of relief washes over me. Roe is the first person to ever know the history between Lennon and me.

My night with him has been a secret I've had the burden of carrying for the past six years. I haven't even been able to talk about it with the one I shared the night with.

Lennon.

My heart feels lighter when Roe and I step inside. Seas of white dresses stretch along each wall. Various bits of lace and sequins peek out from white chiffon and silk. Roe elbows me, and I turn to catch the largest grin I think I've ever seen on her. I'm grinning the same way. We've shopped in stores of this scale all our lives, but never a bridal store, and never for a wedding dress.

"I didn't realize until now how exciting this is," she says, hooking her arm in mine. "We didn't get to do this for your first wedding. Actually, I wasn't even there. This is nice, isn't it?"

I nod, unable to speak. It is nice. I feel like a princess, and I haven't even tried any of the dresses on yet, which are a far cry from the red bikini and white sarong I was wearing the day I married David.

"Hello." A woman with long, curly brown hair greets us. "Do you have an appointment set up with us?"

"Um." I nervously look at Roe. "No, I don't think I do."

"I'm sorry." She frowns. "We aren't able to have you try on any of the dresses unless you have an appointment."

"Oh. Are we able to make an appointment? My wedding is in five days, and I really need to find a dress."

"Five days?" The curly haired woman gasps, placing her hand on her chest. "I'm sorry. Even if I were to get you an appointment, there is no way we could have a dress ready for you in five days."

"Well, shit," Roe mutters.

Panic starts to course through my veins. I should have known better. There's no way a store such as this one could have a dress ready for me by this weekend, or any of the other stores on Olivia's list.

I'm ready to leave the store when my phone rings from my purse. I pull it out, reading Lennon's name flashing across the screen.

Roe eyes my phone and gives me a knowing grin. I stick my tongue out at her and answer.

"Lennon," I say, keeping my voice as even as possible.

"Good afternoon, Mrs. Black Heart." His voice is deep and low, vibrating my insides. Butterflies fill my stomach.

I roll my eyes at his new nickname for me. Roe's eyebrow lifts, and I shake my head at her.

One day, I'm Mrs. Harding. Now, I'm Mrs. Black Heart.

"I apologize, ma'am." The curly brown-haired woman interjects, stepping closer. "I don't mean to interrupt, but I have a bride arriving soon for her appointment. Maybe you could try a department store or a secondhand shop. They'll likely have wedding dresses you can buy off the rack."

"Wait a minute." Lennon growls through the phone and into my ear. "Are you wedding dress shopping?"

"Yes," I tell him, clearing my throat. "My sister Monroe is here with me, and we just walked in."

Roe turns her attention to the woman long enough to shoot her a glare before she looks back at me, leaning in to listen in on our conversation.

"Why did it sound like the woman was asking you to leave?" he asks. "Were you able to find a dress?"

"Not exactly." I wince. The woman still hasn't moved, refusing to walk away until she's sure we've left her store before her next client arrives.

"What do you mean?" He's lowered his voice again, but this time it's darker.

"I went to the first store on the list Olivia sent, and the lady who works here says I need an appointment before trying anything on. Plus, she says they can't get a dress done for me in time for our wedding."

"What the fuck?" Lennon asks. "Did you give her your name?"

"I didn't realize I was supposed to."

Before my parents died and Kellan destroyed our reputation, our family name held meaning and importance like Lennon's does in this city. But I never liked using it to get what I wanted. Lennon clearly doesn't take issue with it.

"Tell her you're Lennon Harding's fiancée."

"Lennon," I sigh. "It's fine. I can go somewhere else."

"Laurel. You're going to be my wife, and you deserve to pick whichever dress you fucking want. It shouldn't matter which store you go to." He pauses, his breath blowing through the phone to my ear as if he were here with me. My body heats.

"Is the woman who works there with you now?" he asks.

"Yes."

"Good. Put me on speaker."

"Lennon." His name falls on a sigh again.

I'm not even remotely embarrassed by Lennon wanting me to put him on speaker. The butterflies in my stomach and the heat radiating across my body is simply from the shift I sense in his tone. He's irritated the woman is giving us a difficult time, but at the same time he's being protective. Like he cares if I'm happy. And knowing that does all sorts of things to my chest and stomach.

"Laurel," he grits out. "If you don't put me on speaker right now, I won't be able to control myself so easily the next time we meet in my conference room. Next time, it'll be more than just your shoes."

This time my stomach does a full somersault.

My heart hammers in my chest, and my body may as well burst into flames.

I momentarily consider not following through on putting him on speaker to find out what he means, but I decide against it.

"My fiancé would like to speak with you," I tell the woman, eyeing the name tag attached to her black pants suit. "Erica."

Erica crosses her arms over her chest as I pull the phone away from my ear and click the speaker button.

"You're on speaker, Lennon," I tell him.

Roe's hand covers her mouth, and her eyes are spread wide in shock.

"Is this Erica?" Lennon asks.

"Yes, sir." She eyes me, sending me a narrowed, annoyed gaze. "As I told your fiancée, she will need to find a dress at another store. Our bridal store runs on an appointment only system. You must have one to shop here and place an order for a dress. Besides, your wedding is on such short notice there's no—"

"I don't remember asking you to repeat to me the exact same excuses you told my fiancée," Lennon cuts in, anger dripping from his voice. "This is Lennon Harding. I believe my assistant Olivia spoke with you earlier telling you that you should be expecting my fiancée in today, did she not?"

"Oh." Erica's face is as white as a ghost. She nervously looks down at my phone, reading his name. Her neck bobs as she swallows deeply, realizing the mistake she made. "I'm sorry, Mr. Harding. I wasn't aware—"

"No," he cuts her off. "You weren't aware. Because if you were, you would be showing my fiancée any dress she requests instead of standing here talking to me, denying my fiancée of the dress she deserves. You would also know that there is no budget. The future Mrs. Harding will get whatever dress she falls in love with, *and* my assistant was also informed that we were able to make special arrangements for any alterations that might be needed for the dress to be ready by Saturday. Am I correct, Erica, or were we all misinformed?"

"No, sir. You weren't misinformed. I should have asked your fiancée her name when she entered the store. Of course, we have special arrangements set in place for you."

"Good," he says, satisfied. "I expect you to treat my fiancée and her sister with respect and give them the best dress buying experience."

"Be assured, our team here will get whatever the future Mrs. Harding requests."

"Great," he says. "Oh, and Mrs. Harding?"

He's already back to calling me by my future name. My cheeks heat with Roe's increasing stare.

"Yes, Lennon?" I pull my phone closer, no longer keeping it

outstretched for everyone to hear, even though I keep him on speaker.

"I look forward to seeing you in the dress that was made especially for you," he teases. "And to meeting you at the altar."

He doesn't give me the opportunity to answer before he ends our call. I didn't even get to ask why he called in the first place.

Dropping my phone in my purse, I'm still reeling from the past few minutes when I trade glances between Roe and Erica. Erica's face is mixed with both fear and hesitation. Roe is buzzing with excitement.

Her grin stretches all the way up to her bright blue eyes as she wags her finger in the direction of my phone sitting in the bottom of my purse.

"Oh, yeah." She beams. "This isn't just business. That man loves you."

THIRTEEN

Lennon

I doubt this is the type of wedding my father had in mind when he'd given me thirty days to marry Laurel. I'm sure he assumed I would be scrambling to make this work. I bet he's scowling up at me from Hell, pissed I didn't struggle nearly as hard as he thought I would at convincing Laurel to marry me. I don't doubt he entrusted me to make this marriage happen or else he wouldn't have put the risk of the company falling out of our family's hands under such a ridiculous condition. But I also know he expected me to work for it, spending the entire thirty days panic stricken.

My father was sick and twisted like that. He liked to watch others squirm under his power. Me included.

Fucking asshole.

Our house along the Cape is almost unrecognizable. Gold-painted pots of white and cream-colored roses are planted down the stretch of lawn, jutting out the coast behind me. This end of our land stretches out, creating a cliff overlooking the expansive ocean. Each flowerpot creates a makeshift aisle leading straight to the altar our wedding planner scrambled to put together at the last minute. A tall, white-painted, wooden arch stands above me, with the same white and cream flowers wrapped around it like a strand of garland. Pops of green leaves poke through the flowers, breaking up the overwhelming blanket of white covering the yard.

Laurel was detailed in her vision for her dream wedding, including only inviting ten of our closest friends. I agreed, knowing we didn't need to make a spectacle of our big day. Word is bound to get out to the press regardless of whether we invited a thousand half-strangers or ten of our closest friends.

Now, five white chairs are situated on either side of the aisle.

Sitting on my side are Jude and his wife Victoria. Straddled across Jude's lap is their daughter Abbey. She smiles at me, her dimple pressing into her still-fresh baby cheeks. Shy of a year old, she's still unsteady and erratic with her movements, especially when she gets excited. On a giggle, she rocks back, her head landing hard against my brother's chest. She winces but doesn't cry. He gently runs his hand over the top of her head followed by a kiss. He gives me a smile, letting me know he's supporting me even though he doesn't agree with my decision to follow through with our father's condition. Despite our disagreement, I'm glad he's here.

Beside Jude, Perry crosses one leg over the other and clears his throat, distracting himself with whatever he's reading on his phone. He hasn't moved from his chair since he first arrived. In his lap, he cracks open the familiar leather-bound folder I've seen him toting around every time I see him. I'm sure there's some bullshit in there along with my father's will about how Perry is tasked with gathering as much evidence as possible to prove my marriage with Laurel today is official and legal.

Sitting on the opposite side of the aisle is Laurel's sister, Monroe. I recognize her from the night I met Laurel outside the club. At the time, she was dating a frat brother of mine. I'd barely spoken to her that night, drunk out of my mind before deciding to leave, which eventually led me to meeting her sister.

I turn my attention back to the house.

Our photographer stands off in the distance, snapping pictures of me waiting at the altar before Laurel walks out.

Standing beside me is our justice of the peace, a man Olivia found when researching ones who were able to officiate on such short notice.

If I didn't know the details behind our wedding, I'd think it was planned months, even years, in advance. Not a single detail has gone undone.

"A wedding and a funeral in less than a month," Micah says, clapping his hand on my shoulder. "Must be a new record."

"Shut the fuck up," I tell him, hiding my irritation behind a grin.

Micah is only teasing, but I don't like thinking of this place as the venue for my father's funeral. I thought it was twisted he'd requested to have his funeral here considering the weight of memories this place holds.

Up until his funeral, I hadn't been here in years. I refused. Not since the last time I saw her. This house was no longer the bright happy home it once was. A dark cloud rolled in and refused to move, covering this place in darkness. My father's presence didn't help matters, even in his death. But when Laurel said she wanted to be married in a spot surrounded by flowers and the ocean, it was the first and only place that came to mind.

Micah joins the rest of our family and sits beside Victoria. I look over at Monroe sitting by herself and wonder if Laurel invited anyone else besides her. I don't have to wonder for too long before her Uncle Frederick waddles in. The chair creaks when he sits down before he bounces back up, quickly standing long enough to shake my hand.

I return his gesture and then he falls back into his seat.

My attention is pulled away from our limited number of guests when I catch a glimpse of pure white in the corner of my eye.

Laurel takes her time walking down the three paved steps off the elevated deck attached to the back of the house. Music plays from the speakers scattered throughout the courtyard. She weaves her way through the maze of bushes and flowers. She's entirely too far away. My stomach drops, and my heart hammers in my chest like never before. I go weak in the knees, drowning in the urge to bend and give in to the temptation of falling at her feet when she reaches me. Somehow, I force myself to stay standing. No one here knows how much power Laurel holds over me. Not even Laurel.

When she finally reaches the end of the aisle, she pauses, her shoulders visibly rising as she takes in a deep, steadying breath. She has no one standing beside her. Her father isn't here to walk her down the aisle, and I see the hesitation and realization meet her eyes.

The breath is knocked from my chest when she walks toward me. Her long chestnut hair is curled and pinned back, with a few wistful strands hanging loose, framing her gorgeous face. She lifts her arm and nervously adjusts her veil, straightening it on the crown of her head. The sheer fabric cascades down the length of her exposed back. Her dress is simple, with no intricate detailing, lace, or sequins. A long slit drives up the length of her leg, exposing her bare thigh with every step. The smooth, white fabric clings to her body, accentuating and hugging every curve. A deep 'V' cuts down the center of her breastbone. This dress was fucking made for her.

When she takes her last step and stands in front of me, she turns to hand her sister her bouquet. I take her shaking hand in mine and hold it, leading her to face me. She bends, adjusting the train of her dress behind her.

She smiles when she sees me, taking in my all-black suit.

"Hi," she whispers, cracking a nervous smile.

I don't answer her. I can't. I let her go and keep my hands held together in front of me, flexing my fingers together to keep me from reaching out and touching her.

"Is something wrong?" she whispers, leaning forward and giving our officiant a nervous side glance.

"No." I clear my throat. "It's just..."

"What?"

"You're beautiful." I dig my fingers into the back of my hand. I don't have the strength to hold back from telling her truth.

"Oh." She blushes and lifts one shoulder as if she isn't convinced, which is a fucking shame. "Thank you."

"Welcome, family and friends," our justice of the peace announces. I keep my eyes on Laurel.

The music has stopped, replaced by the continuous clicking of the photographer's camera. The sun reflects off her shimmering skin, the setting golden glow shining in her indigo eyes as she stares up at me.

"We are gathered here to witness the marriage between Laurel Eleanor Branford and Lennon James Harding. Two souls who have found one another."

I take her hand in mine again as our officiant continues his speech about the weight of true love and the importance of marriage. I don't think Olivia made him aware of the details surrounding our relationship. A few words stand out here and there, but all I can focus on is Laurel standing in front of me and all the things I could do to her in this dress.

"Now, the rings," the officiant says, holding his hand out, gesturing for us to present them.

Laurel's eyebrows raise. "I don't have yours."

"I told you," I whisper back, tugging my ring free from my pocket. "I had them covered."

I drop the platinum ring in her hand, and she curls her fingers around it.

"Slide the ring onto Lennon's finger and repeat after me," the officiant recites. "I, Laurel Eleanor, take you Lennon James, to be my lawfully wedded husband."

"I, Laurel Eleanor," she begins, turning my hand over and holding it between her small, delicate fingers. She slides the ring on my finger and finishes her vows.

When she's done, the officiant turns his attention to me.

"Same for you," he says. "Repeat after me."

I pull the ring from my pocket and cradle Laurel's left hand in mine. Placing my thumb over her fourth finger, I pinch the diamond ring between my fingers and slide it onto hers. An audible gasp escapes her red-painted lips. The emerald cut diamond is large, practically taking over Laurel's finger. The ring is a statement piece for sure, but I know that's why it was bought in the first place. It was meant to shine. Meant to let the woman who wore it know they belonged to a Harding.

"I, Lennon James, take you Laurel Eleanor to be my lawfully wedded wife. I promise to love you, take care of you, and protect you. In sickness and in health. For richer or poorer. As long as we both shall live."

It doesn't matter in this moment that this is an arranged marriage. The words fall from my mouth without effort.

After placing the ring on Laurel's finger, I hold her hands in mine once again.

Our officiant grins, holding his arms out.

"For the first time, I proudly present Mr. and Mrs. Lennon Harding. I now pronounce you man and wife." He looks at me. "You may kiss your bride."

Laurel's neck bobs as she nervously swallows. Staring at me with widened eyes, the indigo color in them deepens. We haven't kissed since the night we were together on her nineteenth birthday. I wonder if our mouths will react, immediately falling into muscle memory.

Whether she's conscious of it or not, she quickly sweeps her tongue across her lips and squeezes my hand, giving me the signal to go ahead and get through this part of the ceremony. I release one of her hands and wrap it around the back of her head, pulling her body flush against mine. She steps forward and wraps her arms around me. My fingers thread through her soft brown curls when my lips meet hers. She tastes sweet, like a sugar cookie mixed with her strawberry lip gloss. I breathe her in, and she moans against my lips when I don't pull away as fast as she expects me to. I can tell by the way her body relaxes against mine.

It's been years since I've kissed her, but my reaction remains the same. It feels as if my body is going to explode from the sheer liquid heat pumping through my veins. With my other hand, I cradle her face, running my thumb along her jaw. Her arms tighten around me as she fists my suit between her small fingers. She opens her mouth enough for me to massage my tongue with hers. She must think the kiss has gone on too long for the first kiss, or because the entirety of our guests knows this marriage hasn't been born out of love. It's born out of contract.

Unraveling her arms from me, she grabs onto my hand, pulling it away from her face. I immediately feel her absence.

I want to say fuck it, I don't care if everyone is watching. The fire in my chest is no longer a flickering spark. It's a full-on raging bonfire at this point.

With heat blooming in her cheeks, Laurel looks at me with a similar fire in her eyes. She didn't want our kiss to end either, and the fear in her expression tells me she wasn't expecting to feel this way. She only ended it before giving others a reason to ask questions.

She trails her tongue across her lips again, tasting the taste of me on them.

I clear my throat, silently telling myself to remain calm and pull myself back down to earth. But it's difficult when Laurel hooks her arm in mine and my eyes fall to my ring wrapped around her finger.

Reality sinks in. Laurel is officially mine. *My wife.*

We walk down the aisle with her arm still hooked around mine. This wasn't part of the plan. We were supposed to stay outside, chatting with our family and friends until our brief reception, but I can tell by the way Laurel's arm stiffens around mine that she needs to take a breath.

I lead her through the garden until we've reached the greenhouse standing in the farthest corner of the property. We don't speak a word until we're inside and I've spun her around so her back lands against the glass wall.

We're surrounded by plants and mounds of dirt. The air is thick with the scent of wet earth and fresh, unplanted flowers.

My hand is quick to go to her bare thigh peeking through the slit in her dress.

"I don't think we're supposed to be in here," Laurel whispers over the hiccup in her breathing. My finger has managed to inch its way higher up her leg.

"I own this place. We can be anywhere we want to be."

"Well, for a marriage that's only meant to be on paper, I don't think we should be in here. Like this..." Her eyes fall to my mouth.

I'm still thinking about our kiss and how I'm left unsatisfied. I want more. I crave more.

"Are you okay?" I ask her. I feel like it's an unusual question to ask your bride, but this entire marriage is unusual.

"I'm fine." Her gaze is still bouncing back and forth across my face.

I move my hand from her thigh and grab a flower from the wooden workbench beside us; a short green stem full of lavender colored petals. One of the gardeners must have left it behind without giving it a home.

Laurel watches as I bring the flower between us and drag it down the center of her chest.

"Lavender," she whispers.

"Is that what this is?" I ask, the corner of my mouth curling into a smirk.

She rests her head back onto the moisture-covered glass. I'd forgotten the watering system my mother installed in here years ago. Every few hours, sprinklers bolt into the ceiling to spray water on all the plants along the back wall.

"My back is wet," she says. "Among other things."

My cock swells in my black pants. She slides her other leg between mine, pressing it against me. I groan, lowering the flower to her leg.

"The thoughts that ran through my mind when I saw you walking toward me in this dress." My confession swirls in the damp air between us.

Her skin prickles with goosebumps as I lightly drag the flower up her leg. "This dress wasn't cheap," she adds, her eyes half closed. "It cost over twenty thousand from what Olivia told me."

"Twenty thousand *is* cheap," I tell her, grinning like the Cheshire cat.

"You sound like a rich, arrogant snob when you say things like that." Her hands wrap around my arms. The pressure of her fingers gripping me deepens.

"Well, this rich, arrogant snob is now your husband, and you belong to me." I drag the flower over her pussy.

She shivers with the motion, pulling in a short gasp of air between her glossy lips. I drag my thumb across her bottom lip.

"I want you to taste yourself," I command.

She starts to lower her hand between her legs, but I stop her, clicking my tongue in disapproval. "No, no, no. Not with your own hand. I want you to taste yourself on my fingers."

She flicks her gaze up to mine, looking up at me through her mascara-coated eyelashes. She's wearing more makeup than usual, but it isn't enough to hide her natural beauty.

I'm still playing the flower along her pussy, knowing it's only making her wetter for me. She rocks her hips, pushing herself deeper into the motions of the flower. I move my hand along the flower, holding it closer to the petals. My fingertips graze her bare skin, and I grin with delight.

"Is this because it's our wedding day or are you always this bare, Mrs. Harding?" I ask, fighting the urge to rip my suit off and fuck her hard against the glass wall until she screams my name.

"Only when I'm around you."

"Why is that?" I tease my finger between her slick folds. She's drenched as she lifts her hips off the glass. My finger slides deeper, landing against her swollen clit.

"Because," she breathes. "I was tired of having to change my panties after every time I was near you. You make me so fucking wet, Lennon."

Her confession makes her cheeks turn red.

"Fuck," I tell her, stroking her clit. "I think that's the hottest thing I've ever fucking heard." I slide my fingers from her clit, burying two of them inside her. The flower is still held in my hand but off to the side. I cup her pussy and pump both fingers in and out of her, pressing my thumb against her clit.

She moans, fisting the sleeves of my suit tighter. Her long, pink fingernails dig into my muscles.

"Rock your hips with me," I order. "Is this what you imagine every time your pussy is wet after you see me?"

"No," she whimpers, her eyes closed now.

"Open your eyes," I instruct, wanting her to clarify her answer. She does as I say. "What do you mean, no?"

"I didn't imagine this." She moans, rolling her hips. "I imagine you fucking me."

I'm wanting to free my cock and slide into her. My body remembers what it's like to be buried inside her. It's begging to relive that night. But I can't stop watching her writhe against me. My single touch has Laurel forgetting how, at the very core, our marriage is business. She's replaced it for pleasure. At least temporarily. Thrill courses through my veins with her confession. I love knowing I'm able to bring this side out of her.

Her body hums and vibrates as my strokes move faster and harder. I hook my fingers inside her, finding the spot that makes her thighs clench around me.

"I want you to fuck me, Lennon."

"Not now. We have guests waiting on us."

Her mouth falls open. I'm unsure whether it's because she's close to her orgasm or it's from my answer, denying her what she desperately wants. It might be both.

"Besides," I add. "When you come on my hand, I want to ensure your pussy spends the rest of the night wishing it had more than just my fingers inside it."

"Lennon..." she gasps, her head slamming against the glass. Her shoulders tense, and she inhales a sharp breath.

"That's right, Mrs. Harding." I growl. "Come for me."

She lifts her chin and squeezes her eyes shut, riding my hand a few more times before she quivers against it. Her thighs clench, and she screams my name.

I wait until her body has relaxed, and she's opened her eyes before I slide my fingers out of her.

She's catching her breath when I pull my hand out from between her legs. As promised, I lift my hand and hold it between us. I'm still holding onto the flower with my glistening fingers.

Without a word, she takes the flower from my hand and tucks it into the front pocket of my suit. She keeps her hand pressed against my chest. I smirk, swinging my eyes back to hers.

"Like I said," I tell her. "I want you to taste yourself. Open your mouth."

She breathes heavily and swallows before allowing her lips to part. Her mouth pops open as she waits for me.

I place both fingers against her tongue. She closes her mouth and sucks on them, her red-stained lips tightening around my fingers.

"Fuck, Laurel."

She moans, closing her eyes again. I pull my fingers out and slowly back away. My erratic heart hasn't slowed. I only want her more. But seeing her here, knowing what we just did, it's like reality is settling into my bones. I just finger fucked my wife in my mother's greenhouse.

My eyes fall to the flower in my pocket, the scent a mixture of Laurel and lavender.

Laurel hasn't even been my wife for less than thirty minutes, and I've already given in. We acted like two teenagers sneaking off together, hoping not to get caught. I didn't want to rush things with her. In honesty, I didn't expect to be with her this way. I knew Laurel only agreed to marry me for reasons she still hasn't shared, but the fact that I've just received confirmation she's feeling the same as me scares me.

It wasn't supposed to be like this. I've been naïve believing it was going to be simple when my feelings for Laurel have been anything but simple since the moment we met.

When I take another step back from Laurel, she pushes

herself off the glass wall. Her skin is still flushed as she straightens her wedding gown, adjusting and twisting the fabric around her hips. The slit along her thigh closes.

"We should get back out there for the reception," I tell her. "We still need to get back to the city tonight."

"Oh." She snaps her head up. "We aren't staying here tonight?"

I rub my fingers along my mouth and swipe my tongue across my lip, tasting whatever is left of Laurel on my skin. What feels like an anchor dropping to the bottom of the sea floor is my stomach lurching, and I bite down on my molars. "No, I told you before. We'll be staying at my apartment in Boston from now on."

Laurel's gorgeous face relaxes as she studies me. I can see the thoughts working in her mind. She knows there's a reason I don't want to stay here. She still looks at me like I'm a puzzle needing to be solved.

"Okay," she says quietly.

"Let's go, Mrs. Harding." I wrap her hand in mine and lift my other to trail my finger down the side of her warm cheek, resisting the urge to kiss her. "We don't want to keep our guests waiting."

FOURTEEN

LAUREL

I haven't stopped staring at the ring on my finger. Although Lennon told me he was taking care of the rings, I didn't think too much about what it would look like. In the back of my mind, I assumed it would be a simple gold band. Our marriage wasn't born out of love, so I didn't expect Lennon to put much effort in finding an elaborate ring. Especially one that looks like the one I have wrapped around my finger. In a way, it reminds me of my mother's. Hers was destroyed in the accident, but if I close my eyes, I can picture it. Like hers, the emerald cut is large. At least four carats—probably more if I were to guess. The weight of it is the perfect symbolism for the way I'm feeling after telling Lennon 'I do'.

I'm watching him from across the courtyard, pretending as if his constant stares aren't burning a hole straight through me.

He hasn't kissed me since we were standing at the altar. It's a silly notion to be hung up on considering what we did in the greenhouse on the far side of the property. But I can't help noticing the small detail. Reluctantly, I pick it apart, obsessing over it more than what would be considered normal.

I can still feel his long fingers inside me. The heat of his breath wafting against my skin. His deep voice vibrating as he orders me to lick his fingers, tasting what he did to me.

I guess he's successfully delivered on the promise he made. I've been spending the entire night wishing I'd had more than just his fingers inside me.

I'm still eyeing him from across the courtyard, noticing the absence of the flower I'd slid into the front pocket of his midnight black suit before leaving the greenhouse. I stand beside the small cocktail table feeling conflicted. Lennon gave more to our kiss on the altar than I expected. He threaded his fingers in my hair and held me against his lips until I heard Roe gently clearing her throat, clearly telling me she wasn't expecting it either.

I couldn't help it. Walking down the aisle with his eyes trained on me, I'd allowed myself to fall down the rabbit hole. Lennon had given me my dream wedding, and having him stare at me with his striking blue eyes, signature black on black suit, I realized I was treading in waters I wasn't expecting to.

By the time he'd slid the ring on my finger and placed his lips to mine, I was finished.

His kiss had done something inside me. It's as if my soul had been caught in an unknown slumber, awakened only by Lennon's kiss. Sounds like a fucking fairy tale. I'm the princess freed from an eternal sleep by a single kiss. Ridiculous.

I was relieved to know when he'd pulled me to the greenhouse and immediately put his hands on me that I wasn't alone. He'd felt it, too. But now he's back to the Lennon I've come to know. Before he became my husband. He hasn't completely let his black heart take control tonight, however. Every now and then, he'll walk over and place his hand on the small of my back while we make conversation with his family.

I guess that's him fulfilling our agreement that we would act as husband and wife in public.

But the most difficult part about tonight were the pictures. Just like any other typical wedding, Lennon and I took newlywed photos. He didn't hold back with his touches, but still, refused to kiss me, resorting to nuzzling my neck and brushing his lips against my cheek instead. By the time we were finished, I gave myself another pat on the back for deciding not to wear panties today. But I haven't been able to make head nor tails of Lennon's hot and cold nature with me.

Maybe he was afraid of losing control again. Maybe he doesn't want me to feel like he can suddenly touch me whenever he wants simply because I'm now his wife, regardless of whether it's transactional or not.

But all those possibilities haven't stopped the unrelenting thoughts from clouding my brain. It's maddening.

"How did you get this so dirty already?" Roe asks behind me.

I twist, looking down the train of silk. "Lennon showed me the rest of the grounds earlier." I'm quick to answer. I didn't think this lie through. Roe immediately catches on, but she doesn't press me further. I'm just thankful she came in the first place, considering how she's been feeling.

She arches an eyebrow, unconvinced. I ignore it.

We stand side by side and take in the beauty of this place. Frederick left five minutes ago, telling me he was proud I'd taken the plunge and strengthened our bond with the Harding family. I think he was less concerned about the logistics of my marriage and more concerned with the benefits that came from it.

I spent a few minutes talking to my new brothers-in-law. They didn't say much outside of asking the typical basic questions of getting to know one another. Most of our conversations centered around our school rivalry. Boston College versus Harvard. Since Jude's wife Victoria was a Boston College graduate as well, Roe and I were outnumbered. Micah stuck around a while longer than Jude, but that's only because Jude's daughter spit up a large puddle of formula on Victoria's sequined dress.

The sun has set behind the horizon in the distance, and goosebumps spread across my arms from the ocean breeze.

"You didn't have to stay this long if you weren't feeling up for it," I gently tell Roe.

Her small shoulders relax as she tilts her head to the side. "If I wasn't up for it, I wouldn't still be here. But it's okay. Steven is on his way to pick me up from the hotel."

"I'm sorry he wasn't feeling well." I frown.

"It's okay." She shrugs, lifting her hand to tuck my loose strands of hair behind my ear. "You make a beautiful bride, and Lennon is fucking lucky to be married to you."

"Maybe." I laugh, letting those unsettled thoughts about earlier back into my mind.

"I just want to remind you of that, considering Mom and Dad couldn't be here. And with Kellan..." Her soft voice trails off.

"Please, don't," I beg. "For completely different reasons, I don't think I can handle thinking about the three of them. This day has gone better than I expected considering the details of why I married Lennon, and I don't want to ruin it with depressing thoughts. There's no sense in being upset over a situation I can't change, or being angry over someone who's already being punished for the choices they made. Makes it easier to not be angry knowing justice has been served."

"You're right," Roe concedes, giving me a meek, apologetic grin.

"I like to believe Mom and Dad would be happy today." I smile, but it doesn't last long. "And as far as Kellan is concerned, well, he can go fuck himself, I guess."

"Laurel Harding!" Roe says, shocked by lack of restraint. Whereas she's slightly more sympathetic to our brother's situation, I am not.

But hearing her yell my new full name flips my stomach upside down. Like the ring on my finger, it's a foreign sound, but one I think I'll easily get used to.

"I apologize, ladies." Lennon comes up behind me, once again placing his hand on the small of my back, pulling Roe's attention away from me. "I don't mean to interrupt, but the helicopter is ready."

"Helicopter?" Roe asks, her mouth turning down in surprise. "Fancy."

"Taking my helicopter is the quickest way back to the city from here." Lennon smiles. "Thank you for coming, Monroe. It was great to see you again."

"You, too." She smiles in return. "Take care of my sister, okay?"

"I will." He nods.

"Are you sure we can't give you a ride back to the hotel?" I ask.

She giggles. "I'm fine, Laurel."

Misty eyed, I wrap my arms around Roe and pull her into a deep hug. I want to squeeze her, but I'm conscious of the way she's been feeling lately, as well as the port implanted into her chest.

"I love you," I whisper in her ear. "I can't tell you what it means to me that you were here."

"Are you kidding?" she asks, laughing. "And miss my sister marry the infamous Lennon Harding?"

I laugh, resting my head on her shoulder. "I love you," I tell her again. I feel like I need to say it more often nowadays.

"I love you, too."

I leave Roe where she's standing and follow Lennon to the

back end of the courtyard. We pass the greenhouse and walk around a large stone wall, revealing a helicopter waiting for us.

Lennon holds my hand, steadying me as I step up into the helicopter. I sit in the seat on the opposite side from the open door, pulling my veil in behind me. He bends, gathering the train of my dress in his arms. Specks and streaks of dirt cover the bottom hem, reminding me of being in the greenhouse with Lennon.

Ignoring the swelling in my chest, I lean forward and tug on as much of the train as I can, swishing it off to the side, out of Lennon's way. He slides in beside me, dropping the rest of my dress onto the floor, then he shuts the door and twists in his seat. He reaches above me, grabs a pair of headphones, and gently places them on my head, ensuring each side is covering my ears. I'm conscious of his touch, the brush of his fingers on my cheeks, the heat of his skin touching mine. His piercing blue eyes look anywhere but at my own, even when he turns in his own seat, placing his headphones over his ears.

The helicopter starts to lift off the ground, when he leans over, buckling my seat belt. I inhale a sharp breath and hold it. His scent surrounds me, and fuck if I don't want him to take me right now. We fucked in the back seat of his car years ago. How different would it be if we repeated history in his helicopter?

His face is close to mine as he reaches between the inner wall of the helicopter and my hip. The buckle snaps before he sits back down.

Once he buckles himself in, he finally looks me in the eye. "We should be home in about twenty minutes."

I nod and give him a small smile, then turn my head to look out the window. The golden lights of the towns between here and Boston shine bright. Unsure if this is the normal route or if it's a special one, considering it's my wedding night, we fly over the coast. I watch in fascination as the waves lap and recede onto the shore. Small, white wooden buildings and cottage style houses line the shores of Massachusetts.

I've never seen New England from this view before. It's breathtaking.

"It's beautiful, isn't it?" Lennon asks.

Did I just say that out loud without realizing it or was Lennon thinking the same thing?

I snap my head in his direction, the weight of the headphones wobbling on my head before evening out. "It's gorgeous."

"The view is best in late summer."

"Why? Is it because of the fireworks for the fourth of July?"

"No." He looks out the window on his side. "I don't know why, but with every passing day, more boats can be seen floating in the harbor. It's like a hundred glowing lights sprinkle the moonlit ocean. I think everyone realizes the summer doesn't last long, so they try to soak up as much time on the water as they can."

"I bet." It's true. New England summers don't last long, but I think there's beauty in that. It only makes us appreciate the sunny, warm weather even more.

Lennon and I don't speak the rest of the ride home. We sit in silence, keeping our distance. Hope tugs on a string attached to my heart, wishing he'd reach out and touch me in some way. Place a hand on my knee. Brush his finger along my cheek like he usually does. But when the helicopter lands, he doesn't touch me until he's helping me step out of the helicopter.

We've landed on top of his building, and when we reach the door leading off the roof, I find a familiar face holding the door open for us. The helicopter turns off, allowing us to talk without having to yell.

"Laurel, this is my personal assistant, Ray," Lennon says.

"Nice to see you again, Mrs. Harding." Ray smiles.

I gasp. It's the first time a connection to the night Lennon and I shared has been acknowledged. Relief and excitement balloons in my chest as if all my doubts have been validated. Not that Ray's recollection and acknowledgement supersedes Lennon's, but it's nice to know I'm not alone with my memories.

"You as well." I give Ray a smile then turn to Lennon, hoping he'll make a comment about Ray's introduction. But he doesn't. He simply wraps his hand around mine.

"If you ever need anything, Ray will be here," Lennon tells me. "I've already given him your phone number, and I'll give you his so you can reach him at any time."

Ray congratulates us on our marriage before Lennon leads me inside the doorway. We ride the elevator down two levels. When the doors slide open, I drop the train of my dress and step into my new home.

Lennon drops his keys and loosens his black tie. He spins around, walking backward as he talks.

"Ray's already arranged to have all your clothes from the bags you left at the Cape Cod house this morning put away accordingly in our bedroom." He points down the hallway.

I lean forward, eyeing the single bed situated along the farthest wall. Lennon requested I pack a bag with as many clothes and toiletries as I wished to bring to his place and bring it to the house in Cape Cod when I arrived this morning. I'm amazed he asked Ray to take them from the Cape house just to bring them back to the city.

Lennon's city apartment is exactly how I imagined it to be: oak-stained walls, slate countertops covering a similar shade of oak cabinets. The kitchen looks untouched. The outer wall of the apartment is floor to ceiling glass overlooking downtown Boston. In the distance, I can see mine and Lennon's office building.

I'm surveying the living room, noting a large TV in the far

corner, along with one couch and one large leather chair. Other than that, there isn't much to his apartment.

Lennon inches his way toward the front of the hallway and cocks his head to the side. "Come on. I'll show you the rest of your new home."

Hope tugs onto that string, once again, as I follow my husband down the long hallway. I step into the bedroom and play with my new wedding ring, twirling it around my finger. The sensation is foreign.

"Wait," I say, eyeing the large bed. "Is this the only bed in the apartment?"

"Of course," he says while removing his tie. He tosses it onto the bed and removes his jacket. "I've never needed more than one bed, Mrs. Harding. Not when it's only been me living here. Is that a problem?"

Heat blooms in my cheeks. I still haven't wrapped my head around the fact that we aren't staying at the house on the Cape. He surprised me when he said we would be leaving. It only made sense for us to stay there before heading back to the city. But I could see the darkness coming over him when I brought up staying. I didn't push him any further. Part of me thinks it could be because it's the same place where his father's funeral was held.

But it still doesn't stop the nagging question bouncing around in my brain.

Why would Lennon have us stay at a place where there's only one bed when we could have stayed at the house that had over a dozen to choose from?

"No, it isn't a problem," I whisper, my gaze falling to Lennon's chest. "You're my husband. I guess it's actually the least problematic situation for us to be in."

He's already removed half his suit. His black button-down shirt is partially unbuttoned, revealing his fully tattooed chest. I swallow, following the sharp lines and shapes taking form along his tan skin. My stomach bubbles with heat.

"Everything okay?" Lennon asks. He hasn't moved from where he's standing on the side of the bed.

I stay where I am near the foot of the bed and look down at my feet and the bottom of my dirt-riddled wedding dress.

"Yes," I mutter, wanting to get out of this dress and get my mind off Lennon's exposed chest.

How the fuck am I supposed to sleep with him and keep our marriage strictly business when he looks like this?

"I think I need a shower." I remove my veil, folding the sheer mesh fabric over itself and placing it on top of the dresser behind me. I don't know if the dresser belongs to Lennon or me. In fact, I don't know what is mine and what isn't.

Overwhelmed, I spin around, turning away from my husband. I reach behind my back, fumbling to find the zipper. I bend my hands, contorting my wrists until I've got a grip on the tiny metal teardrop pull. My fingers burn as I try to pull it down, but it doesn't budge. Seriously, why do they make these zipper pulls so goddamn tiny?

I grunt in frustration when two large hands cover mine. A shiver works its way down my spine when I feel Lennon lean forward, bringing his mouth to the hollow of my ear.

"Having a little trouble? Let me help you."

I don't hold back. I lean into him, turning my face toward his mouth. His heavy breaths brush against my skin like the lavender flower he brushed against me in the greenhouse.

"Thank you," I whisper, allowing my arms to fall at my sides.

Fire shoots between my legs. I'm a mess.

He's towering over me, keeping his face close to mine. My eyes flutter before closing, breathing him in. He's a mixture of cologne, lavender, and dirt.

He manages to get the zipper undone. My shoulders instinctively fall, the relief of my tight dress releasing its hold on me. Lennon's body is pressed against mine as he runs his fingertips across my bare back, widening the opening of my dress. The thin silk straps of my dress fall off my shoulders.

"Better?" he asks. His fingertips feel like a feather being dragged across my skin.

I lick my lips and bite down on the bottom one. "Mmhmm." I nod.

I'm tired and exhausted, but I'm also craving more of Lennon's touch. I don't want him to stop.

It's as if he's caught me in a trance. I'm stuck on a loop, getting high with every single touch. The more he presses, the more I let him in. I'm like Alice falling down the rabbit hole, having no fear in taking a giant bite of cake.

Our marriage vows were lies. Does that mean every dirty word and every heated touch is a lie as well? I can't make sense of what's right or wrong, up or down. All I know is how it feels when I'm with him. How it's always felt.

Our wedding has broken down a wall we've built up until this point. The moment Lennon led me to the greenhouse, and I willingly went with him, was the moment everything changed. Lies blurred into releasing all of our inhibitions. Our kiss at the altar opened the floodgates. We either haven't been able to shut them or we don't want to. We don't fight the current, allowing it to take us with it instead.

Sliding his hands underneath my dress, Lennon pulls the fabric away from my back, allowing the dress to fall off my shoulders. The straps slide down my arms as Lennon's hands work their way around my back to the side of my ribs. His fingertips leave a blazing trail across my skin as he grips both of my breasts in his large hands.

I gasp and tilt my head back, resting it against his chest. He's taller than me, at least by ten inches. I've always been short and haven't grown since I was in the eighth grade. But even with him towering over me, I feel safe with Lennon. His touch is gentle yet measured with purpose, taking care to know it means more than just a simple touch.

He cups each of my breasts in his hands, allowing them to fill his large palms. His hands are only on one part of my body, but I feel him everywhere. I moan, rolling my hips back until I press against his hardened cock straining against his pants.

Gliding his thumbs over my pebbled nipples makes me gasp again.

"Do you like it when I touch you like this?" he asks quietly.

"Yes." My straps fall out of my arms, and my dress bunches around my hips. The upper half of my body is completely exposed. Lennon's hands continue to massage my breasts. He glides his thumbs over my nipples, pinching them ever so slightly before he repeats the cycle.

"I want your mouth on me," I admit, wishing he'd kiss me.

"Like this?" he asks, gently placing his lips on my shoulder. I roll my head away from him, exposing more of my neck.

"Yes," I whisper. "Like that."

"And this?" He drags his tongue down the curve of my neck.

"Yes."

"Tell me..." He kisses my neck. "Mrs. Harding." He kisses behind my ear.

"Oh, God," I moan. "What?"

He pinches my ear lobe between his teeth, careful not to bite down on the five-thousand-dollar earrings he insisted I buy with my dress.

"Did your pussy spend the rest of the night wishing it were touched by more than just my hand?"

My heart expands as I place my hand over his right one, guiding him lower. I pull his hand down along my stomach, over the bit of dress wrapped around my hips until we hit the top of the slit in my dress.

He allows me to take the lead until I bring both our hands between my thighs. I press his fingers against my hardened clit, cupping myself with his large palm, making sure he feels my wetness. I'm soaking for him, the memory of his hand on me in the greenhouse amplifying every sensation.

"What do you think, husband?" I ask, jerking my hips backward into his cock.

"Fuck." He hisses. "I'm thinking we need to rectify this situation. Don't you agree?"

"You shouldn't..." I swallow, catching my breath as he works his fingers against my clit and his thumb over my nipple. "You shouldn't ask questions you already know the answer to, Mr. Harding."

FIFTEEN

Lennon

I want to tear at the remaining bit of dress standing between me and my wife. My cock is begging to be free from the constraints of my black pants. It's a fickle thing to both want to make something last but hurry to the finish line at the same time.

I try to remind myself that Laurel isn't going anywhere. We live together now. She's my wife, and if this is what she wants every night, fuck, even every single day, then that's what I'll do. I could touch Laurel like this forever and never tire of it.

The way her body reacts. The way her hips rock into me and her head rests on my chest. She feels safe and protected. Cared for. And something in the way I caught her staring at me across the courtyard earlier, after our moment in the greenhouse, tells me she isn't used to being cared for.

For the first time since undoing her dress, I take a step away from Laurel. I let her breasts go, but not before giving her nipples a small pinch, causing her to yelp. I smirk, delighted in the sound coming from her throat.

I don't say another word when my hands make it to her hair. I pull a thousand bobby pins and clips from her dark brown strands. Each one allows another curl to cascade down her back.

A moan escapes Laurel's mouth.

"Now, I know I can be quite arrogant at times, Mrs. Harding." I laugh. "But I don't even think *I* can give you an orgasm by simply touching your hair."

She laughs, turning her head and looking up at me. Her indigo eyes widen under her long dark lashes, and I'm fucking done for. "Maybe not, but with the way you put your hands on me, you come pretty close."

My heart pounds beneath muscle and bone. I'm certain if we stayed quiet, the both of us could hear it. When she says things like that, I think about pinching myself just to be sure I've heard her correctly.

"Turn around," I order, my cock swelling.

She does as I say, and I drag my thumb down the length of her jaw before dropping to my knees in front of her.

I wrap my hands around the bunched silk fabric around her waist and pull it over her hips. With it pooled at her feet, she steps out.

Looking up at her, I nearly lose my breath. She's completely naked. Peaked nipples, smooth tan skin. Her stomach is in line with my face, but I keep my focus on her eyes.

She steps forward, running her fingers through my hair. My dark brown strands aren't as stiff as they were at the start of the wedding, most likely due to Laurel's hands and the wind caused by the helicopter.

"Are you sure this is what you want?" I ask her. I need to know before continuing. "Being with you like this wasn't part of our terms and conditions."

"I know." There's a distant look in her eyes, as if she's remembering the terms of our marriage, but it only lasts for a second before it's gone. Gripping the ends, she looks down at me with fire in her eyes. "I want your mouth on me."

She repeats the same words to me she said earlier. Wrapping both arms around her legs, I grab onto her ass, cupping each of her full cheeks in my palms. She gasps as she stumbles forward. Her stomach lands against my mouth, and I plant a kiss below her belly button, then over her sweet pussy.

I keep my left hand on her ass cheek and bring the other behind her knee. I lift her leg, bending it over my shoulder, exposing her to me.

Keeping my eyes pinned to hers, I stick my tongue out, sliding it between her wet slit.

She tugs on my hair again, crying out when I run the tip of my tongue to her swollen clit.

"Oh, fuck, Lennon," she cries. Her mouth falls open as she rocks her hips, pressing into me. "More," she begs. "I need more."

"Fuck, Laurel. You taste so fucking good." Her right leg bends slightly, letting me know she's already getting close.

I don't want to stop, knowing this is what Laurel wants. Release. But I don't think I can watch her have another orgasm without being inside her. I'm a greedy motherfucker.

Without warning, I drop her leg from my shoulder and stand. With her jaw dropped, she watches as I bend down, wrapping my arms around her legs, lifting her over my shoulder.

She yelps as I carry her toward the bathroom.

"Lennon!" She grips the back of my shirt for support.

Her bare ass is next to my face, and my arm is wrapped around her smooth legs. I run my left hand up and along the back of her thigh, stopping on her round pillowy cheek and giving it a squeeze. I slap her ass. She squeals and writhes against me.

"This isn't fair." She whines. "My entire body feels like it's going to explode with all your teasing."

I carry her through the doorway to our bathroom and don't let her down until we're standing in front of the large shower.

She holds her breath and keeps her eyes on me as I reach behind her to turn the water on.

"I only thought it was appropriate I carry you over the threshold." I smirk. "Tradition and all..."

She holds her breath. I can tell when something I've done or said is unexpected. She inhales a sharp breath, and her body tenses. The look on her face tells me she's worried she's allowing herself to go too far with me too quickly—the same fears I felt earlier in the greenhouse—but I stop those thoughts as soon as they creep back in.

Laurel is my wife. I'm attracted to her. I have been for a long time. If it wasn't for her giving me the signal she's okay with it too, I'd have left her alone, agreeing to suffer sleeping on my stiff leather couch if that were the case. We wouldn't be standing here.

I empty my pockets, pulling out the lavender flower I'd rubbed against her in the greenhouse. Her eyes follow it as I turn to lay it on the marble sink.

"I thought you got rid of it."

"Absolutely not. This one is mine." I pick up the flower and bring it to my nose. Laurel's cheeks flush red. "I couldn't risk it blowing away at the reception or when we got in the helicopter."

A breath falls between her parted lips, and I lose all resolve. My eyes dance between hers and her pretty mouth.

Steam billows from the large, stone-walled shower beside us. I place my hands on either side of her face, pulling her mouth to mine.

She kisses me back, leaning into me on a moan.

I haven't kissed her since the greenhouse. I was afraid if I did, I wouldn't be able to stop. And I was right. I can't stop.

She opens her mouth, moaning once more. She swipes her tongue against mine. I walk her back into the shower until her body lands against the tiled wall. She shivers and prickles with goosebumps. I place my hands on either side of her head, caging her in.

She bites my bottom lip, tugging on it before pulling away. Her delicate hands work to unbutton my soaking wet shirt. She peels it off me, followed by unbuckling my belt.

Once she's removed my belt, pants, and boxer briefs, she stops. Her eyes roam over my chest, surveying every tattoo inked into my skin.

"I have a slight addiction," I say over the streaming water.

"Slight?" She pops an eyebrow and giggles. She stares at each one in fascination, dragging her fingers over them, tracing the various lines.

"Some have meaning, most don't." I hold my breath when she touches the one beneath my heart, hoping she doesn't see the one on my back. Not yet.

Her lips part as she silently reads the words on my chest, tracing them with her left hand. The bright lights of the bathroom shine against the large diamond on her finger.

"Take a sad song and make it better," I whisper.

Laurel looks up at me as droplets of water stream down her face.

The corner of my mouth curls, but my chest aches. The reason behind my tattoo sits on the tip of my tongue, but I hold back. I'm too focused on Laurel to dig deep into the parts of my soul I've refused to acknowledge for the past six years.

I want to tell her I haven't forgotten about our night together and I carry the proof with me on my skin as a reminder. Because for so long, I was convinced I'd never feel the way I felt that night.

My father made sure of it. Injected it into my bones.

But I've been determined not to forget. I want to open up to

Laurel, but every time I've been given the opportunity, I freeze. The words get stuck in my messy, unorganized heart.

"It's from a Beatles song," I tell her, focusing back on the tattoo she's seen.

She accepts my answer without further interrogation, trailing her fingers down the center of my chest. She's moved on, desire sparking in her gaze. My cock has sprung to life, hard as a rock and begging to be inside Laurel.

"What do you want?" I tease.

Wrapping her hand around my length, she tugs on it, jerking me forward. I grunt, pressing my fingers into the wall.

"I want my husband to fuck me," she whispers, tilting her chin up. Her filthy words fall on her innocent voice.

"We can make that happen." I bend my knees slightly, grabbing onto the back of Laurel's knees. She inhales that familiar sharp breath again when she wraps her legs around me. I push her back against the wall. Her arms drape over my shoulders, and when I pull my hips back and slide my cock inside her, her nails cut into my flesh.

"Oh, my God." Her head tilts back against the tile. Black streaks of mascara and bits of shimmering glitter from her eyeshadow cover her cheeks, dripping down to her faded red lipstick. She's bared herself to me. Open, raw, and gorgeous.

Once I've slid my entire length inside her, we both remain still, allowing the feeling to settle between us.

"Fuck," I breathe out. "Your pussy feels fucking amazing, Mrs. Harding."

"I told you I've been wet for you all night," she pants, tightening her legs around my waist. "You weren't kidding when you said you wanted me begging for you."

"Right. Beg for it." I grunt, sliding myself out of her before pushing myself back in. I pump myself into her a few more times, watching as her face transforms with every thrust. I'm holding her up, pressed against the wall. She tilts her head back, exposing her neck to me. I press my mouth to her neck, licking her wet skin.

"Please, Lennon," she cries out, clawing at my chest.

"Please, what?"

"Faster," she moans. "Harder."

I do as she says. Being with Laurel now is different than the night we fucked in my car. Not because it's been six years, but because this time I haven't been drinking. I'm completely fucking sober. My mind is clear and focused. And now, being inside Laurel is even better than I remember.

I wrap one hand under the bottom of her leg, holding her up. I drive my cock into her again and try my best not to slam her body too hard against the stone tile. The full curve of her body fills my hand. Her full breasts are pushed against my inked chest. She's soft and supple, wet and smooth. I thrust in and out of her, and the faster and harder I move, the tighter she gets.

"Fuck, Mrs. Harding." I grunt. "I'm about to come, so you'd better come with me."

"Why?" she asks, rolling her hips off the wall. "You watched me come without you in the greenhouse. Don't you think it's my turn to have the privilege of watching you come undone beneath me."

"Fuck that." She yelps when I slip myself out of her. Her feet fall to the floor. I quickly plant a kiss on her swollen mouth before gripping her hip and spinning her around.

She places her hands above her head, against the wall, breathing heavily in anticipation. Reaching up, I grab the shower head, adjust the settings to the one I want, and bring it to her front. Her head is dipped low, but when I press the pulsating jet of water to her clit, she lifts her head and gasps.

"Oh, my God, Lennon," she breathes.

Pulling her hips back, I find her entrance, driving my cock

into her from the back. Pushing against the wall, she presses her hips into me, taking my full length as I continue to work her clit from the front.

The air in the shower grows cold. The chill creeps along our skin as I keep the stream of water pressed against Laurel's swollen clit. All the blood rushes to my cock.

I've spent so much time teasing and playing with Laurel, I didn't realize I was also doing the same to myself. I lean forward, keeping the showerhead in front of her and rocking my hips.

"Are you close to coming?" I growl.

"Is that a real question?" she softly whimpers, unable to stay still. She's writhing under me. "I've been close to slipping over the edge this whole time."

"Then, do it, Mrs. Harding," I tell her, pressing my lips to her back. "I want to watch you quivering from my cock. I want to watch you take me as my cum spills inside you."

I press the entire showerhead harder against her and move my hips quicker. I look down, watching as I slide into her thrust for thrust. A beautiful sight I want to remember.

"Lennon, I'm coming." My name falling from her open mouth pushes me to my limit. Her pussy contracts around me as she reaches her climax, screaming out my name.

Blood rushes to the base of my cock and I groan as I come inside her. The showerhead drops at my feet, spinning and spraying water against the far wall. But we don't care. Feeling me reach my orgasm, she rolls her hips against me. I run my hand along the length of her back, admiring the shape of her. I catch my breath as she straightens herself and looks over her shoulder.

With satiated eyes, she gives me a small smile.

I place a gentle kiss on her cheek and slip out of her, then pick up the showerhead and set it back on the holder.

"I'm going to be sore tomorrow," she says, resting her back

against the wall. She's leaning against it, looking up at me. I step toward her and reach beside me, grabbing the purple pouf I only assume to be hers since I've never seen it before. Ray must have put it in here when he was unpacking Laurel's bag.

"Don't worry." I squeeze a dollop of body wash onto the pouf and massage it until bubbles form. I lower the pouf between Laurel's legs, gently rubbing it over her center. "I'm your husband now. I'll make sure you're taken care of. But I can't say I'm not pleased knowing the effect I have on you, Laurel."

With her half-hooded, indigo eyes staring up at me, she stands on her toes and kisses me on the lips. "You have no idea the effect you have on me, Lennon."

SIXTEEN

LAUREL

I've always known this was the plan.

Lennon and I get married. We stage it to look like a real, whirlwind wedding. Then we both go back to work the next day as if it never happened. After all, that's the whole reason he married me in the first place. He has a business to run, and now that he's secured his inheritance, he's effortlessly slid into his new role. Long days and nights keeping him at his office. But knowing the facts hasn't deterred the feelings I've come to realize since our wedding day.

I've fallen for my husband.

I'm not delusional in thinking we'd have the honeymoon of my dreams, or even a honeymoon at all, but disappointment has burrowed itself into my bones, refusing to let up. Over the course of the past three days since our wedding, I've woken up alone, with Lennon already at work. After the second day, I began to question if it's his normal routine to wake up before the sun has begun to rise, or if he's doing it to avoid me.

Reassuring myself he's an early riser to his core, I shove aside the negative thoughts invading my mind.

I rely on the memory of his mouth against mine. His voice

rumbling in my ear, telling me he wanted me to want him. And the moment he reached into his pocket and pulled out the flower he'd stolen from the greenhouse before placing it on the bathroom counter.

I tell myself none of those moments have been lies even if this marriage is one. Because since the night of our wedding, Lennon has infuriatingly kept his distance. He hasn't touched me. He hasn't laid another finger on me.

He's even gone as far as falling asleep in a T-shirt and his signature gray sweatpants. As if the gray sweatpants weren't enough visual torture, it's been impossible not to look at him without my eyes falling to the ring he now wears on his fourth finger. A ring to signify to the rest of the world he belongs to me. But does he really?

Frustrated both mentally and sexually, I toss the bed sheets aside, hoping work will take my mind off Lennon. I swing my legs over the edge of the bed only to immediately regret it. My head pounds from my forehead down to the base of my neck. Snot drips from my nose. I frantically fumble for a tissue, pulling one from the small box sitting on my nightstand. I blow my nose. One nostril is completely clogged, and when I swallow it feels as if I've eaten a thousand knives.

"Shit," I croak in a voice deeper than usual.

Feeling like my head is the size of a hot air balloon, I shuffle to the shower before another string of snot drips from my nose. I stay under the stream of hot water longer than usual, hoping it will clear my sinuses enough to think clearly and go to work.

After a long shower, I head straight to my closet like a zombie and get dressed in a simple baby pink blouse and black dress pants. I've blow-dried my hair and swept some mascara over my lashes before heading out into the kitchen.

Ray, Lennon's, scratch that... *mine* and Lennon's jack of all trades, is waiting for me in the kitchen, his laptop open as usual.

I call Ray a jack of all trades because I haven't been able to pin down one single job he's responsible for. It seems he does most everything for Lennon, other than Lennon's actual job of working at Harding Holdings. And now, it seems he does the same for me.

Driver. Assistant. Bodyguard. Friend. A jack of all trades.

Since I only see Lennon in the evenings, I've come to know Ray quite a bit more over the last few days. I haven't brought up the night we first met when I'd mistaken him for my rideshare six years ago, or how it appeared he remembered me when we met again. Considering Lennon and I still haven't talked about it, I figured it's best to keep it as the elephant in the room between us. Knowing it's there but never speaking it into reality.

"Good morning, Mrs. Harding." Ray grins. "I've taken the liberty of making you a fresh cup of coffee. Two creams, no sugar, just the way you like it."

"No coffee for me this morning, Ray." I sniff. "I don't think my throat can handle it."

"Are you okay?" His forehead wrinkles as he lifts both eyebrows at me. "You don't look very well."

"I feel like my head is going to explode," I say, passing him in search of medicine. Starting with the farthest one, I open every cabinet, hoping to discover pills or some sort of liquid hidden behind the coffee mugs or sauté pans.

"Can I help you find something?" Ray asks, looking up from his laptop.

"Medicine. I need medicine. Preferably something that will numb whatever is going on up here." I wave my hand over my face. "But not strong enough to cause me to pass out and wake up a week later. Please tell me my husband keeps medicine here. There was none in our bathroom."

Ray slides off his stool and opens the cabinet to the right of the sink. He hands me a bottle of bright orange liquid.

"Thank you." I sigh, sniffing again.

"Are you sure you want to go to work today, Mrs. Harding?" Ray asks. "Maybe it's best you stay home."

"I can't." Taking a swig of medicine, I walk over to the large dining room table and slide my laptop into my black leather work bag. "I have an important case that goes to trial in a few months, and I have a ton of paperwork I need to sift through."

"Okay, but if you need to come home, just give me a call."

A tickle reaches my nose, and I tilt my head back, preparing myself for a sneeze. The reaction causes me to squeeze my eyes shut, which only adds to the pulsating pressure in my head. I sneeze five times in a row while Ray watches on with a mixture of sympathy and disgust.

"I'm not sure Mr. Harding is going to be pleased when he finds out you went to work like this."

I roll my eyes, waiting in front of the elevator doors. Ray presses the call button.

I cross my arms over my chest, grinding my teeth from the echo of pain vibrating in my bones. "If my husband can go to work as easily and early as he appears to daily, then there's no reason I can't as well."

Ray presses his mouth into a tight line and nods once in understanding, dropping his argument. The elevator doors slide open, and he holds his arm out, allowing me to step in first. It's strange having someone escort me everywhere. I'm no stranger to bodyguards. My parents used to have one: Lewis. We were close when I was growing up, and at times, I caught myself thinking of him as the cool uncle. But he was always more attentive to my parents than he was to me or my siblings.

But Ray is different. He is to me what Lewis was to my parents.

I let my bitterness for Lennon's scarce presence fill the air in the elevator. I'm unsure whether Ray notices. If he does, he doesn't tell me.

By the time I make it to my office, I've used nearly every tissue I shoved into my purse before leaving the apartment. I also have only one text from Lennon, letting me know he's going to be in meetings all day, but he'll call me after his first one ends. I haven't responded. Mostly because doing anything involving moving my body is painful, and partly because I wouldn't know what to tell him. It's hard to know how much I'm able to open up to Lennon about when he keeps his feelings to himself. Sometimes at night, I lie in bed and watch him sleep, wondering what he's dreaming or what his life looked like growing up. I want to know more about him and how his heart works, but I don't want to push him, either.

He opened himself up to me the night of our wedding. Vulnerability filled his dark blue eyes as I traced my finger along his tattoo. But I've come to learn Lennon doesn't allow his vulnerability to show for long. I'm hoping, with time, he'll let me in. But until then, we'll stay sitting in this limbo of sorts. Wavering back and forth of letting each other in just enough before shutting the door again.

I decide to leave his text unanswered, hoping to distract myself with work.

I fail miserably. An hour later, I've struggled to respond to even two of my emails. My fingers and bones hurt, and my eyes are fighting to stay open.

Three knocks on my office door pull me away from my computer screen.

"Busy?" Frederick asks, raising his eyebrows. The moment he catches sight of my appearance, he jerks back, scrunching his nose. "Are you all right?"

"I'm fine." I brush him off. He sounds like Ray.

"You don't sound it."

I cut him a glare and click out of my emails, resting my head in my hands. After a few seconds of silence, I look up at my uncle. He's still staring at me wide eyed. Only now, he's standing noticeably farther away than when he first walked in here.

"Really." I clear my stinging throat, crossing my arms on my desk. "I'm okay. I just have a little cold. I'm not even sure where it came from."

"If you're sick, you should have stayed home."

Irritation pricks at my chest.

My uncle's uncanny ability to flip between being boss on the verge of letting me go to a concerned father figure makes my head spin.

"It's astonishing, Frederick," I clip, my annoyance boiling over. "It's astonishing that you beg me to land more clients and remind me on a daily basis how our firm is on the brink of collapse but complain when I actually come in and do the work."

The wrinkles in his forehead deepen, and sadness fills his eyes as he frowns. "I'm sorry, Laurel. I never meant to place that much pressure on you."

I suppress the mock laughter fighting to come out of me, but I hold it back, knowing it would only make my throat feel worse.

Every single day since my parents died, Frederick has done nothing but put pressure on me. Thinking back on it, I'm not even certain he grieved the death of his brother and sister-in-law. At least not publicly.

I shake my head and bite my bottom lip. Tears well behind my eyes, and I'm unsure if the reason for them is from this conversation with my uncle, the stress of Roe's cancer, Lennon's distance over the past three days, or the sickness that has managed to knock me out both physically and mentally.

But my beaten down heart tells me it's a combination of all four.

I look up at Fred. "I don't think I can talk about this right now."

"Okay." He nods in understanding, pulling a newspaper from under his arm and slapping it on my desk. "I just wanted to let you know The Boston Globe has published the news of your wedding this morning."

With trepidation, I pick it up and read the headline.

A SECRET LOVE, A SECRET WEDDING

BOSTON ELITES LENNON HARDING AND LAUREL BRANFORD TIE THE KNOT IN UNDIS-CLOSED INTIMATE WEDDING

Below the headline is a picture of Lennon and me kissing. The only kiss we shared that day in public. The one right after we said, 'I do'.

We look happy and in love. It's strange seeing us from this perspective when I'm the one who lived it. Lennon's hand is wrapped around the side of my face, pulling me close. His head is tilted as he presses his lips firmly to mine, like he won't be able to breathe if he pulled away. We look like a couple who've been together for years.

In the bottom corner of the photograph is our photographer's name. It's no surprise finding the story of mine and Lennon's wedding in the paper. It's always been part of the plan. At the urging of Lennon's attorney, Perry, and my uncle, we all agreed publicity was for the best.

Lennon's marriage would show stability and strength for his family's company. Even though the public isn't aware of the stipulations placed on his inheritance, they knew the story of his marriage to me would quieten the speculation around the future of the company, considering Lennon's reputation. It appears I wasn't alone in thinking Lennon was like his father when it came to relationships.

As for me, Frederick couldn't wait for the announcement. He was more than convinced my marriage to a Harding would increase our public image. I guess after today only time will tell if my fake marriage has bettered our reputation.

Looking at mine and Lennon's kiss at the altar has my heart twisting in ways I didn't know it could. I've fallen for my husband, and I've fallen hard. But have I fallen harder than him? Judging by the photo on the front page of the Boston Globe, I would say I haven't. But pictures can be deceiving. I want to believe everything Lennon said and did the other night, but it's difficult when he's hot one second, cold the next.

I hand the newspaper back to Fred, but he waves his finger and points at my desk. His lip curls in disgust. "You can keep it. I can find another copy."

"Thanks, I guess." Reaching for a tissue from the box on my desk, I blow my nose and wipe it before tossing it into the trash.

"Before I go, I meant to ask you. Has Monroe said anything to you about what's going on with her lately?"

My stomach drops. Roe asked me not to tell Fred. I've respected her wishes, but I can feel the blood draining from my face at the prospect of where this conversation is headed. I'm not prepared to handle the conversation if Fred tells me he knows or if he guesses.

"What do you mean?" I cautiously ask.

"I don't know." He shrugs his large shoulders. "She's been quiet lately, and it's very unlike her, if you know what I mean."

"I do." I give him a small smile.

"I was just curious if maybe her and Steven were going through anything, or if it might have to do with her work at the museum."

I frown, shaking my head. "Not that I'm aware of."

"Okay." his eyes wander in thought before swinging back to me. "Well, if you see her, let her know I'm worried about her." He begins walking out of my office but stops in the doorway. "On second thought, maybe don't see her until you're better. You might be contagious."

My heart sinks into my stomach. Frederick leaves my office, and I'm quick to grab my phone. Panic settles in, overriding all the pain I've felt since waking up. I scramble picking up my phone, nearly dropping it as I call Roe.

She picks up on the first ring. "Hey, sis."

"Roe," I croak, clearing my throat. I swallow my breath and shove aside the pain.

"Are you okay? You sound sick."

"I am sick," I blurt out. "And I just realized what that could mean. I don't know how or when I got it, but I'm worried I might have passed it on to you. You aren't feeling sick, too, are you? Sore throat? Stuffy nose? Feeling like your head might explode?"

My pulse quickens. If Roe is sick, it could lead to any number of complications. It might compromise her chemo schedule and even her surgery. Her immune system can't be put at any more risk, and the guilt I would have for being the one to give it to her would shatter me.

"No," she whispers. "I'm fine. I'm actually at my weekly chemo session right now."

I breathe a sigh of relief and pinch the bridge of my nose. Silent tears stream down my face. An avalanche of emotion crashes against my chest, and the floodgates have opened. Roe. Lennon. My head. It's all too much all at once.

"How's it going?" I ask her, trying my best to not let her know I'm crying.

"As good as it can be," she whispers again, sadness laced in her wispy voice.

"I told you I wouldn't mind sitting in with you one of the days you're at the hospital. You're there for eight hours, Roe. It must be taxing." I don't tell her about my conversation with Fred. The last thing she needs is to feel like I'm pressuring her to tell him when I know it's not what she wants. I don't want her worrying whether I'm going to spill the beans or not.

"It is, but I have Steven," she reassures me. "Besides, you just got married, and I don't want to hold you back from spending time with your new husband. Regardless of the reasoning behind your marriage."

"You're not holding me back," I tell her.

Lennon's doing that all on his own.

"Good," she whispers again. "Listen, it's a little difficult to talk in here since there are other patients getting their treatments, too. I'll call you when I feel up to it later. Okay?"

"Okay." I blow out an exasperated breath.

"Feel better soon, Laurel." I can practically feel her warm smile through the phone. "I know you're at work, but consider going home. You sound terrible."

I chuckle. "Thanks."

"I love you."

"Love you, too." When Roe hangs up, the silent tears I shed when I was on the phone only get worse.

My heart is incredibly heavy, and it does nothing to help the weight radiating across my body for varying reasons.

I reach for another tissue, wiping away my tears and then swiping it across my nose. My eyes hurt. My chest hurts. Everything hurts.

Reluctantly, I pick up my phone. It's nine in the morning. Lennon's probably still in his first meeting, but I don't think I can make it until then.

I click on Ray's number and type out a message before

packing up my laptop and heading down to the main lobby of the building.

> Laurel: You win, Ray. I need to go home. I'm on my way down to the lobby.

I step into the elevator and fall back against the wall, watching the numbers go down with every level. My body aches as I close my eyes, ready to hibernate in bed and not wake up until this sickness is gone. But I know even then that's not what I truly need to feel better.

What I need is all those things... but with my husband lying beside me.

SEVENTEEN

Lennon

"Fucking unbelievable." Micah slaps his hand on the table, wearing the largest grin I've ever seen. He swings his wide eyes at me. "You've been CEO of Harding Holdings for only three days, and you've managed to close nine of the contracts that were held off the past month. We didn't lose a single client."

"Great job, Lennon." Tyson, our accountant, taps on the tablet he's holding between his hands. "If you keep this up, you're on track to match your profits from last year."

Leaning forward and resting my arms on the edge of the table, I can't help but side eye my phone for the millionth time since I sat down in this conference room an hour ago. It feels like I've been living here the past few days, but all I want to do is talk to my wife.

I haven't heard from Laurel today. We've only been married for three days, but we've managed to pick up a routine. A routine of sorts. But to secure these accounts that Tyson and Micah are raving about, I've had to sacrifice my time with Laurel by way more than expected.

Not having accounted for a honeymoon, I immediately headed into work the morning after our wedding. It took all the strength I had to leave her lying in my bed completely naked and sore from the night before, but my father's words echoed in my mind, reminding me of the legacy he left behind.

Call it greed.

Call it ambition.

Call it ego.

I want to be better than my father. I want to take his company and increase our profits and footprint tenfold. But I know to get there, I can't risk taking a break. Even if only for a day. I'd already left the company in limbo for thirty days.

Jam packed with meetings from morning until night means I haven't seen much of Laurel. I've relied on her texts. I've relied on seeing her in my bed, sleeping as if she's belonged there all along. Because she has. My body aches for her, and my cock is pleading to be inside her again, but I've also allowed the fear to creep in again. The same fear I had the night of the wedding. I don't want Laurel thinking I've taken our arranged marriage as permission to touch her whenever I want if that isn't the kind of marriage she had in mind.

It's been a battle between my heart and my dick, but I don't want her thinking she's going to get the Lennon she's known in the past, so I've slowed things down a bit. Though even I have to admit it's too slow.

"Lennon?" Micah calls me, pulling me from my thoughts.

I look around the room. Tyson is no longer sitting beside Micah. Everyone else has already left. It's just my brother and me.

"Oh, shit." I run a hand down the side of my face. Exhaustion settles in my bones. "I didn't realize everyone left."

"Tyson said he was going to compile a spreadsheet of all the financial details of these new accounts and email them over to you."

"Good." I sigh, flicking my wrist to read the time. "Our next client should be here in an hour. I have a few emails to send off, so I'll meet you back here." I stand from my place at the conference table and head back to my office with my phone in hand.

Micah follows me, sliding his hands into the pockets of his suit as we walk.

"Do you remember Archer Mayfield?" he asks.

I nod. "Isn't he your childhood best friend or something?"

Unlocking my phone, I check to make sure I didn't miss any messages from Laurel. I didn't. The last message I have from her is the one where she sent me a picture of the lavender flower I'd taken from the greenhouse. She slid it into the sleeve of one of the vinyl records she'd found on a shelf in the living room, next to my mother's old record player. I laughed at the picture of the album cover under a heavy abstract marble statue one of my decorators must have bought to make my place appear more personal. Or some shit like that.

Laurel told me it was the only solution she came up with when she realized I wasn't lying when I told her I didn't own a single book—a problem she said she was going to rectify immediately. I sent her a message this morning letting her know I was going to call her after my first meeting of the day, but she never responded.

"Dude, are you listening?" Micah asks, annoyed. "I've been wanting to talk to you about this for the past week. Now that you're out of your sticky situation, we can."

"I'm sorry. I haven't heard from Laurel today."

"How's that going, by the way?" Micah prods. "How's married life been?"

I take a deep breath, not wanting to pour my heart out to my little brother. I can't tell him I've fallen for my wife. Not when said wife isn't supposed to mean more than our signatures at the bottom of a certificate.

Hardings don't do marriage and commitment.

A wire snaps in my chest, and I inhale a shaky breath. Laurel has completely fucked me up in the best possible way. It's as if I'm forcing myself to live the life I did when my father was alive before I proposed to her.

"Married life is fine." I shove the feelings aside temporarily, treading as carefully as I can with my brother. Transparent lies are better than bold faced ones. At least that's what I tell myself. "What were you saying about Archer?"

"Oh, right." He scratches at the stubble lining his chin. "Archer is my best friend from high school. I don't know if you remember him, but he lived next door to me when my mom had that house out in Cambridge."

"I remember him." I nod, recalling the night Micah had brought him along on one of our weekly family dinners at my father's favorite restaurant, Eclipse. One of the only nights we would see him when he was still living with his mother. And I remember the night I bailed Archer and Micah out of jail after they got arrested.

"Well," Micah starts, pulling me from the memory. "Archer runs a giant tech firm out along the West Coast after moving out there last year. But he wants to start expanding his way to the east, so I thought maybe we could set up a meeting with him."

"Sure." I don't hesitate. Helping Micah's best friend isn't a problem. My little brother has dedicated enough of his time to our family business and fought tooth and nail to be a voice in this company. "See when Archer can schedule a meeting to present his business plan. Preferably next week sometime, but double check with Olivia because at this point, I have no fucking clue what I'm doing. I'm running on fumes, and we haven't even made it halfway through the week."

"Perfect." Micah beams, screeching to a halt in the hallway. "I'll see you back in the conference room in an hour."

"Great," I mutter. I don't know why, but a prickling sensation plays at the back of my neck with Laurel's silence. Like a knife, an ache twists in my chest.

Once Micah turns his back to me, I'm hot on my heels to my office. Olivia is sitting at her desk, the sound of her long nails meeting her keyboard echoing down the hallway.

"Hello, Mr. Harding." She stands, grabbing a stack of papers from her desk. The usual list of notes and messages she took in my absence.

I hold my hand up. "Unless any of those are from my wife, I don't want them."

"Oh." She blinks. "Um." Her body twists as she holds the papers, unsure whether she should still hand them to me or place them back on her desk.

"Have you heard from her?" I ask.

Olivia's eyebrows arch across her forehead. "Your wife?"

"Yes, Olivia." I grind my molars. "My wife."

"No, sir. I haven't. Would you like me to call down to her office and let her know you would like to speak with her?"

"Yes." I place my hands on my hips, my face heating with irritation. Or fear. Fuck, it might be both. "I want you to send her call straight to me, and if she's in a meeting, leave a message telling her to call me immediately."

"Of course." Olivia sits back in her chair and picks up the receiver of her desk phone.

I slam my office door, disappointed to not find Laurel sitting at my desk half naked.

I pull out my phone again and call her. She doesn't pick up.

Walking over to the far window of my office, I stare out at the city. There are plenty of explanations as to why Laurel might not be answering: meeting with a prospective client, sitting in at a hearing downtown, accident on the way into work.

It's irrational and stupid. Foolish. My throat starts to swell with every passing second. I loosen the tie around my neck. My hands are clammy, and it feels as if my veins have been injected with liquid heat again. It feels like when I wake up from a nightmare. I haven't had one since Laurel moved in. I wasn't sure why, but I hoped maybe my subconscious knew she was there, casting out the nightmare.

Although the panic attack I'm suffering from right now feels the same as when I wake up from a nightmare, my fear multiplies, because this time is different. I'm not asleep or caught in a dream state, imagining the guilt and hopelessness. This is real. I'm aware of every beat of my heart and every breath squeezing through my constricted lungs.

The intercom on my phone beeps, letting me know Olivia would like to speak with me. My legs carry me swiftly across my office, eating up the space between me and my desk.

"Yes, Olivia?"

"I called Mrs. Harding's office."

"Okay, does she plan on calling me back?"

"I didn't speak with her," Olivia explains. "I spoke with her secretary. He told me Mrs. Harding left for the day about an hour ago."

"An hour ago?" I ask incredulously. I look up at the clock hanging beside the door to my office. "It's still morning. Did her secretary say why she left?"

"He said she went home sick. He also said she mentioned on her way out that her driver was taking her home."

I inhale a deep breath and swallow. "Thank you, Olivia."

"You're welcome," she says, softly. I hear the sympathy in her voice. "By the way, Erik Larsson is waiting for you in the conference room."

"Great," I grit out. "Tell him I'll be there in five minutes."

I hang up and immediately call Ray.

"Yes, sir," Ray greets in his usual tone.

"Did you take Laurel home earlier?" I ask, cutting to the chase.

"Um, yes, sir. I did."

My nostrils flare in anger. "Why didn't you inform me?"

"I apologize, sir. Mrs. Harding was adamant on going to work this morning, but shortly after, she requested I take her home. I asked her if she wanted me to inform you and she said no considering you were in meetings all day."

"Is something wrong?" I ask, trying to tone down the panic in my voice.

The beeping of the monitor. Her sad, weary eyes. Her last gasping breath. The single tears sliding down her cold cheek.

I force the sickness down my throat.

This isn't the same. This isn't the same.

I can't breathe. All sorts of disturbing images play in my mind—ones that are nauseating and heart-wrenching. Ones no normal, sane person would conjure up unless they had good reason. There's no in between in my mind. I go from zero to a thousand, immediately darting to the worst possible scenario.

"She woke up with a head cold, Mr. Harding. Sore throat, stuffy nose, headache. She climbed into bed as soon as we got home and hasn't emerged since."

"Oh," I sigh, my stomach relaxing. I place my hand against my chest. "Let me know when she wakes up. I don't care what she said about me being in meetings."

"Yes, sir."

"Oh, and Ray?"

"Yes?"

"Next time my wife leaves work because she's sick, I want to fucking know about it."

"Yes, s—"

I cut Ray off before he can finish his sentence. My phone slips from my hand, dropping on my desk with a loud thud.

A twinge of guilt hits me. I've never talked to Ray this way. Although he's worked for me the past ten years, I've always treated him with respect and valued his friendship. But my shaking hands and hammering heart couldn't take the conversation. Anchoring myself, I sit at my desk and bury my face in my hands. Pressure builds behind my eyes.

Minutes pass before I'm able to collect my thoughts and clear my mind.

When I open my eyes again, I stare at my desk as one single tear drop slides down my cheek, dropping onto the glossy wood. It splashes and pools as my heart sinks like an anchor plummeting to the bottom of the sea.

I place my hand on my chest and count my heartbeats.

Laurel is okay. She's at home, in *our* apartment, wrapped up in the safety and comfort of *our* sheets on *our* bed.

I need to get a fucking grip.

EIGHTEEN

LAUREL

Crinkling plastic and a dull thud wake me from a dead sleep. I crack my eyes open, unsure of what torture the sickness will inflict on my body when I do so. Will it be my head? My nose? If I swallow, will a searing fiery pain make its way down?

The pressure in my nose has subsided only a little. I sniff. The nostril that was clogged this morning is now clear, the sickness moving on to the other one. I groan, cracking my eyes open to the bright midday sun.

A beautiful Boston day. Summer will do that to the city. During the winter months, clouds descend over the city and make a home until summer forces its way in, waking Boston from deep hibernation.

But even though it's summer, my body wears this sickness like it's the dead of winter. My skin flashes with heat, but a shiver ripples across my body.

Closing my eyes again, I roll over and slide my arm out across the mattress. Lennon's side of the bed is still empty.

Sadness mixes and mingles with my sickness. The memories of my conversation with Roe and the absence of Lennon have my heart constricting once again.

It's difficult to love someone but not have the ability to fix them. Love can make you powerful while also making you weak. A beast with two faces. The hero and the villain. A paradox not seeking to be solved.

I want to save Roe, but I can't. I want to love Lennon, but it's difficult when he keeps me at a distance.

I open my eyes again and press my hand to my forehead. Sticky with sweat, my skin is on fire. I pant and stare at the far wall on Lennon's side of the room.

A large, brown, wooden dresser stretches from one wall to the other. Lennon's dresser. I've seen him pull socks and under-wear from the top drawers when he gets dressed for work, thinking I'm still asleep.

I gasp when I see the items covering the entire top of the dresser. Items that weren't there before.

With my broken heart and weakened body, I force myself to crawl out of bed. Searing pain radiates in my bones as I tug on the throw blanket at the foot of the bed, wrapping it around my shoulders.

I walk the few steps over to the dresser and eye every item. Bottles of water enhanced with electrolytes. Every brand and type of flu medicine in both liquid and pill form. Headache and pain medicine. A heating pad. Ice packs. Chicken noodle soup. Saltine crackers. Ginger ale. I lose track of what's in front of me. It's as if an entire pharmacy has been delivered to not only my doorstep, but my bedroom.

With watery eyes, I gasp when I see a book sitting at the end of a dresser. It's a romance novel—one I haven't read yet. I find myself smiling through my fevered state, wondering if I ever told Lennon I liked to read romance novels. I can't remember a time when I did. I flip the pages of the book before placing it back on the dresser.

Pulling the blanket around me tighter, I venture out of the

bedroom for the first time since coming home. I step over my abandoned pink blouse and black dress pants, not having the energy to pick them up.

I'm wearing only Lennon's T-shirt from last night and my panties. When I came home, I saw his shirt laid out across his dresser and felt the pull inside me, telling me to wear it.

Unsure if anyone is here, I slowly walk down the hallway, peeking into the kitchen before fully committing to entering. I'm standing at the foot of the hall as Ray sets two large tote bags on the counter. He begins emptying them, placing bags of vegetables and meat on the counter.

He twists his head in my direction when he sees me.

"I'm sorry, Mrs. Harding. I tried to be as quiet as possible. I didn't mean to wake you."

"It's..." I croak, pausing long enough to attempt to clear it without screaming out in pain. "It's okay." I nod toward my bedroom behind me. "Did you get all that stuff for me?"

"I picked it up." He nods, moving to the refrigerator. He organizes the items and places them in their proper place before shutting the door and turning around to face me. "But your husband asked me to go to the pharmacy and pick up everything you might need."

My eyebrows shoot up, and my jaw drops. I point my thumb back over my shoulder. "He asked you to buy all that?"

"Yes," he says resolutely. "He wasn't able to break away from his meeting this morning, but he wanted to make sure you had everything you might need so you were well taken care of."

A tear slips from my eye. I quickly wipe it away, not wanting Ray to see the effect Lennon's unexpected gesture has on me.

My husband brought the entire pharmacy to me.

My knees feel weak, but I'm unsure if it's from my fever or from Lennon.

I leave Ray in the kitchen and shuffle back to the bedroom. Dropping the throw blanket on the floor, I inhale another shiver. Reaching for the book, I shove it into the crook of my arm and grab the heating pad, a bottle of water, and two of the pain pills before climbing back under the sheets. This time I lay in the middle, resting my head on Lennon's pillow.

After plugging in the heating pad, I swallow the pain pills before settling in and cracking open my new book.

I don't even make it through the first page before my eyes grow too heavy to stay focused. And when I fall asleep, the pain in my body is almost erased by Lennon's presence surrounding me.

When I wake up again, darkness has descended upon my bedroom. A moan escapes my throat when a large hand slides along my bare thigh, inching toward the hem of Lennon's T-shirt I'm still wearing.

"Holy shit, Laurel. You're burning up."

I open my eyes to find Lennon's deep blue ones staring back at me. It feels like it's been forever since I've seen them.

"I know," I groan.

My throat isn't as painful as it was earlier, but the echo of it still lingers. I swallow, hoping it will soften the heat.

"Why didn't you tell me?" Lennon pleads, the corners of his mouth turning down in a frown.

"You've been so busy at work," I whisper. It's easier and less painful to whisper. "This week was too important for me to bother you."

"You're my wife, Laurel." His fingers lift the hem of his shirt I'm wearing, his fingers circling the side of my ribs. "It's my job to make sure you're taken care of and that you're protected." Guilt settles in his expression. "But I'm sorry I couldn't get out of my meeting earlier. I came home as soon as I could."

I look behind him to the cornucopia of medicine and gifts sprawled out on the dresser. I'm still in shock. Although I haven't seen much of him lately, knowing he took the time and effort to make sure I had all the medicine I would need stirs something deep inside me. A hole I didn't know existed started to fill when I saw the pharmacy in my bedroom.

When you've been used by so many others throughout your life, especially when that someone is an ex-husband, the sweet gestures are more apparent. David would never have done anything like this for me.

I look back at Lennon.

"Thank you for bringing the pharmacy to me." My shoulders quake with a gentle laugh, and I give him a small smile.

A grin spreads across his face, lighting his eyes. "Since I couldn't be here to take care of you, I wanted to make sure you had everything you needed to get better."

He pauses, the corner of his mouth curling into a playful smirk. "At least until I got here."

"I was beginning to think you were avoiding me," I admit. "You haven't really touched me since the day of the wedding."

I expect him to deny his distance, but he doesn't. He swallows, shifting his eyes to the side before looking back at me. "I didn't want you to think that just because we were married now, I thought it meant I could touch you whenever I wanted. It wasn't part of our agreement."

"Oh, that makes sense." I nod apprehensively.

He hooks his fingers under my chin. "But that doesn't mean every second of not touching you hasn't been complete and utter torture."

Heat blooms across my cheeks. "It's been torture for me, too," I confess. "You force me to sleep in this bed with you while you lay next to me in those fucking gray sweatpants."

"What's wrong with my gray sweatpants?"

"Please." I roll my eyes, refusing to believe he's never heard about what women think of men in gray sweatpants. "You can't tell me you don't know." When he doesn't answer, arching his eyebrows waiting for me to elaborate, I giggle. The motion makes my chest hurt. "They leave nothing to the imagination, Lennon."

"Huh." He juts his smooth bottom lip. "I owe you an apology, then. That must have been torture."

I laugh again as lines form in the corners of his mouth as he smiles.

Gathering what little strength I have, I place my hand to his chest, pushing gently. "You shouldn't be this close to me. I might be contagious."

"I don't care." His velvety voice glides over me like a soft blanket, pulling me closer. "Besides, you're contagious even when you aren't sick."

My pulse quickens at his words. My teeth chatter. With cold as ice toes, I slide them between his legs, attempting to warm them up.

"I think you have a fever," he points out. All I can focus on is the tiny circles he's drawing on my skin.

"Hmm." I nod in agreement. "I don't even know how I caught it. Maybe at the wedding? But it's June. I didn't think the flu was common in June."

"It's usually not." He lifts the corner of his mouth into a

smile. "But then again, nothing about this month has been normal, right?"

"Right." I get lost in his eyes. My insides melt from them. Or it could be my fever. "I feel terrible," I admit.

I blink and run my tongue across my lips. It's impossible not to want to kiss him when he's this close. My eyes fall to my hand on his chest, covering the Beatles lyric tattooed into his skin.

His eyes cast down, following my hand.

"*Hey, Jude* was my mother's favorite Beatles song," he whispers. "It's the reason why my brother is named Jude and I'm Lennon. I'm named after her favorite song writer. He's named after her favorite song. I can't remember a day that went by where my mother didn't sing at least one Beatles song."

"It's a beautiful song." I give him a warm smile. His admission wraps around me and comforts me. He's giving a piece of himself I've never seen before. The vulnerability has reappeared, and I can see it in the way he looks at me. The way his hand continues to draw delicate circles on my heat-flushed skin. "What happened to her?" I ask, swallowing my nerves. "Your mother."

He closes his eyes, and when he opens them again, he doesn't look back at me. Instead, he's lost, looking off in the distance. A different type of ache settles in my bones.

"She died six years ago." His voice is so small, so distant, I almost think I didn't hear him. The words take a few seconds to catch up to me before his admission settles in the air between us. Something tells me he doesn't talk about his mother often, if at all. Me bringing up the tattoo on his chest has forced him to talk about her.

"I'm sorry," I whisper, my hands continuing to roam over his chest, touching every single tattoo. My apology is twofold. One for bringing up his mother. Another for him losing her. It's clear she meant a lot to him.

He doesn't speak another word. His jaw twitches as he keeps his mouth closed, shutting down the conversation before it's barely began. Guilt washes over me. Lennon doesn't open himself up very easily, and I'm afraid if I begin asking too many questions too quickly, he'll start to pull away. Just like he has since our wedding day.

I decide to open a part of myself to him, testing the waters.

"Three years ago, my parents went on vacation to celebrate their twentieth wedding anniversary." I swallow the heat rising in my throat, pausing every few words to catch my breath. I adjust my head on the pillow and tip my chin higher, looking up at Lennon. His eyes dart downward, staring into mine while his finger continues drawing invisible circles on my skin. "My father had pretty much taken my mother wherever she wanted to go. I don't think there was a country or continent left they hadn't visited. Being the adventurous woman she was, my mother wanted to go mountain climbing. My father wasn't too thrilled with the idea, and neither were me and my siblings. I mean, none of us were the outdoorsy type. We all grew up in the city, Boston specifically."

Lennon lets out a light laugh, understanding.

"I guess my mom was itching for a new kind of thrill or adventure," I continue. "All her kids were out of the house, and she'd spent years as a stay-at-home mom. Of course, she organized all my father's business dinners and fundraising galas, but she never had a career for herself. I think maybe she was searching for what she loved outside of her family. Wanting to make her happy, my father begrudgingly agreed to the mountain climbing trip. They were on their second day of the trip when I got the call from one of the members of the group that they were climbing one of the crests when a large boulder broke loose above them. My mother's line got stuck on a branch sticking out from the stone, and my father went to go help her.

They tried to move out of the way in time, but they didn't make it."

A tear slips from my eye, warming my already heated cheek. Lennon's thumb catches it, his eyes filled with more sadness than they were earlier. I've never talked about my parents' death. No one in the family speaks of it, their loss too great for all of us to accept. But not only was it difficult losing them, but thinking of the fear and pain they must have felt has been entirely too much to bear.

"I'm sorry you lost them." Lennon breathes. "I can't imagine what that must have been like."

My eyes fall to his mouth, spilling words for me more delicately than I've ever heard from him before.

"I know this doesn't take away the pain of losing them," he whispers. "But your father went to rescue your mother, risking his own life in the process. True love is selfless. And if that isn't the purest form of true love, then I don't know what is."

I give him a small smile, my heart growing a thousand times bigger. To my father, my mother was the love of his life. I'd always hoped to experience that kind of love. It makes me happy knowing Lennon could feel the love they had for each other just from that one story.

I slide my hand across his hardened muscle and wrap it around his neck. I scooch closer, entangling my legs with his, and I don't say another word. Nothing else needs to be said.

"Fuck, Laurel," he breathes, pressing his lips gently to my forehead. "I'm not kidding. You're on fucking fire."

He stops drawing circles on my skin and wraps his arm around me underneath my shirt. He pulls me close, pressing the tips of his fingers into my flesh. The pain I woke up with only minutes ago is starting to disappear with his touch. But I guess in the time it took me to tell him the story of my parent's death, my fever has reached a pitch. His eyes widen as they search my face.

"When was the last time you took medicine?" he asks, concern laced in his deep voice.

"I don't know." I close my eyes and breathe him in. "I don't even know what time it is."

"Here," he says, pulling himself away from me, panic rising in his voice. His leg unravels from mine. "You should take some more."

"No." I quickly tug him back. "This is making me feel better. Being with you is making me feel better."

Lennon is the cure to my weakened soul. Every touch is a remedy for my broken heart and my injured body.

The grief surrounding Roe's cancer vanishes momentarily when I'm in his arms. Life isn't as ominous and tragic when he's with me. He's a light in my world of darkness.

My husband rolls back to me, returning his hand to the same place as before. Spreading his fingers across my back, he massages me. Tiny bursts of electricity spark across my skin, my fever accelerating.

"Is this okay?" he asks.

I nod, closing my eyes and bringing my forehead to his mouth. He kisses me again, his hands moving faster with every breath. My pulse quickens.

"More than okay." I start rolling my hips, begging to have him closer.

I keep my hand pressed against his chest, my fingers resting over the lyrics on his chest.

Take a sad song and make it better.

Today has definitely made it to the top ten worst days of my life, and Lennon is making it better.

I lift my leg and wrap it over his. Slipping his long, muscle-filled leg between mine, his thigh presses against my hot center. I rock my hips again as his hands continue exploring my body.

"I like my shirt on you, Mrs. Harding," he whispers. His chin is resting on the top of my head. I can't see his face or his gorgeous blue eyes, but I close mine, imagining the fire that must be in them when he makes his confession.

"I like wearing your shirt," I muse. "It's soft and it smells good."

I don't even care if I sound creepy at this point. I haven't felt this good since I came down with this stupid fucking flu.

"It smells like me." His voice lowers, his chest vibrating against my mouth. I press my lips to it, kissing the tattoo on his hardened pec.

"Exactly."

Moving his hand from behind my back, he glides it around my ribs to cup my breast. His thumb grazes over the small pebble. A small whimper escapes my chest. I thought my fever was cooling off, but I was wrong. So fucking wrong. My entire body could combust from Lennon's touch.

"Are you sure you don't care I'm this close to you?" I ask him. I'm writhing more beneath him, rocking my pussy over his leg. I need to feel him. I want to feel him inside me.

"No," he groans, his hard as stone cock pressing into me. He hooks his other hand under my chin, lifting me to look up at him. "But I've never had sex with someone with a fever. I don't want to make you feel worse."

"Impossible."

"As painful as this is to fucking say," he grunts. "And trust me when I say painful, I mean *excruciatingly painful*, I'm not sure it's a good idea."

"Please," I beg. I don't care how weak or pathetic I sound. "Please, Lennon…"

"Laurel." My name falling from his gorgeous mouth incinerates my insides. He doesn't often call me by my first name.

"Please," I beg again. "I need to feel you inside me. It's been too long, and I'm too sick to care how pathetic I sound. I think you're the only medicine I need right now."

My lower belly blooms with heat. It's hard to discern how much of the heat across my body is from my sickness or from my proximity to Lennon. I think even if I weren't sick, I'd still be just as hot.

A thin film of sweat coats my skin as Lennon moves his hand from my breast to the side of my face. I love when he holds me like this. It reminds me of our first kiss. Well, not exactly our *first* kiss. That kiss was six years ago in the back of his car.

This type of kiss reminds me of our first as husband and wife.

"Only if you do something for me first." Our faces are so close, I feel like I'm stretching to reach him. He holds back, using his hand on the side of my face to keep me just out of his reach.

He doesn't allow me to answer. Placing a gentle kiss on my forehead, he pulls away from me. The air he leaves behind is cold. Shivering, I curl myself into a ball and wrap the sheets around me. I watch as Lennon leaves the bedroom. He returns a few minutes later with a glass of ice water. He sets it down on his nightstand and walks over to the personal pharmacy he brought home. After finding what he's looking for, he turns around and holds his hand out to me.

"Please take these." Another smile emerges across his mouth. "I know you said I'm the only medicine you need, but just in case..."

Although his words are playful, there's sincere concern woven into his blue eyes. Clouded by the darkness in our bedroom, his worry is still obvious. I do as he says and pull my arm out from under the sheet, uncurl my fingers, and hold out my hand.

"Fine," I mutter. "If you insist."

He drops two pills into my palm. I sit up enough until my head is upright, then pop the two pills into the back of my throat. Lennon hands me the glass of water. I drink nearly all of it, not realizing how dehydrated I must be. The water is cool and soothes my throat on its way down. I sigh, still shivering with a fever as I slither back under the blankets.

I watch him as he climbs into bed beside me. Shadows and darkness cover his entire body, and I'm sad I can't see him clearly from here. I still feel like there's so much of Lennon to explore. So much I still don't know, both inside and out.

Hope deflates in my chest when he doesn't return to the same position as before. He's only inches away from me now, but he doesn't link his legs with mine or lift the hem of my shirt to touch me.

"Feel better?" he softly asks.

"A little," I admit. "I didn't realize how thirsty I was."

"Good." Still not moving to touch me, he twists, shifting to face his nightstand. He reaches inside the glass, pulling out a cube of ice.

I inhale a sharp breath when he reaches his hand out, placing the cube of ice on my neck, directly on my pulse.

More goosebumps spread across my skin. Part of the ice melts, a trail of water gliding down my neck and over my chest.

"Does this feel better?" he asks, delight mingled with the concern in his voice. He inches closer to me again, but still not close enough for my legs to wrap around him.

"Yes." I quiver. It's a conundrum being both hot and cold. My body is melting but I can't seem to shake the shiver refusing to give up.

After holding the cube against my pulse for a few seconds,

he reaches behind him and grabs a fresh cube. He lifts his hand and slinks it back under my shirt. I hiccup a sharp breath when he circles the fresh cube around my hardened nipple.

"How about now?" His voice has grown considerably deeper, as if the thrill of my reaction is now a conquest he must explore. Each new destination with an ice cube pushes him further. I must admit, though, his ice cube trick is working.

"Definitely," I moan, my eyes fluttering. I can't decide whether to keep them closed or open, focused on the fire in Lennon's gaze.

He glides the ice cube over my nipple, coating my breast in cool water. I turn away from him and lay on my back, facing the ceiling. I arch my back as he drags the ice cube to my other breast, repeating the same motion. He's coating my fevered body in iced water.

Once the second ice cube has melted, he reaches for another one. This time, he doesn't hesitate before placing it between my thighs and slipping his hand under the front of my black lace panties. He parts my folds with the tip of the cube, pressing it firmly against my swollen clit.

I arch my back again, sucking a breath in between my teeth. Lennon's mouth is against the hollow of my ear.

"What about now?" He growls.

"Lennon," I whimper, unable to describe how I'm feeling. I know I'm still sick. I know the illness is still coursing through my bones and veins, wreaking havoc, but something about being touched this way when I feel like dying inside makes me feel alive.

As he would his fingers, Lennon circles the ice cube over my clit. I moan again, bucking my hips to the ceiling.

"Please," I beg, turning my head to the side. I open my eyes and stare into his. He stares back at me, watching me with piqued curiosity. I can tell he's enjoying watching me like this.

"Tonight is about you, Mrs. Harding." He removes the half-melted cube from between my legs. "Tonight is all about making you feel better."

Our bedroom is covered in shadows. I watch him as the small amount of light causes his eyes to flicker.

My mouth pops open, and I'm gasping for air as he places the half-melted cube between his teeth. His lips wrap around the cube, sucking on the end. Moving himself over my body, he slides off my panties, pulling them down my legs. He tosses them over his shoulder, then parts my legs. He bends forward and hovers over me.

I gasp when a drop of water lands on my stomach. My shirt is pushed up, exposing my wet breasts to the cool air. Arching my back again, Lennon leans down, looking up at me as he places the cube against my lower stomach. With my legs bent, my thighs are at either side of him. He lowers himself until his head is between them. Turning, he drags the cube down the length of my inner thigh, flicking his hungry gaze up to catch my reaction. A deep moan escapes my throat, and I bite down on my bottom lip.

I can't keep my legs still. My entire body is buzzing in anticipation. Lennon drags the ice down my thigh, from my knee until he brings it to my hot center. He teases my folds, running it down the length before using his fingers to open me. The cube has melted to half the size it was when Lennon first started. When he places the frozen cube to my clit, I'm met with both ice and fire. His lips are warm, but the last bit of ice on his tongue is cold as he slides it over my swollen bud.

I place my hands on his head, threading my fingers through his hair. I grip on the ends, tightening my thighs around his face as he continues to work his icy-hot mouth on me.

The rest of the ice cube doesn't last long, and neither does Lennon's gentleness. His soft, delicate tastes are now firmer. He sucks and licks and bites my clit. I can't stop moving under him, my mind growing hazy. My legs tingle as I buck my hips. I'm losing control.

Lennon is quick to slide his arms under me. He grips onto my hips, keeping me pressed against his mouth. My blazing flesh molds between his long fingers as his voice rumbles from his chest, vibrating against me.

"Lennon, I'm coming." I want to say more but my throat won't let me. I move my hands from his hair and stretch my arms out at either side of me, grasping onto the sheets. Anything to anchor me to the earth. I feel like I'm going to float away. I've never been touched when I've had a fever. Honestly, the last thing I could think about eight hours ago was being touched. But with Lennon, it's different. It's almost as if my body knows this is what I needed.

My chest expands, and my thighs press against Lennon's head harder. One more lap, suck, and bite, and I'm coming against his mouth. Digging his fingers deeper into my flesh, he holds me against him as I ride out my orgasm. Bursts of electricity shoot across my skin.

My legs finally relax, and Lennon pulls himself away from me. He places a gentle kiss on the outside of my folds, then another on my hip, then another along my ribs. After kissing one of my nipples, he's made his way back up to my face.

"How do you feel now?" he asks, dragging his finger down the length of my cheek.

My chest is still rising and falling as I try to catch my breath. I lick my lips and grin. "Better."

My eyes are heavy, the fever having gone down. My entire body is wet both from ice and fire.

"Good." He chuckles. "Now, get some sleep." He leans forward and kisses me for the first time in days. His lips are warm and soft. They comfort me in a way I wasn't expecting.

But when he lays beside me and silence fills our bedroom, my thoughts wander back to his question earlier of why I didn't tell him I was sick.

"I want to tell you something first," I whisper. Softer than earlier. My throat is still sore, and my body is still warm and buzzing from Lennon's touch. But I know the tone of my voice isn't just from being sick. It's because I'm sharing another piece of myself with Lennon.

"What is it?" he asks, resting his head on his pillow. His tattooed arm is stretched out beneath me.

I want to tell him about Roe. The pain and weight of her diagnosis is taking a toll on me, and keeping it to myself is eating me alive. Living with a secret is a solitary existence. Especially one as dark and emotional as Roe's. My insides are tangled, pulling, and constricting around each other. Woven into knots I know will never come undone.

But I keep this secret to myself. I won't break my promise to my sister. Even if it's devouring me.

Instead, I tell Lennon a secret that *is* mine to share. One he deserves to know.

"I've been married before." I freeze. Holding my breath, I wait for his reaction, not knowing what to expect. My eyes bounce back and forth between us in the shadows. I still haven't been able to make sense of his feelings toward me. It's hard to discern which acts and roles he's playing as the contractual husband, or what he does because he cares for me. Right now, I feel like he cares for me, but there's still nagging doubt living in the back of my brain.

"You have?" he asks, raising a brow. Surprise is written all over his beautiful face. I bite down on my bottom lip, expecting him to start asking other questions, but he doesn't. He simply lets me tell my story.

"We met in college. In Torts class, to be exact." I sigh, the memory of my short-lived marriage to David no longer affecting me physically. Not like it did even a few months ago. Talking about my previous marriage is like reciting a vague memory from my childhood. The inner workings in my heart have changed. Parts have been rearranged and replaced. I keep my eyes locked on Lennon's chest. "One day he surprised me by asking me to marry him. I figured he wanted to spend the rest of his life with me. He was an expert at convincing everyone he had a good heart. We were only married three months before I found out how he used me to get to my uncle's firm. It started with him asking me to get a meeting set up with my uncle to get hired on as a low-level attorney. Frederick hired him, but one day, I came home and overheard him on the phone with one of his buddies we went to school with. He was explaining the entire plan he'd concocted since the day we met. I stood down the hall, in the doorway of our bedroom, with my hand over my mouth. He laid out the whole plan as if he were executing a bank heist. The next morning, I kicked him out and filed for an annulment. David and I were only married for three months."

Lennon stays silent as I watch my hand move up and down against his chest in tandem with his breathing. He hasn't said a word, and for a moment, I'm worried I've freaked him out. Bad thoughts seep into my mind. Maybe Lennon doesn't want a wife who's been married before. Maybe he'll search for a way to get out of our marriage before our year is up.

Fear rolls in like an uninvited guest.

I inhale a sharp breath and look back into his eyes, answering his initial question of why I didn't tell him I was sick. "I'm no stranger to being used, Lennon. It's hard for me to trust others when they've only ever seen me for their benefit rather than my own."

My confession settles between us, heavy and weighted.

There's the truth of it. The only reason Lennon and I

married in the first place was for his benefit. Mine only came later. For Roe. But his initial proposal was self-serving.

"That's why I didn't tell you I was sick," I confess, shrugging. "I never had a husband who cared before."

Lifting his free arm, he places his thumb on my lip, staring at his own finger as he traces my flesh. "Everyone has always assumed I've had a black heart, and I don't care about anyone but myself. And after what you just told me about your marriage with David, I don't blame you for not telling me. Your silence just worried me. That's all."

"Oh." I nod, tucking my bottom lip under my teeth.

Lennon pulls his hand away. "But now you do," he adds, lifting my chin.

"Now I do, what?"

"Have a husband that cares."

My heart hammers away in my chest. I look at the mountain of medicine behind him and then into his eyes. I can't help but smile.

"Are you going back to your office?" I ask , sniffing. The pressure behind my eyes and in my nose returns. Reality of my condition slowly creeps back in, the humming of my orgasm now completely gone.

"Fuck, no," Lennon says, tucking my hair behind my ear. "This is the only place I need to be right now, Mrs. Harding."

Wrapping his arm around me, he pulls me toward him until I'm pressed against his chest.

With heavy-lidded eyes, I read the lyrics tattooed below Lennon's heart one last time and allow sleep to take hold, dragging me under.

NINETEEN

Lennon

I don't want to do this.

I can't walk into that room and see her, knowing what I'll see. I want to remember her with the sun in her hair and her fresh dirt-coated fingers. I want to remember her dancing among the flowers with the ocean crashing onto the shore behind her, singing along to her favorite Beatles song, Hey, Jude.

"She lost consciousness last night. We've seen episodes like this in cases such as hers. Sometimes the chemo does more damage to other organs in the body before it can eliminate the cancer," the doctor explains. His words are muffled and suffocating. "Her housekeeper found her this morning and called the ambulance. Luckily, she kept breathing even though she fainted, but we haven't been able to wake her since she was brought in. We believe she was left too long and there's been some damage to her brain."

I swallow the lump in my throat and wring my black tie around my fingers. I squeeze until my knuckles turn white.

"She's named you as next of kin," he tells me, almost as dryly as if he were ordering a cup of coffee.

I snap my head up, and the world crumbles under my feet.

"What?" I ask him, running my hand down my face. "What does that mean exactly?"

"It means you have to make a choice."

"What choice?"

"The choice whether to keep her on life support or to let her go."

"Let her go?" I tilt my head and narrow my eyes. "What do you mean, let her go?" I'm genuinely confused. I don't understand.

"We can discuss her condition further and you can weigh your decision, Mr. Harding," he explains. "But ultimately, you will have to decide."

I swallow the lump in my throat, feeling like my body is going to implode.

I leave the doctor standing outside the room and push through the door. She's lying on her back with her head turned to the side. The machine rhythmically beeps in the background—apparently the same machine that's keeping her breathing.

Her head is turned toward me, but her eyes remain closed. A tube is connected to her mouth, pumping her lungs with oxygen. Her chest rises dramatically. Unnaturally. I swallow the heavy, thick lump in my throat, and with a shaky hand, I reach out for hers but stop when the door opens behind me.

Jude walks in. His hair is messy and his tie hangs loose around his neck. I narrow my eyes at him, wondering where the fuck he's been.

"Where were you?" I yell, unable to keep my anger back. I know it isn't him I'm truly angry at. I stand and face him, curling my hands into fists at my sides.

He runs an exhausted hand down the side of his face, tears welling in his bloodshot eyes. "I'm sorry. I was at this fundraiser for the fraternity."

I charge toward him, the sour scent of alcohol hitting my nose inches from his face. "Are you fucking drunk?"

His blood shot eyes wobble, unfocused as he sniffs. Pain, guilt, fear, and too much alcohol. That's all I see.

"Yes." He sighs. "Dad urged me to go."

"No." I point an angry finger at him. "You don't fucking blame this on him."

"Everything is his fault!" he yells back. He runs another exhausted hand down the side of his face.

"Trust me when I say the man deserves to burn in Hell for every single fucking thing he's done, and I want to blame him for it all. But you're responsible for your own fucking choices, little brother. Get a fucking grip."

"Where is he?" Jude asks, venom clouding his blue eyes. The same eyes as our mother.

"Dad?" I ask, lifting a brow. "Fuck if I know. You're the one always trying to crawl up his ass just to please him."

"Fuck you, Len," he spits, the veins in his neck bulging. "You're just as much of a suck up to Dad and you know it."

"Yeah, well, I never let it get in the way of taking care of Mom, did I?"

"You're an asshole," he says, quietly.

I pinch the bridge of my nose. "I'm sorry, Jude. I didn't mean it." I look up at my brother apologetically.

He steels his face and sniffs, hardening his drunk eyes.

"We shouldn't be arguing right now." He looks over my shoulder, his eyes immediately softening when he sees her.

"No, we shouldn't."

"What did the doctor say?" He moves to the other side of the bed. Jude grabs her other hand and holds onto it. He gently sits beside her.

I choke on the words, unable to get them out. My vision blurs, and I sniff, holding back the tears from suffocating me. I shake *my head. I need to be strong for my brother. I need to be strong for her because my father never could be.*

"I have to make a choice," I manage to choke out.

"What?" Jude gasps, looking over his shoulder and twisting to look up at me.

"She put me in charge of deciding. The doctor says there's nothing they can do."

"What the fuck?" My brother runs his hands through his hair. My heart shatters as I watch his face transition, the reality slamming into him. His neck hardens, and his mouth turns down in a frown as he chokes on a sob. His shoulders quake, and the sound of his voice as he cries breaks me. If I wasn't already broken, I know I am now.

"No, Mom." He leans forward and rests his head on her hand. "I'm sorry I wasn't there. I'm so sorry."

I watch my mother, willing her to react. Anything to prove to the doctors she isn't as damaged as they say she is. I want her to prove they're liars.

When I look at her, I swear I see her large, round, midnight blue eyes open. A kaleidoscope of fear and love swirling in them.

"What are you going to do, Lennon?"

"What?" I ask on a breath, darting my eyes to my little brother. Even in his drunken state, his eyes are wide open. It's as if I can see straight into his broken soul. I wish I could reach inside and fix him. I wish I could grab my mother's hand and she'd magically wake from this nightmare.

"What are you going to do?" Jude asks again, desperation in his voice. "What are you going to do?"

MY ENTIRE BODY IS RIGID, hard as stone. I want to scream, but the sound gets caught in my throat. At least momentarily. I work around the panic, and before I realize it, my voice is bleeding into the shadows of my bedroom. White knuckled, I clutch onto my bed sheets, hoping they'll anchor me. But the panic comes back in an unrelenting and unforgiving wave, the sound of the beeping machine echoing in my brain.

"Fuck!" I scream into my pillow. Tears stream down my face, and my neck tightens. I can feel the veins bulging from my skin, begging to burst.

I see his face, looking at me, asking me what I'm going to do. I see her head lying against the pillow, but she isn't sleeping. No. She's looking at me with her large, round eyes, asking why I did this to her.

"No." I shake my head, squeezing my eyes shut, willing the images to disappear. "No!" I scream. "Stop!" I want to get them the fuck out, but they refuse to leave. I don't know why this happens time and time again with them just staring at me, begging me to fix what's permanently broken.

Is there something wrong with me? Did I truly fuck up in my decision to let her go? Is this a choice I'm going to have to live with for the rest of my life? Is this the price I paid for my sin?

The echoing sound of the pen scribbling my name across the thin paper attached to the hospital clipboard rings in my ears, and I swear, it's all it takes for my heart to stop beating. Just like hers.

Good.

I fucking deserve it.

TWENTY

LAUREL

Lennon's screams immediately wake me up. My eyes snap open and I'm gasping for air when my head jerks away from my pillow. My back is turned on him, but I immediately feel him stiffening behind me.

I quickly roll over. His back is facing me now, and he's curled in on himself. The sharp planes and ridges of solid muscle strain against his tattooed skin. I swallow my panic when he releases another scream.

"Lennon," I whisper, pulling him to face me. But he doesn't move. He's frozen solid. A statue. I sit up and lean over him, urging him to turn around. The death grip he has on his pillow is merciless. White-knuckled, he clutches his pillow as if it is the only thing keeping him afloat.

I say his name again, but this time it comes out quivering and unstable. The blood drains from my face. I'm lost and confused as to what's happening. The veins in his neck are swollen, and his jaw is clenched tight.

"What's wrong?" I ask, tugging on his arm again, but he still doesn't answer. He doesn't flinch at my touch. The screams eventually stop after a few seconds of my hand on his arm. At first, I wonder if he's fallen back asleep. His hand still grips the pillow. I lean over him farther, noticing his eyes blinking slowly. He's staring at the wall. But despite the quiet that's descended upon our room, Lennon's body hasn't caught up. His chest rises and falls rapidly. Heavy breaths push out of his lungs faster than he's able to take them in.

"Breathe, Lennon," I soothe him. "I'm right here. I'm here."

Oxygen catches in the back of my throat when he jolts. Twisting, he rolls over to face me. His shoulders are hunched, and for the first time ever, I see fear in his eyes. He's scared and vulnerable. It's a strange sensation. Lennon Harding commands every room he walks into. Brooding and moody, clients both fear him yet admire him.

But all I see in front of me is a man haunted by the night. Haunted by the memory of a nightmare still alive in his mind. Panic stricken eyes stare back at me.

"Tell me something good," he chokes out.

"What?" I whisper, quickly swiping my tongue across my lips. My body is humming. Wide-eyed, I look at him, not knowing what to expect.

"Tell me something good," he repeats, pleading as he places his hands around my face. "I need to hear something fucking good. Something sweet."

His breaths are shallow and rattled.

"Sweet?" I ask, my heart sinking into my stomach.

The sound of him uttering the word he'd whispered into my ear the night we met stirs something inside me. It's like a raging storm. The wind rattles between my stomach and my mind. Maybe he does remember. Maybe he remembers every single fucking second of that night as I do. Every touch. Every kiss. Every word he'd whispered that night.

I hold my breath as he pulls my face to his until our foreheads meet. His rushed hot bouts of breathing fill the tiny space between our mouths.

He squeezes his eyes shut. "Please," he begs on a whisper. "I need to hear something sweet."

"Um." I scramble to think of something sweet, flipping through the catalog of memories I keep locked away. "Okay, I heard about this man in Italy who graduated from college at the age of ninety-six. He grew up poor and served in World War Two. He never expected to make it, but he finally lived out his dream of going to school. He achieved his lifelong dream."

A small smile lifts the corner of my mouth, remembering how my roommate from college told me this story one night when we were drunk and studying in the library. I'll never forget the way her face lit with pure joy at the time.

But my smile doesn't last long because Lennon still hasn't relaxed. His shoulders dramatically lift with every breath, but this time he lifts his gaze. His eyes meet mine as he runs his hands down my cheeks before feathering them along the length of my neck.

"Another one."

Seeing his desperation, I wrap both my hands around his, keeping him from pulling away. A torrent of waves float in his eyes, begging for an anchor to keep him close. I press the tips of his fingers against my pulse. I'm hoping this will bring him back to the room with me.

"The other day," I start, "I was walking down Newbury Street and saw this man holding up a cardboard sign asking for money or food. He looked like he'd been standing on that same intersection for weeks. But I found myself grinning when this woman came up to him and handed him a grocery bag and a large reusable bottle filled with water. I don't think I've ever seen someone so grateful."

Lennon's breathing slows. The effects of whatever nightmare he had is now fading. I release his hands. He runs them down across each of my collarbones and over my chest. As if he can't decide where to begin and where to stop, he keeps going. Down my arms, across my chest. Everywhere he can reach, his hands go. He touches me as if he's trying to memorize me. As if I might disappear. His hands explore me as if it's the first time he's touching me. Like he can't believe I'm here. An image his mind has created to play a trick on him.

Small bouts of breath pass between my lips as his hands smooth over my body. A tiny tremble of fear still vibrates beneath his touch.

I let Lennon's hands roam over my body, being careful not to rush him. Something tells me this isn't the first time he's experienced this nightmare. He's used to doing this alone. The storm rolling in his distant eyes begins to fade.

Reality settles in the air between us. Wide eyed, he stares at me.

"Laurel, I..." He blinks, glancing down at his hands.

I inch closer. "It's okay. Everything is okay."

"I, um." He blinks again.

"You don't have to say anything."

His face relaxes as he rolls back. With a heavy breath, he looks up at the ceiling. "I'm sorry," he croaks. His voice is small, and the difference from his usual tone doesn't sit well with me.

This nightmare has shown another side to Lennon I've never seen before. I see the toll it's taken on him, his embarrassment evident in the way he's pulled away from me.

Feeling his absence, I climb over him, straddling his waist and pressing my thighs against his strong frame.

"You have nothing to apologize for."

The moonlight and city lights below peek through the window, casting a bright glow on Lennon. I lean down, bringing my face closer to his. Reaching up, he ghosts his fingertips along the length of my jaw. Tracing invisible lines, he makes a trail all the way up to my forehead.

His breathing has slowed, our connection bringing us both back down to earth. Gravity pulls on us like a magnet, anchoring us to our bed, to each other.

His finger dances slowly across my forehead. "Your fever is gone."

"It is." I crack a smile. "You nursed me back to health, Mr. Harding."

I hadn't noticed my fever was gone until now. My nose is still a little clogged, but other than that I feel normal. My fever has passed, and my bones are no longer aching. Instead, I only ache for Lennon.

He must be feeling the same because he wraps his hand around the back of my neck, slamming our mouths together. It's the first time we've kissed since the night after our wedding. I moan, leaning into it and breathing it all in. His soft mouth is warm. Hungry for more, he coaxes my lips apart, slipping his tongue against mine. His hand stays at the back of my neck, massaging me.

"Mm," I moan, my body wanting more. I pull away. "I can tell you another sweet." I tease, sitting up and lifting my shirt over my head. Correction. *His shirt.*

"Yes, please," he whispers, running his hands up and down my bare thighs. "Tell me another one."

I smirk, loving this game of his. A warm sensation seeps into my bones.

"One day, this lawyer got sick in the middle of the summer." I roll my hips and lean forward, bringing my face close to his. He tucks my long, loose strands behind my ear, revealing the side of my face. My cheeks grow sore from my large grin. "Three days after her wedding, in fact."

"Sounds awful," he teases. "I mean, who gets sick in the

summer anyway?" He scrunches his nose, and I bite back the giggle in my chest.

"I know, right? And it was awful." I nod, popping my bottom lip into a mock pout. "Their marriage was a little unconventional, having done it to save his family's business."

"Now that doesn't sound very sweet." He frowns back, continuing to slide his hands up and down my thighs.

"Well..." I roll my hips. Heat expands in my lower belly. "She went home without telling her husband, but when she woke up, in a fever I might add, he'd brought the entire pharmacy to her just to make sure she had everything she needed."

"You're right." He grins, his nightmare far behind him in the rear-view mirror. "That was a sweet story."

My pussy is pressing against his swollen cock. He grunts when I rock my hips again, rubbing myself along his length.

I lift my hips away from him and easily slide his cock into me. My walls clench as I gasp, pausing to savor the sensation of taking him completely. He tilts his head back, pressing it into his pillow, grunting. A warm buzz radiates across my body when he looks back at me, his eyes catching the moonlight. He grabs my hips, pulling me down until we're completely connected. His chin is nearly pressed to his chest, his eyes focused on the place where our bodies meet. He looks up at me with a salacious grin, hungry for me. I slowly lift myself, keeping my eyes pinned on his.

"I've missed this." I plant both hands on his chest, digging my nails into my skin as I move above him. I roll my hips as I lift myself again, making sure I move at a slow pace.

"Missed what?"

"You." I tilt my head up, closing my eyes as another moan escapes my lips. "This."

I don't care if my admission goes against the terms and conditions of our marriage. We were only supposed to act like a married couple in public. But the separation from Lennon these past three days has awoken a sleeping beast inside me. My feelings for Lennon can't be tamed. It's torture trying.

"I've missed this, too," he grits out, apparently not caring either. "I've missed your sweet pussy taking my cock. All of it. But I want your eyes open." He growls. "Looking at me."

I open my eyes and do as he says. He reaches down to where our bodies are connected. Pressing his thumb firmly against my clit, every nerve in my body expands.

"Oh, fuck," my voice trembles as I catch my breath.

"Play with your tits, Mrs. Harding."

I reach up and grab my breasts. The soft flesh molds between my fingers. I graze my thumbs over my peaked nipples.

"Fuck, yeah." Lennon growls. "You're even more beautiful like this, Mrs. Harding."

"How?" I ask, arching my spine and tilting my head back. I swallow down the heat rising

"You're even more beautiful with me inside you. Watching your body move against mine does something to me," he confesses. "I love when you're completely naked and raw for me. I love watching your body reacting to mine." He sucks in a breath between his teeth. Sitting up, he wraps his hand around the back of my neck and pulls me close. He keeps his hand between us, working my clit as I rock my hips.

He bites down on my lip, and I melt against him on a moan.

I drape my arms over his shoulders, pressing my chest against him. I lift myself higher as Lennon tightens his grip around my neck. He fists my hair between his fingers, tugging on it. He's gentle enough not to hurt me but strong enough to make me gasp with every tug.

Between his hand on my neck, his thumb against my clit, and him filling me, my heart expands and my legs tingle. But I'm not sure if those are the only reasons. Looking into Lennon's eyes, I think about how he was only minutes ago. Vulnerable and afraid. Guilt and sadness mixed with pain. I've never seen him this way. But I think the arrow shooting straight to my heart is the way he looked at me with need. I'm the life raft he'd been desperately searching for, begging to bring him home.

And I did.

But he isn't alone. I realize Lennon has been slowly stitching me back together, too. Every time I've been with him since finding out Roe's diagnosis, I've never felt more at home. The world seems less dark and isolating. Even if he doesn't know my life is collapsing outside of our small bubble.

"Laurel," he whispers, pressing his lips to mine.

I run my fingers through his dark hair, rocking my hips faster. I bury my face into his neck, fire building in my stomach.

"Come with me," he whispers. His cock twitches inside me.

I cry out, my voice muffled by Lennon's warm neck. My walls clench around him as his cock pulsates inside me. His hand runs down the length of my back, letting go of my hair, massaging me in rhythm with my orgasm. I keep my face buried in his neck. Unsure why, emotion gets stuck in my throat. Pressure builds behind my eyes, tears threatening to spill. I can't explain it, but I feel closer to Lennon.

It's a foolish notion to fall for your fake husband. On paper, he's real. He isn't supposed to be more than that. But here we are. Here he is with his arms around me, healing me without even knowing it.

TWENTY-ONE

LAUREL

The flu or whatever it was that possessed my body for a full twenty-four hours is gone. I'm one hundred percent back to normal when I crack my eyes open and face the morning sun. Bright yellow rays reflect off the buildings of the city below. I expect Lennon to be gone as he has been every morning since I've been sleeping here.

Maybe it's a foolish notion to believe we turned a corner last night. Not that I blame him if he did leave. He is running a multi-million-dollar corporation. I'm sure this is normal. But with the way his concern bled in front of me yesterday, a sliver of hope played in my heart hoping he'd stay. At least until I'd woken up.

So, I stay where I am, close my eyes, and soak up the sun, not ready to turn around and face whether he's still with me or not. I'm not sure I could handle the way my heart will react when it finds Lennon is gone. I keep my eyes closed and breathe in, thinking back to yesterday. My legs are sore, and my center is still warm from having him buried inside me. But the most significant moment of last night crashes into my thoughts.

Lennon had a nightmare. I'm still unsure whether it's a regular occurrence, but I've never seen so much pain in his eyes.

I wonder if his nightmare has to do with his mom. He's kept the details about her short, never wanting to discuss her for more than ten words. He's always quick to shut down the conversation.

But then again, I'm harboring secrets just as dark and deep. I've kept the truth about why I married Lennon more than close to my chest. I've kept it locked under the splintered bone and the aching muscle that my heart has turned into. I don't know when Roe will feel comfortable enough to share her diagnosis with the public, but her secret is eating me alive. And the closer I grow to Lennon, the more difficult it will be to keep. Drowning in thoughts of my sister, I decide to face what the day might bring.

The balloon that's made a home in my chest doesn't deflate as it usually does when I turn around. Lennon is still here. In bed with me. He's turned on his side, facing away from me. The muscles on his back contract with every slow and measured breath he takes.

I study the tattoos inked on his skin, one by one. A large tree is sprawled out across his left shoulder blade. Leaves fall from the tree like burnt ashes. Similar to the one on his hand, a dark purple rose runs down the middle of his back. Thorns and loose petals swirl around the stem. There's a darkness to Lennon's tattoos but there's also truth in them. He told me some of his tattoos hold meaning, some don't. I wonder how many have meaning.

My eyes continue to roam over his back until one knocks the oxygen from my lungs. On the right side of his torso, along his ribs is a large lavender-colored feather. The wisps of the feather are delicate. Intricate. The feather is as big as the size of my hand, the top disappearing under his arm.

Watery eyed, I cover my hand, gasping when I read the script tattooed underneath the feather.

Sweet Nothings.

My hand trembles when I reach out, wanting to touch the words. Like a magnet, I feel drawn to them. My heart craving to make them tangible and real.

The feather looks exactly as it did on my nineteenth birthday tiara. I close my eyes as a tear slips between my lashes. The memory of Lennon holding the feather between his fingers playing in my mind. The way it danced against our breaths as he whispered in my ear.

My fingers ghost the length of the feather. My vision blurs as tears slip from my eyes.

"Good morning, sweet nothings."

TWENTY-TWO

Lennon

Laurel gasps when I turn around and face her. Her eyes flutter shut as she allows the sound of my voice uttering the nickname I'd given her six years ago to settle in her chest. She inhales a shaky breath as she opens her eyes again.

"I told you the other day," I remind her. "Some of my tattoos have meaning, some don't."

Honestly, I'm surprised she hasn't seen the feather tattoo until now. It's not that I was hiding it from her, but maybe I was hoping she would see it at some point. Though I have been keeping her at a distance the past few days. Along with the fear of the depth of my feelings for her, I haven't wanted Laurel to think I suddenly thought it was okay to touch her now that we're husband and wife. But when I felt her still behind me, her hand reaching out to touch the feather, I knew she'd seen it.

Our marriage has been unconventional in all ways. Finding out your contractual husband has a secret tattoo for you could have been received in many different ways.

A small smile plays on my lips, but it fades when a tear slips from Laurel's eye. I reach out, a concerned expression tugging between my eyebrows.

I frown. "Please don't cry."

Slowly, she removes her hand still covering her mouth. "But..." She swallows, trying to come up with the right words. Her eyebrows pull together. "I didn't think you remembered."

"Of course I do." I let out a small chuckle. "I don't think you can have a night like that and not remember it."

"You were drunk," she argues, clearly still in disbelief. "I thought you'd forgotten. The night we saw each other again at Eclipse, you acted as if you didn't know me."

I hold back the emotion climbing up my throat. Everyone always assumes I don't have feelings. It's part of the reason I've kept Laurel and sweet nothings to myself.

"I was an asshole that night," I admit, my chest squeezing. "The look in your eye tore my guts out. I could tell you were smiling your way through dinner, playing along as we all were. But I didn't want my father to know we'd already met. If I did, he never would have let it go. He'd have asked a million questions. He would have stalked you and forced me to manipulate you to get to your law firm. I knew that's why we were there, but admitting I knew you would have made it worse."

Her chest quakes with a shuddering breath. "All this time." She chokes out. "Why didn't you tell me? You could have told me after that night."

I press my mouth into a thin line, knowing I need to tell her. She deserves to know my deepest secret. She deserves to know the darkest parts of my soul I've kept buried.

"I, um." I scratch my chin in thought, coming up with the best place to start. I allow myself to fall on my back and look up at the ceiling. It feels like we've been in bed forever. But honestly, I could stay like this forever wrapped up in Laurel. "It's hard to show others who you truly are when they only ever see you as James Harding's son." I turn my head to look at her.

She rests her head on my arm, looking down at the feather

tattoo. She's now seeing the front side of it. The entire feather stretches from the backside of my ribs to the front. She presses her palm against it, feeling my lungs expanding under bone and flesh.

"My father raised me and my brothers to be unfeeling." I clear my throat. "Well, he wasn't exactly successful with Jude. Because of my father's greed and selfishness, he made Jude suffer in ways I couldn't possibly imagine. In ways I didn't learn about until recently. Eventually, Jude stepped away from our father and running the business. I was proud of him because stepping away from my father wasn't an option for me. At least, it never felt like it was. The city heralded him as a savior. They placed him up on this pedestal and no one ever challenged him. Even his children. Until Jude did. I think for my father, he knew even if Jude stepped away from the business, he could still rely upon me. I was always meant to follow in his footsteps." I smirk. "Cold, black heart and all."

"I don't know," she teases, trailing her fingers across my ribs. Across the feather. "Your heart doesn't seem very cold these days."

I smile, her words shooting an arrow straight for my heart.

"I think Jude's betrayal stung worse for my father because he knew I was staying out of obligation. If my brother had stayed, it was because it showed loyalty to him in a different way than I could ever provide. He couldn't control Jude."

"I knew your father was arrogant and calculating," she quietly says. "Being in his presence alone was intimidating. I couldn't imagine what it would be like being his child."

"The earliest memory I have of my father is sitting at the dinner table with my mom and Jude," I start, replaying the memory in my mind. "My dad hadn't come home in time for dinner, even though he promised our mom he would. But often, he usually didn't show up until we were fast asleep in bed. We were eating when he stumbled through the door, clearly drunk. His bloodshot eyes met ours as he walked in with a stranger on his arm. I didn't know who she was at the time, but when I got older, I realized she was one of the dancers from the club he frequented downtown. He'd walked in with her and sat her on the table in front of my mother. With a glare, he laid the woman back on our table and snorted a line of coke down the length of her stomach. Keeping his dark eyes pinned on my mother the entire time. He'd done this in front of his wife and kids."

My stomach sours at the memory.

"Lennon…" Laurel's soft voice says beside me. I run my fingers up and down her back, focusing on the ceiling fan above us. I stare at each blade, watching as they spin continuously.

"That's the first memory I have of my father." My voice cracks. "But it's also the first memory of my mother telling me something sweet."

Laurel sucks in an audible breath. "Sweet nothings?"

"She didn't call them that," I point out with a weak smile, circling my fingers across her smooth skin. "I only coined that nickname the night we met. But that night, after my father walked away with his stripper, my mother stared at us wide eyed. I don't think she knew what to do. Tears streamed down her face when she turned to me and Jude. She inhaled a shaky breath and said, 'When John Lennon was growing up, he used to play in a field near his house called Strawberry Field.' I recall sitting there looking at her wondering why she would bring that up after watching our father snort cocaine out of a stripper's belly button, but then when I watched Jude's face brighten, I understood."

I turn my head again, looking down at Laurel. I hadn't realized but tears now line my eyes. Laurel places her hand on my cheek. "Whenever I would have a bad day or life turned to absolute shit, my mother would always tell me something sweet. A random fact that has nothing to do with the dark thoughts clouding your mind. She would turn something that seemingly meant nothing and make it sweet."

Laurel's cheeks flush pink, and a dimple presses into her soft skin when she smiles. "I love that."

"The night we met," I tell her, turning on my side, "was the night after my mother died." I slide my hand down her ribs, circling my fingers across her bare hip. She's completely naked lying next to me, the sun shining a warm glow on her pale skin. Thinking back to the night I found Laurel in the back of my car is a mixed bag of emotion.

Laurel's indigo eyes fill with tears. I hate seeing her cry, but I know I need to tell her. I've never opened myself up to anyone. Until her.

"I'm so sorry, Lennon." Her chin quivers. "I had no idea."

"The night before I met you at the club, I'd just made the toughest decision of my life. It's haunted me ever since."

"Your nightmare?" she asks, swallowing.

"Yeah." I trail my finger along Laurel's hip bone, focusing on the good. The sweet. I can't allow my nightmares to control me. Not like they have been. Being here with Laurel helps.

"Is it the same every time?" She wipes her thumb across my cheek.

I nod. "It's of the night I had to let my mother go. She was in a coma after collapsing at home by herself."

"Your dad wasn't there?"

"No." I shake my head. "He never was. I never understood why she stayed with him all those years, but I guess love doesn't make sense sometimes. After she'd collapsed and fell into a coma, though, the doctor told me she wouldn't survive if she were taken off life support. She'd left me as her next of kin, so I had to make a choice. The doctor assured me she no longer had brain activity, but making that decision, with my brother begging me for answers, broke me. I was shattered that night."

"I'm so sorry." Her cry comes out strained on a whisper.

Pressure swells behind my eyes as I look at Laurel. My eyes fall to her hand and the ring wrapped around her fourth finger. "I killed her, Laurel. I killed my mother, and it's haunted me every day since she died."

"Oh, Lennon." With flushed cheeks and concern woven into her beautiful eyes, she grabs my face. "You didn't kill her."

I sniff, the guilt still eating away my soul. "I did. She was breathing until I signed that piece of paper."

"No," she says, tears slipping down her cheeks. "If anything, you saved her, Lennon. It might not feel like it, but you did the right thing."

With my chest tightening, I pull Laurel closer. She wraps her arms around me, hooking her leg over my waist. Warm limbs and soft skin, she cries into my chest.

But I don't want to stay like this too long. I don't want to dwell on the decision I made that night and how it's tortured and haunted me since. I need Laurel to know what she means to me.

I place my hand on the back of her head, threading my fingers through her long brown locks. "I went to the club that night to drown myself in my guilt. I wanted it to eat me alive. I wanted it to chew me up and spit me out. I deserved it. All I kept debating that night was if I made the right decision. Even if the doctor said she wouldn't have ever been able to live without life support, I wondered if there was a slim possibility she could. And I'd robbed her of it because I'd chosen wrong." I look into Laurel's eyes, wanting to get lost in them. My heart hammers in my chest, and my body warms with her around me. It's strange. For so long, I've lived in the dark, detaching myself from everyone in my life. I've never been committed to any other woman because none of them were Laurel. "But then there you were. Sitting in the back seat of my car like a princess in your tight, shimmering dress, with your fucking birthday tiara and large, hypnotic, indigo eyes. Your cheeks flushed in embarrassment, but I was drawn to you. I didn't want you to leave. I wanted more time with you. We had only one thirty-minute ride together, but it was the best fucking thirty minutes I've ever had. And it was a euphoria I never stopped chasing."

She lifts her hand and places it over mine. Lifting our arms up, she looks up at them. Our fingers mingle and intertwine in the sunlight. She watches them over and over, her delicate hand in mine.

"I thought you would hate me for never telling you I remember our night together," I confess.

"I don't." She frowns, still watching our hands.

"You should." My confession drops in the air like a rock sinking to the bottom of the ocean. It's quick and unforgiving.

"But I don't," she repeats.

She shakes her head, sadness drowning in her eyes. I've seen the same sadness in her beautiful gaze before when she thinks I don't notice. It's as if she's stuck in her own head, standing too close to the edge of giving in to whatever sadness she allows to sneak in.

"I figured that was why you were so adamant on not marrying me when I first proposed. Because you hated me for not remembering."

"No." She faintly smiles. Her pink lips twitch. "At least not completely. But mainly because you broke into my office and proposed marriage as casually as asking me to join you for lunch."

I laugh. "You eventually said yes, though. I still don't know what it was that changed your mind."

She doesn't answer. Her face softens and the sadness

returns. We let the silence descend upon the room until she decides to break it.

"That night has stuck with me ever since," she whispers, turning to look back at me. She continues to keep our hands in the air, never explaining what made her accept my proposal. "You marked me, Lennon Harding. You scored my heart and claimed it as yours long before you broke into my office and proposed to me."

"I blame it on my enormous black heart," I admit with a smirk.

She smiles, but it quickly vanishes. She presses her lips to mine, selfishly and delightfully stealing the air from my lungs. When she pulls away, she slides her hand under my side, pressing it against my feather tattoo.

"Maybe it isn't so black after all," she teases. "But I do think you underestimate the size of your heart, Mr. Harding."

TWENTY-THREE

LAUREL

If Lennon and I had a honeymoon, this is the closest we've come to it.

Over the past four weeks, since the morning I'd discovered his feather tattoo, Lennon and I have easily fallen into married life.

Unofficially revising our terms and conditions, we've slipped into our roles as husband and wife in more ways than in front of the public eye.

We spend all our nights tangled up in the sheets of our bed. I scream his name while he keeps one hand expertly around my heart. We fuck wherever possible, kicking Ray out of our apartment as soon as we make it to our front door. Every surface of the apartment is now marked with the memory of Lennon slipping his cock inside me or his mouth devouring me between my legs. And when he's asleep, I stare at the feather tattooed across his ribs, still wrapping my head around the fact he got it for me. Some nights, my eyes close, with his tattoo being the last thing I see, forcing myself to believe it's real.

For me, it's difficult to come to terms with making a seismic impact on someone's life in the matter of thirty minutes. But I mattered to Lennon that night. Enough for him to get a tattoo, permanently marking the memory on his body.

Although our relationship shifted the night he confessed about his nightmare, doubt and uneasiness still sits in the bottom of my stomach.

I'm waiting for the last string to snap or the ball to drop. I'm waiting for the moment I'll wake up and this will all have been a dream. Or Lennon will come home telling me he wants a divorce before we've even made it to the twelve-month deadline.

I know the reason I agreed to marry Lennon is still the elephant in the room, though. I see it in the way he looks at me across the dinner table, studying me and hoping I allow him a glimpse into my soul, searching for the answer. He hasn't outright asked me, but I can sometimes see it resting on the tip of his tongue. Pleading and begging for the relief of an answer.

Every few days, he'll drop a not-so-subtle hint about wondering why I agreed to marry him. It's fair for him to question my motives. Especially when he thought I'd hated him for not remembering our one-night stand. How or why would I agree to marry the asshole who couldn't remembering fucking me in the back of his car?

That's how Lennon thought I'd felt. But as with him, appearances are experts in presenting falsities instead of the truth. Reality effortlessly wears a mask.

He knows I didn't agree to marry him for the money, considering I come from a wealthy family as well. Maybe he thought I was marrying him to restore my reputation. But if that's his theory, he hasn't said as such.

Aside from the constant worry our bubble of marital bliss will suddenly pop, I'm also constantly concerned for my sister.

My stomach wobbles as I hold my phone in my hand, staring at our text thread.

I quickly type out another message, my pale pink nails clicking across my screen.

> Me: Roe, I know you said you weren't feeling well, but you can't ignore me like this. I thought we set up a schedule for you to message me every day at a certain time letting me know you're okay.

I immediately regret my text coming across as harsh.

> Me: We're treading unfamiliar waters, sis. I'm just worried about you.

My thumbs hover above my screen, indecision weighing on my mind to wait for Roe's response or simply cut to the chase and call her.

Roe's chemo treatments have been wearing her down the longer she takes them. I wanted to vomit when I read a post in one of the cancer support groups saying beating cancer is a savage, unforgiving race. A race to beat the disease with chemotherapy before the chemotherapy kills you.

A never-ending, vicious cycle.

Since Roe has been growing weaker over the course of her treatments, we came up with a system in order for her to check in with me. It helps knowing she has Steven to take care of her, but I'm still her sister.

I also don't know when her money is going to run out. Roe told me she could pay for the treatments up until the surgery, but I don't know if that's changed. The driving reason for me agreeing to marry Lennon was to make sure I didn't drain my account helping Roe pay for her treatments, but she still hasn't answered me on whether she needs me to help pay or not. I'm chewing on my thumbnail, willing my sister's name to pop up on my screen.

"We've got it."

I snap my head up as Frederick slaps a stack of paperwork two inches thick in front of me.

"We have what?" I ask, blinking away the nausea making a home in my stomach. I place my phone on the table beside the stack of papers and lean forward in my chair.

"Ryan Perrish has filed an official complaint. I've agreed to take up the case, and will be delivering it to the court this afternoon."

"That's great." I give him a small smile and sit back in my seat, picking my phone back up.

Frederick snaps his fingers gleefully and spins on his heel. He points to the bar I have set up in the far corner of my office. He pours himself a glass of vodka, knocking it back before refilling it again. Sucking on his teeth, he turns back around.

"I thought you'd be thrilled," he mutters, his grin melting from his round face. I love my uncle but sometimes I feel like my love for him has diminished over the years. Corporate greed has changed him. He isn't the same man I used to look up to when I was a kid.

"I am." I cross my arms.

"Huh." He pops an olive into his mouth, smacking his lips as he chews. "You should be. This is all because of your marriage to Lennon."

I lift my eyebrows and inhale a deep breath. "It still amazes me how one person in our family nearly ruined us, and now, because I simply married someone, it's as if Kellan's misdeeds and crimes have been forgiven."

"His misdeeds and crimes aren't forgotten, Laurel." He schools his face. "No one has forgotten what he's done. He's serving his ten years, and he will have paid for his crimes. I've forgiven him. Perhaps you should consider doing the same in the future, and maybe you will in your own time."

Venom and poison sit at the tip of my tongue. Frederick is playing both sides of the coin. Devil's advocate. But there's a major difference between me and Fred. Kellan isn't Fred's brother, and Kellan didn't betray him as deeply as he did both me and Roe.

Growing up, my brother was always the first to act without asking permission. He never felt the need. Being the eldest child and only boy went straight to his head. He'd used it as ammunition to gain access to everyone and everything for his own benefit. Aside from the drugs, Kellan is a lot like Lennon's father. The kind of man who takes and takes. The kind of man who sinks his claws in so deep, feeding themselves on everyone they love like a parasite until there's nothing left.

"Yes." Frederick sips on his drink. "He knows where he stands with our family, considering the last time I spoke with him on the phone."

"You still talk to him?" My jaw drops. I shouldn't be shocked. Frederick was always closer to Kellan than he was to either me or Roe. But I am. I snap my mouth shut and stare at my uncle, wide eyed. Kellan not only stole my trust and thousands of dollars through the finance business he was running, he also siphoned money from Frederick's accounts.

Kellan had interned for Fred during college and was given access to all of Frederick's bank accounts linked to the firm. Stealing money from the firm was rolled into only one of the many charges Kellan was convicted of.

"Of course, I do." Frederick sets his glass down on the bar and snaps the lapels of his suit, straightening them. He smooths his hands over the silky fabric. "You should, too. He's still your brother."

I shoot him a sharp glare. "Just because he's my brother doesn't mean I should forgive him for what he did. He took everything from me, Fred."

I swallow the nausea that comes with thinking about the inheritance Kellan stole from me. The inheritance I could have used to help Roe.

"I'm not saying you should forgive him," he argues, narrowing his eyes. He pinches the bridge of his nose and sighs before looking back at me. "But one day, he will get out of prison, and what will happen to him?"

I grind my molars. "I don't give a shit what happens to him."

Fred clicks his tongue against the back of his teeth in disapproval. "This is why I avoid talking about Kellan with you, Laurel. You can't see past your anger."

"I don't think I need to," I grind out, curling my fingers. My nails cut into my palms. "My life isn't unfulfilled because my brother is no longer in it."

Fred swipes his hand across his mouth in thought. "Considering what our family has been through, I just hope you don't regret cutting him out of your life."

"He's the one who cut himself out. Not me," I remind my uncle. He's too forgiving for someone who doesn't deserve it.

"He told me he still cares for you," Fred says in a noticeably quieter voice. "He asks if I can convince you to talk to him. He wants to attempt to rebuild your relationship."

This time I really do feel fucking nauseous.

I roll my eyes. "I doubt he wants to rebuild a relationship with me out of the goodness of his heart, Fred. Kellan always wants something. His love isn't free."

I chew on the inside of my cheek and uncurl my fingers. I look down and run my finger over the half-moon indents I've left on the skin of my palm.

My breath catches in my throat as realization dawns on me. I snap my head up. "Did you tell Kellan I got married?"

Fred pauses, allowing the silence to fall between us. Any

seconds that pass after the last word falls from my mouth already confirm the answer I know to be true.

My uncle stuffs his hands into his pockets, already knowing how I'll receive his answer. "I did. I figured he had the right to know."

"Why?" I ask, trying not to raise my voice. My relationship with Fred has always been on the rocks. I've always wondered why I've put up with his bullshit for as long as I have. Perhaps it's fear of the unknown. Even before I graduated, I became a junior attorney at this firm. But perhaps it's complacency. Emotion constricts my throat, and I swallow around my anger.

"I told you," Fred defends. "He's your brother, and I thought he had a right to know."

"That wasn't your decision to make, Fred." I scoff. "It also wasn't your news to share." Now I understand where Roe is coming from. Some secrets aren't meant to be told by others. We have a right to decide when and how people find out our darkest truths.

Fred waves his hand flippantly. "He'd already seen it on the news, anyway. The New England region talked about your wedding for a solid week."

I catch my breath, swallowing my anger. Fred has a point. Every news station and newspaper column in the region was covering our wedding. But it still doesn't negate the fact Fred felt the need to discuss it with Kellan, knowing where my feelings stand.

"Still. . ." I grit. "I would appreciate it if you wouldn't talk to Kellan about me in your little phone calls. I'll decide when and *if* I ever choose to speak to him again."

I don't allow my brother to take up too much space inside my head. He doesn't deserve it. The only thing that comes out of thinking about Kellan is a massive headache and anger that won't ever fade.

"Mrs. Harding?" my assistant, Trey, says through the intercom on my desk.

"Yes, Trey?" I ask, peering up at my uncle, thankful for the interruption.

"Your husband is here to see you. He says you were supposed to meet him in his office for lunch."

"Right." I clear my throat. "Send him in, please."

"Of course."

Frederick waddles over to my desk and points his finger to Ryan Perrish's complaint. "I've made this copy for you to read over. I want you on this case as well."

"Okay." I nod, thankful Frederick is no longer so desperate for money that he's picking up cases that have no merit. At least Ryan's case is legitimate. Or so I hear.

Apparently, I'll find out when I read through the two-inch file sitting on my desk.

Lennon knocks on the door to my office before peeking his head around the large oak. He's wearing his signature black suit today, but this time, he's paired it with a dark gray tie instead of his usual black.

I smile the instant I see him, the worry for my sister slightly subsiding. At least enough to where the sight of Lennon makes my body hum with excitement.

"Good morning, Mr. Harding," Frederick greets Lennon, holding out his hand.

Lennon returns the gesture. "I told you, Frederick. You can call me Lennon. Please."

"Sure, Lennon. Bad habit since I never addressed your father so casually, but I guess it's different now that you're married to my niece." Frederick sighs, patting his hand against his stomach. "Anyway, I was just finishing up here with Laurel." He swings his gaze in my direction. "Let me know when you've read through that complaint. I want you on this case with me."

"Okay." I push out from my desk and move around to the front of it, standing beside Lennon. He's several feet away, but his scent immediately surrounds me.

Frederick gives us each a nod before stuffing his hands inside his pockets and sauntering out of my office.

"Everything okay?" Lennon asks. I snap my head to the left, Roe's silence returning to the forefront of my brain. Like a magnet, I'm drawn to my phone. Did I miss her text while I was busy talking to Frederick? She might have messaged me when Lennon knocked on the door.

"I'm fine." I wave him off.

He gives me a look that tells me he knows when I say I'm fine that I'm anything *but* fine. The knot in my stomach returns when his eyes meet mine. I feel exposed, as if my eyes are windows he's peering through. I'm open and vulnerable, with Roe's secret laid out for him to see.

I want to walk away, only to get the weight of his concern for me away from my hammering heart. He stops me before I have the chance, gently wrapping his fingers around my wrist.

"Hey." He gently tugs me toward him, pulling me to his chest. "You would tell me if something was wrong, right?"

I swallow. I want to tell him, but how do I tell him a secret that isn't mine to share? Part of me thinks it isn't fair for Roe to ask me to keep her diagnosis a secret. But then another part of me doesn't think it's fair for me to judge whether her request is fair or not.

If I did, it would make me a hypocrite when I'd gotten angry with Fred for doing the very same.

"I would." My lie stings on the tip of my tongue. I want to spit it out, the bitter after taste only adding to my nausea. I've allowed Lennon into my life and into my heart so easily these past few weeks, I feel like I've been cut open and studied. My mind flickers with the thought that our contractual marriage was easier before we blurred the lines.

I immediately regret the thought when Lennon places his thumb against my bottom lip.

"Are you sure?" he whispers, a deepness woven into it.

His question is a jolt of electricity straight to my heart. He's doing it again. The underlying tone of his question insinuates him wanting answers. Answers I can't give him. I inhale a shaky breath and close my eyes, giving him a resolving nod.

"Yeah," I reassure him, waving him off again. "Frederick just brought up my brother, and I hate talking about him."

I'm not completely lying.

"Oh, what did he say?" Lennon asks, raising his eyebrows. "He's still in prison, right?"

"He is." I sigh, the anger from my conversation with Fred still simmering under my red-hot skin.

Lennon slowly closes the gap between us. "Your uncle may have left your office, Laurel, but the conversation hasn't. Your gorgeous face betrays you."

Despite all the frustration and secrets knotted around my heart like barbed wire, I melt with Lennon's words.

"I told you before, I haven't spoken to my brother since his sentencing." My husband nods, patiently listening. I quickly trace my tongue across my lips, twisting my fingers. "Well, Fred still talks to him. *Apparently.* And he told Kellan about us getting married."

"I'm sorry." He places his hand on my arm and pulls me forward as my bare feet stumble across the floor to keep me from falling off balance.

"I can't be too angry with him," I whisper, my eyes falling to his mouth. "News of our wedding was plastered on every magazine and newspaper. I guess he was bound to find out one way or another."

"Your brother can be angry, but there isn't much he can do from prison, right?"

"You're right." I nod in agreement. "I just don't want my brother to know anything about my life. He lost the right when he stole everything from me and my family."

"He did," Lennon agrees, tugging on me again. His hand wraps around the back of my neck, pulling me to him. He kisses me. His mouth is warm, and his lips taste like his peppermint toothpaste.

I pull away from him when my heart feels like it's going to jump out of my chest. I seriously want to drop the conversation of my brother. I back away from Lennon and turn to walk around my desk.

My eyes dart to my phone, my worry for Roe replacing the anger with Kellan. What a dramatic swing of emotions I'm going through today.

"I'm sorry I didn't go up to your office when I was supposed to," I quickly mutter over my shoulder, changing the subject and leaving him where he's standing. "I got hung up on a call with a client." It isn't a total lie. I honestly lost track of time, my concern for Roe distracting me. I move back around my desk and quickly press the button on the side of my phone. The white bar displaying Roe's name and her tiny message of: *Slept late. Just woke up,* sits in the middle of my screen. My shoulders visibly relax with a sigh, and I drop my phone back on my desk. I fish my stilettos out from under my desk with my bare toes and sit in my chair. I bend down, sliding the first foot in.

"What are you doing?" Lennon's deep voice booms beside me.

I look up. My face is in line with the zipper of his black slacks. I swallow, my mind immediately going to what's hidden underneath and how good it feels to have it driven into me. He's standing directly beside me with his hands inside said slacks. His blue eyes are piercing as they stare down at me.

"I'm putting on my shoes so we can go to lunch," I explain, reaching for the other one.

His eyes darken as he lifts his leg and taps the shoe out of my hand with the tip of his foot. It falls to the floor with a clunk.

"It's ten in the morning, Mrs. Harding."

"It is?" I ask, clicking the button on the side of my phone again, lighting it up. He's right. It is only ten o' clock. I didn't bother looking at the time, only at the message from Roe.

I look back up at Lennon. "But you told Trey I missed meeting you in your office for lunch."

"I might have lied a little." He scrunches his perfect nose.

"Don't you think Trey might find a ten-a.m. lunch suspicious?" I ask, giggling. "He knows I usually don't eat until after noon."

"Huh," he says, twisting his tongue in his mouth. "Do you always eat after noon or are you open to an early lunch?"

My heart races, and my veins pump with liquid heat. Lennon's doing it again. Playing the perfect distraction. The conversation with Fred has finally left my office. My concern for Roe has now faded since she's texted me. My only focus now is Lennon.

But over these past few weeks, I'm learning Lennon is more than just a distraction. My feelings for him aren't simply physical. I think it's a fact I've always known. Deep down in the places of my soul I choose to keep buried. Beneath all the feelings of being used by others and feeling unappreciated and undervalued in the corporate world. There's a part of me that's known Lennon never was a simple one-night stand. He also isn't only my husband on paper. He's more. Much, much more.

I shrug, sitting back in my chair. I lift my hands and unbutton the rest of my blouse. When I walked in here this morning, I shrugged off my black suit jacket and undid the first three buttons of my dark blue silk blouse. Loosening the rest of the buttons, I slide out of my shirt, sitting in front of Lennon in only my black mini skirt and matching black lace, unlined bra. The sheer fabric leaves nothing to the imagination of what's underneath. My hardened nipples are tiny hard as stone peaks under the black mesh.

"I'm open to an early lunch."

Lennon snarls, the corner of his mouth curling into a delicious, satisfied grin.

"Good." He growls. "Then, on your knees, sweet nothings."

I do as he says and bend to my knees in front of him. Looking up at him with hooded eyes, I unbuckle his black belt, unbutton his black pants, and free him from both those and his boxer briefs. I slide them down his legs, freeing his fully erect and swollen cock.

My nails trail up his legs as I stare up at him. He hooks two fingers under my chin, feathering them along my skin.

My heart's still racing, and my skin flashes with heat. I already want to feel him inside me, but I want to do this for Lennon more. Wrapping my fingers around his length, I pull him toward me. I swipe my tongue across my lips and open my mouth. My lips wrap around his mushroomed tip, sucking before sliding him farther in.

He grunts the deeper I take him, letting out one more once he hits the back of my throat.

"That's it." He hisses. "That's it, sweet nothings. I don't think there's anything better than seeing you on your knees for me, ready and willing to suck on my cock."

I look up at him, locking my eyes to his. He reaches down and places his hand on top of my head, guiding me. He pulls himself out, then back in, allowing us to fall into a rhythm. I suck in my cheeks and pucker my lips around his length, moaning when I place both my hands on the back of his thighs, pulling him impossibly deeper. It seems to spark something inside him. He begins moving faster, slamming himself into the back of my throat with every thrust.

"Fuck. I'm coming." His hand massages my hair, creating a tangled mess.

He slams into my throat one more time before he suddenly stops moving. His cock pulsates as warm cum hits the back of my throat, and I swallow.

When he's finished, he pulls out of my mouth and hooks his fingers under my chin again, urging me to stand.

He smiles as he catches his breath. He kisses my swollen mouth before quickly turning me around. Placing his hand on the small of my back, he bends me over my desk. I place my hands on either side of me, above my head and press my cheek to the cool wood.

Gripping onto my skirt, he lifts it up over my full bare cheeks.

"I stand corrected," he drawls, running both hands over my cheeks. I feel his chest above my back when he leans forward, bringing his mouth to my ear. "There is something better than you on your knees in front of me. It's you bare assed over your desk with your beautiful face staring up at me."

I gasp and attempt to grip onto my desk when he rams himself into me. I'm soaking wet, making it easy for Lennon to drive himself down to the base. I stand on my bare toes when he pauses, keeping his hand pressed to the small of my back. I moan, resting my forehead on the desk, attempting to catch my breath. But everything inside me is fully aware of Lennon's cock buried between my legs.

"Is this what you like?" he asks.

"Yes," I cry as he pulls out and drives into me again.

"Don't worry, sweet nothings." His velvety voice slides over me like his hand drawing down the length of my back. "I'll take care of you."

And when he slides his hand along my spine until he's reached my tailbone, I know there's deeper meaning to what he says.

I'll take care of you.

My heart is too erratic, and my body is too focused on Lennon behind me to make out the invisible circles he draws on my back. It's quick, and I try to memorize the shapes he makes. It's almost as if he's a spy leaving me to decipher a secret code in invisible ink. Or begging for me to open the window he's been eager to peek through. The one to my soul that will finally let him all the way in.

I hold my breath when he places both hands on my hips and thrusts back in and out of me. He's slow at first, but with every thrust, he picks up the pace until my walls tighten around him. I stand on my toes as my orgasm rips through me. I dig my fingertips into the wood, hoping they'll anchor me to my desk, but they don't.

Lennon places his hand over my mouth, muffling the scream climbing its way out up my throat. My legs quiver and my blood tingles as my orgasm rocks through my body.

When I'm finished, Lennon leans forward and kisses the spot on my back where he ghosted his fingers in secret code. After he pulls himself out of me and straightens my skirt, I stand, sliding my arms back into my shirt. My stomach grumbles loudly, and my cheeks heat with embarrassment.

"Hunger not fully satisfied?" he teases.

"This is a different kind of hunger." I smile.

"Well, the rest of my day is clear, so whatever you want to do, we can do it." He casually shrugs his shoulders.

I peer at him with raised eyebrows. "Your entire day is cleared?"

"Yes." He nods once. "I couldn't wait until we got home to see you, much less wait until lunch, so I had Olivia clear my entire schedule."

This time, I'm certain my heart bursts.

I step closer to him, wrapping my arms around his neck. I stand on my bare toes again as my stomach grumbles once more. "What did I do to earn such special treatment?"

"You married me." Lennon's words fall effortlessly from his mouth as if he's simply stating a fact, which he is. But there's more to it. More than if he had said those same words to me over a month ago when he proposed.

An adequate response is lost on me when he reaches up and tucks my hair behind my ear.

"But we're having dinner with Micah and a friend of his tonight," he tells me.

"Oh, we are, are we?" I pop an eyebrow, teasing.

"We are."

I wrap his tie around my hand, pulling him down to me. His eyes darken, falling to my mouth. "I thought you said you cleared your schedule for today."

"I did." He growls. "But this is a family dinner, and I owe my brother a favor."

"Well." I smirk, butterflies filling my stomach at Lennon calling this a family dinner. "Who would I be if I were to deny you from delivering on a promise?"

TWENTY-FOUR

Lennon

Walking through the large glass doors to Eclipse brings with it a flood of emotions I'm unprepared for.

I haven't been to my father's favorite restaurant since the night he died, hours before I found his cold lifeless body.

But the wave of emotions crashing in as the valet holds the door open for me is a mixed bag to say the least. Among them, grief is nowhere to be found. Not one ounce of sorrow is felt for the man who made everyone's life miserable. A wave of nausea crashes along the jagged, rocky shore of every memory I have of walking behind my father, and how every person he passed by would either bow to him as if he were royalty or cower away in fear. Ducking their heads or making themselves appear busy. Everyone felt my father's presence, from the valet's opening the front door to the bus boys cleaning off tables on the opposite side of the dining room. Eclipse was my father's domain.

Ground zero. Homebase. In many ways, this place was my father's castle rather than our own office building.

I'm gripping Laurel's hand with more pressure than I realize. I feel her wince beside me before she wraps her hand around my bicep. She leans close, whispering in my ear as we continue walking up the concrete steps and through the glass doors.

"I'm here." Her words hit me right where I need them. Somewhere between my heart and the bitter unresolved resentments I harbor for a man sentenced to eternity of rotting beneath six feet of cold, Massachusetts dirt.

I squeeze her hand in return and smile at the hostess standing near the entrance of the dining room. Large, opulent chandeliers hang from the ceiling. The light reflects off every facet of glass, sparkling onto the marble floor beneath our feet.

"Good evening, Mr. Harding." Hugh, the owner of Eclipse, greets us. He holds his arm out toward the back of the restaurant. His greasy hair is slicked back as usual, but the hollows of his eyes have deepened since the last time I saw him. "We were sorry to hear of your father's passing. We've missed him greatly here and are glad to see you feel it in your heart to return."

"Right." I nod, biting down on the tip of my tongue. I swear I taste blood, but that could just be the sour feeling I have from hearing Hugh talk about James Harding as if he was a fucking god we were all privileged to have known.

I know it's because Hugh misses the business ties he had with my father, though. They often snorted lines of coke in the back office, and my father would get him access to every woman he'd ever encountered. Hugh's haggard appearance tells me he's lost more with my father's death than any of his children have. Now he's looking at me as if he's hoping I'll pick up right where my father left off.

Laurel squeezes my arm again, reminding me she's my anchor.

"Hugh, this is my wife, Laurel," I introduce, figuring I should at least play the part I came here to play.

"Pleasure to meet you, Mrs. Harding." Hugh bows at the waist.

"You as well." Laurel smiles, her red-painted lips stretching to reveal her perfect teeth.

"Your usual table near the back is all set for you," Hugh says, leading Laurel and me through the dining room.

We follow him until we reach our usual booth; a large circle covered in rich crimson leather. I inhale a sharp breath and hold out my arm, allowing Laurel to slide in first.

She sweeps her long curls to the side and over her shoulder, exposing her long, smooth neck. Diamond earrings dangle from her ears and a thin silver chain is wrapped around her neck, the teardrop diamond resting between the perfect swell of her breasts. The subtle shimmer of her dark green dress reflects from the overhead lights almost as brightly as the chandeliers above us. She's fucking stunning. And all mine.

Once Laurel slides in, I follow behind her.

"If I may, Mr. Harding." Hugh nervously clears his throat. His squirrely eyes dart anxiously between Laurel and me.

My nostrils flare with impatience, and I grind my teeth. I know where this is going. "What is it, Hugh?"

"I was wondering if we might be able to talk once you're finished with your dinner. There are a few things I would like to discuss."

Laurel must sense my desire to bite back at Hugh and his ridiculous request. I didn't come here to fucking chit chat with him as he cries over missing my father while asking if I can continue whatever disgusting, dysfunctional arrangement they had going on. I don't know the inner workings of the lengths my father went to secure this fucking booth, but I know it was deep and seedy enough that the crimson wrapped seat isn't meant for casual dinner conversation over an overcooked piece of filet mignon.

My wife's hand quickly lands on my knee. She gives it a gentle squeeze before sliding it farther up the inside of my thigh.

I adjust myself in my seat, telling my cock not to react to the hand making its way toward it.

I clear my throat and blink up at Hugh. "Not tonight, Hugh. Call my assistant, and she can see when my schedule is free."

A wave of disappointment rolls over his face, but it doesn't stay for long. He gives a hesitant grin. "Thank you, sir. Enjoy your dinner."

Hugh finally disappears.

I blow out a heavy breath and rest my elbow on the table. I massage my forehead with my fingertips. Laurel's hand lands on my back, pulling my attention to her.

"Are you okay?"

"Yeah." I reassure her with a small smile. "I just didn't expect to feel like this walking in here. I figured since I didn't give a shit that my father died, this place wouldn't affect me. Instead, all I keep feeling is this bitter, angry resentment. It's like I was a zombie walking through my whole life, never realizing the impact it had on me until now. Now that he's gone."

Laurel doesn't say anything. Her eyes look up as our waiter places two empty wine glasses in front of us before pouring a bottle of my father's favorite red wine. Fucking hell.

The waiter asks if we're ready to order, but I tell him we're still waiting for Micah and Archer. He hurries off.

I turn to Laurel, realizing this is the first time she's been back since my father dragged her here, hoping to hook her up with Jude. Laurel wasn't aware, and Jude wasn't interested. Then I brought Madison, pretending I didn't already know Laurel.

I feel like shit for that night. All of it.

As I have my entire life, I wore a mask that night, hiding who I truly was. A man obsessed with the woman that was sitting across from him.

"Are *you* okay?" I ask my wife. I set my elbow on the table and rest my head in my hand, half-turning to her.

She sucks in her bottom lip, chewing on it in thought. Her eyes fall to the table before she looks back up. Her shoulders visibly rise as she inhales a breath. "I didn't realize I hadn't been here since the night your father brought me."

I wonder if my father had already written the stipulation to marry Laurel into his will then or if he added it after.

Ever since the night Laurel woke up to one of my panic attacks after my nightmare, our relationship has shifted. Our circumstances aren't exactly the same, but she understands what it feels like to lose a parent you love wholeheartedly. One you weren't prepared to lose.

Not that anyone is ever prepared to lose someone they love.

But I saw the emotion in her eyes—the one she held without judgment. It was the first time someone had seen the raw, ugly side I keep hidden from the rest of the world.

I reach under the table and place my hand on Laurel's thigh. A long slit drives up the length of her dress. It reminds me of her wedding dress, exposing the curve and tan skin of her thigh. I drag my finger across her skin, and it immediately reacts to my touch, as it always does. Goosebumps rise to the surface. I lightly draw the invisible words I've been writing for days. It's become a habit of mine.

I think back to that night and the mask Laurel tried her best to wear.

"I don't think I'll ever be able to tell you how sorry I am for not speaking up that night. I should have said something."

"Don't." she shakes her head. "Don't feel bad. I get it now. I didn't then, but I do now."

"No, Laurel." I look her in the eye. "Maintaining appearance for the sake of my father shouldn't haven't mattered. You didn't deserve to be used by him. I only added salt to the wound. I made you feel unseen." I inch my finger to her inner thigh, regret seeping into every muscle. "But I saw you that night. You were all I could see."

Laurel's lips part as she breathes in. She's been sad lately, and I wonder if that's been part of it. Conflicted because she married and fell for a man who acted as if he didn't know her.

"Starting without us already?"

I straighten my back and twist my head to see Micah standing in front of our table. His friend Archer is beside him. He looks older than the last time I saw him, but not old enough to where age has altered his features too much.

"Of course not, brother," I tell him. "The waiter just poured the wine."

"Great." He beams, pointing to Archer. "Lennon, you remember my best friend, Archer."

"I do." I shake his hand, giving him a smile. "I remember having to bail the two of you out of jail the night you were caught sneaking into your high school."

"It was tradition for the seniors to sneak into Coach's office and cover every surface with sticky notes." Archer shrugs, casually.

"We only made it halfway across his desk when the cops showed up." Micah shakes his head, disappointed. The event was only five years ago, but the memory is still very much alive for them.

I move to the side and hold my arm out. "Archer, this is my wife, Laurel Harding. Laurel, this is Archer Mayfield. He's Micah's best friend."

Laurel reaches up from where she's sitting, her smile revealing her white teeth. Her shimmering eyeshadow reflects in the lights as three lines crease in the corner of each of her eyes. "Pleasure to meet you, Archer."

"You, too. Holy shit, Lennon." He grins like the Cheshire

cat, his eyes darting between us. "How the fuck did you land a wife as beautiful as Laurel?"

I laugh. He sounds just like Micah.

But my laugh is hiding my true reaction. Micah clears his throat and slides into the booth, leaving me to answer a question he clearly doesn't want to answer.

"I don't know, man. I got fucking lucky, though." I'm not lying. I did get fucking lucky.

I'm devastatingly, obsessively in love with my wife. The wife my father basically forced me to marry. And I have been since the first night we met. I gladly let Laurel reach inside my cold, hard chest and steal my heart without hesitation. She's owned it ever since.

Archer slides in beside Micah. The waiter returns to our table and takes their drink orders before disappearing again.

I expect Micah to bring up our father, considering he was the one who decided to arrange this dinner with Archer here, knowing we haven't done a family dinner since the night he died. But Micah doesn't, and I don't blame him. The night is off to a decent start. No need to drag it down by bringing up the man we all hope is rotting in Hell.

"Mayfield." Laurel twists her mouth in thought after swallowing a sip of her wine. "Are you related to Felicity Mayfield, the model?"

"Yep." Archer presses his lips into a firm line, nodding. "Felicity is my mother. Since retiring from modeling, she's landed a few roles in some movies releasing soon."

"Wow." Laurel's cheeks blush with pink. "She's stunning. I used to see her when I would flip through my magazines when I was younger."

"She's looking forward to getting back out into the spotlight, so I'm sure she'd love to hear that." He grins. "But if this doesn't pan out for her, she always has my younger sister, Adeline, to live out her dreams."

"Oh," Laurel's eyebrows lift. "Your sister wants to act?"

"Modeling." He explains. "She's wanted to be a model for as long as I can remember but my mother wants her to wait until she's older. She's eleven right now. My mother doesn't want her to be forced to grow up as quickly as she was."

"Understandable." Laurel smiles. "I'll definitely keep an eye out for them both in the future, then."

The four of us continue to make casual conversation. We talk about family life, mostly Archer's, and what he's done since moving out to California. The stories continue until we've cleaned our plates and our drinks have been refilled more than once. Laurel's just taken the last bite of her steak when Micah finally brings up the reason for this dinner in the first place.

"So, Len." Micah relaxes against the back of the booth, draping his arm over the rounded leather. "Remember I was telling you about Archer's tech firm out on the West Coast?"

"Yeah." I nod, swallowing the last bit of wine sitting at the bottom of my glass. "How's that going, Archer?" I lower my hand under the table and draw circles on Laurel's thigh like I did earlier. She doesn't flinch before she leans into me, scooting closer. I never thought of this until now, whether she's doing this for show or because it feels natural to her. It feels natural to me, so I don't question it, even if I feel the dozens of eyes constantly peering at us like we're some sort of spectacle.

Archer shoves the hair off his forehead, slicking it back with his fingers. He leans back in the booth, mimicking my brother. "It's going great. In fact, I've tripled our projected profits for the fiscal year and we're only in the third quarter."

"That's amazing." I trade glances between him and my brother. "So, what do you need me for?"

"Well, I'm looking to expand and build a division on the

East Coast. Most tech firms are located in Silicon Valley. Even Seattle. But I think Boston might make a great home base for us as well. Micah thought your company might be interested in setting us up with some properties for office space as well as investing in the company. You'd have a stake in a market that hasn't given the East Coast a chance."

"You're right about the concentration on the West Coast," I agree. "Boston could use some notoriety in the tech world. Why don't you meet me at my office this week and we can discuss the details?"

Archer grins excitedly. "That would be great."

"I'm interested in seeing some number and data reports. I'd also like it if you gave me a run down on exactly what kind of tech you create and what you envision for the future."

"I can do that." Archer's face flattens to a serious expression.

"This calls for a celebration, don't you think?" Micah claps his hands together, laughing.

"A celebration?" I ask cautiously, mostly because my baby brother's idea of a celebration is to go on a two-night bender in Barcelona.

"Yeah." His eyes bounce enthusiastically between the three of us. He snaps his fingers and points to me and Laurel. "No, you know what? We should celebrate with a post nuptial party."

I turn to Laurel before turning back to Micah. "What do you mean?"

He waves his hands. "You know, since you guys sprung your rushed wedding on the city, maybe it would be good to throw a party. Like the ones Dad used to do every time he'd strike a billion-dollar deal."

I shake my head. "I don't know." Why is Micah suggesting a party for me and Laurel when he knows the circumstances of our wedding? He doesn't know Laurel and I actually have feelings for each other. As far as he's concerned, we're playing the part right now.

Uncertainty and uneasiness wades in my stomach. I don't want to be like my father. Showing up here to Eclipse, at his castle away from his kingdom, has shown me just how determined I am to not follow in his footsteps. Before I married Laurel, I'd felt like a hypocrite. Marrying her was exactly what my father wanted me to do, and it's what he would have done if he were put in a similar position. But as if a major fuck you to my father, I married the one woman I'd only ever dreamed of marrying.

I still don't know her reason for agreeing, but when I look at Laurel, I decide to shove my questioning of her motives aside because she's the only woman to ever knock the wind from my lungs with a single glance.

"We should do it," Laurel says, wrapping her hand over mine that's still resting on her thigh.

"Really?" I ask, shocked she would agree. Between work and whatever it is that holds the sadness in her gaze, I didn't think Laurel would feel up to planning a major party.

"Yeah. I think it'll be great. Plus, it will show everyone you're still running Harding Holdings with just as much strength if not more than your father did."

"I agree with Laurel." Micah wags his finger in her direction. "She's a smart woman."

"Fine," I breathe out, turning to Laurel, then I snap my head back to Micah. "But we're doing it at the house in the Cape."

I feel Laurel stiffen beside me. She hasn't said as much, but I know she still questions why I keep the history of that house under lock and key, and why others like Olivia or Micah look at me as if I've suddenly grown a third eye anytime I bring the house up.

"What?" I ask Micah.

He stares at me, wide eyed. He snaps his mouth shut and shakes his head. "Nothing. I don't know what's changed with you, Lennon."

"What do you mean?"

"It's just, with Dad's asking for his funeral to be there, and you and Laurel getting married there last month, I didn't think you'd want to go back so quickly." Micah's blue-gray eyes soften, turning down in sympathy. "Considering before then you hadn't been there in six years."

Laurel's chest stills, and her hand slowly pulls from mine. I tug her back, not wanting her to let go. I still haven't told her the significance of my mother's house on the Cape, but I figure this party will be the perfect opportunity.

"I know." I nod, straightening my spine and lifting my chin. "But what better way to celebrate a marriage than to hold the celebration where the ceremony took place."

"You have a point." Micah grins.

"I know I do." I turn to Laurel and give her thigh a gentle squeeze. I'm hoping if I finally let her in and tell her what the house on the Cape means to me, she'll finally let *me* in. All the way.

TWENTY-FIVE

LAUREL

Being a billionaire's wife has its perks.

Just like our wedding, Olivia has managed to plan, arrange, and execute a full-scale celebration, only this time, it isn't a small, intimate wedding. Over five hundred guests have been invited. String lights run the length of the long driveway. They run in rows over the expanse of the backyard facing the ocean. It's the third time I've been to this house, and I have yet to see it this lively. This bright.

Hundreds of tables are set across the yard covered in white linens. They blow with the warm summer breeze coming off the ocean beside us. The sound of the waves crashing against the large, jagged rocks below the cliff are muted by the music playing through the outdoor speakers. Caterers and wait staff circle the tables, offering our guests appetizers and drinks. I'm standing on the balcony overlooking the entire yard.

My simple black gown blows in the breeze, the slit parting over my thigh. I've noticed this style of dress is Lennon's favorite. Maybe because it reminds him of my wedding dress. Or it could be the easy access, knowing I never wear any underwear when I know I'm going to be around him.

Two large hands meet my waist. They slide around to my front until his arms are wrapped around me, tugging me back against his chest. His mouth meets the hollow shell of my ear. I melt into him as my heart flutters.

"Don't you think we should greet our guests?" His deep, velvety voice reaches the space between my legs. "We've already kept them waiting long enough."

"We should," I breathe out, my eyes scanning the sea of people below. "I was just admiring the view."

I'm not being entirely truthful. I'm waiting for Roe. I'm expecting her to pop up somewhere in the crowd wearing her favorite red dress, with Steven on her arm. I have yet to see her and wondered if she'd show up at all. It's been a few months since she started her treatments, and I've asked her time and time again when her surgery has been scheduled, but she's reassured me they haven't told her yet. Worry and fear has embedded itself in my bones. As the days pass with ever increasing silence from Roe, the more worried I feel. But I'm at a standstill, caught between wishing I could do more and wondering if I'm overanalyzing. I can only help Roe as much as she's willing to receive it. I've tried. I've offered to stay with her, but she's always told me she has Steven there for the physical support. She needs me for the emotional. The distance she's placed between us has only grown over the past several weeks. Torn and hurt, I'm shocked our relationship has taken this turn. We've always been close. I used to think sharing the same birthday, two years apart, was a coincidence, but as we grew older, I think it was meant to be. I think the stars aligned and we forged a bond that went deeper than sisterhood.

Now, it's as if all of it has deteriorated. Instead of her diagnosis bringing us closer, we've grown apart.

I hate it.

Lennon tightens his arms around me. I cross my arms, placing both of them over his, biting back the tears building.

He towers over me, bent low enough to keep his mouth near the hollow of my ear. "This was my mother's house."

I hold my breath, keeping my focus straight forward. He's talking about his mother. I anxiously wait, blinking away the need to cry. I know Lennon has sensed something off with me, and maybe now he's feeling like him opening up to me will help me open up to him. I want to. My heart is aching to be free of this burden I carry, clawing and digging with its talon, begging to be free.

"It was?" I ask around the lump of emotion caught in my throat.

"Yes," his voice deepens. "My mother didn't gain her wealth from my father. My grandmother was a fashion designer, and my grandfather was a renowned architect in Boston. They built this house after they got married, and this is where my mother was born. After my grandparents died, they left this house to my mother. But when she met my father, he convinced her to have his name added to the deed as well. After years of putting up with my father's affairs and drug use, they separated, and my mother moved back here. But even though they were separated, she remained married to my dad. She spent the last years of her life here going through her chemotherapy treatments. She had staff here, but otherwise, she was alone. Jude and I were drowning in schoolwork and doing whatever we could to please our father, so we didn't come out here as often as we wished we would have."

I spin around in Lennon's arms. He looks down at me with tears lining his dark lashes. One slips, spilling down his cheek when I reach up to cup his face. My hands mold to his sharp jawline, the scruff lining his jaw pricking my skin.

His bottom lip quivers. "My mother was here, at this house

when she'd collapsed. She was alone for hours before someone finally found her. It's why she'd lost all brain activity when she was brought to the hospital. Her brain was starving for oxygen for far too long. After she died, I hadn't been able to bring myself to come here. Or stay here. Until my father, in his own sick twisted way, arranged for his funeral to be held here. In her house."

"Oh, Lennon..." Words fail me. I don't think there's anything I can say in this moment. All I can do is feel and let my husband know I'm here for him.

"I needed you to know," he says, running his thumb across the bottom of my plum-stained lip. "I needed you to know so you could see me. You could see all the pieces of me that are broken and ugly. Every facet at every angle. The darkest parts of my soul that I keep hidden from the world behind an even uglier mask. I needed you to know that was the reason I didn't want to stay here the night of our wedding. I wasn't ready to face my demons just then, but I am now." He wraps both my hands around my full cheeks and looks me in the eye. "I need to tell you something."

I swallow hard, inhaling a shaky breath. His blue eyes cloud over, a storm of emotion swirling inside them.

"I know you're keeping something from me." His words filter through the night air between us. "I have no clue what it is, but I see the sadness you hold in your eyes. This burden you carry with you all day, every day. I still don't know your reason for agreeing to marry me. I want to believe it has something to do with the way you feel about me, because I don't think your feelings for me are new. I think, just like me, you've kept them suppressed, living out your daily life, thinking you don't deserve to be happy. But you do, Laurel. Now, I'm not sure if that's the case or if there's another reason, but I want you to know I'm here whenever you're ready to tell me." He lowers his hand and wraps it around mine, pulling them to his chest. He slides it under the opening of his black button-down shirt, gently pressing my palm over the Beatles quote tattoo. Concern and worry are etched into the three lines creasing his forehead. His dark eyebrows knit, pulling between his gorgeous eyes. "You have my ear and my heart."

"Lennon..." My bottom lip quivers. "I want to tell you but..." A sob escapes my chest. He's pried open the windows I've forcibly kept shut. The secret I've been holding is screaming to be free. But a flash of red coming from below stops the words from leaving my mouth.

Roe is here. She glides slowly and smoothly between the crowd. Her skin is pale in the golden hue of the string lights hanging above. My heart skips a beat and then stops.

Lennon's fingers hook under my chin, tugging me back to face him and look me in the eye. "I love you, sweet nothings."

My mouth pops open. It's everything I ever dreamed of hearing Lennon say. He loves me. I want to tell him I love him, too. The words rest at the tip of my tongue, eagerly waiting for their chance to leave. Because the truth is hanging between us, staring me straight in the face. I do love Lennon. I've always loved him.

The words almost leave my mouth when he places his finger over my lips. "You don't have to say anything back right now. Trust me, I'm not going anywhere. I just wanted you to know, so whenever it is that you're ready to share what's going on, I'll be here." He cups the back of my neck and pulls me to him, then crashes my lips to his, tasting me before slowly pulling away. When I open my eyes again, his blue eyes are all I see. "I'll be downstairs, waiting for you. Come down when you're ready." He kisses me on the cheek before turning on the heel of his black shoe. He shoves his hands in his pockets and glances over his shoulder one more time before disappearing through the open French doors and down the elegant grand staircase on the far end of the hall.

Once he's no longer in sight, I cover my mouth, muffling my cries. My heart is bursting with love for Lennon. I wanted nothing more than to tell him I love him back, but I know he's right. I can't be honest about my love for him when I can't be honest in sharing all the pieces of me. Like he was with me just now. Here I was thinking he was the one hiding half of himself in the shadows. But it's me. I'm the one turning half my back to him.

I stand alone on the balcony and look around with watery eyes. My vision blurs as I take in the exterior of the house. Lennon's mom was here. This was her home. I can see how this was her favorite place. It's beautiful and peaceful. I place my arm over my stomach and bend over in a sob. My shoulders quake, and I hate that I'm feeling this way right now. At a party thrown to celebrate and honor mine and Lennon's marriage. Even if I married him to secure funds to help my sister with her cancer treatments.

The truth is I love Lennon.

I've loved him ever since I was nineteen.

I lower my shaking hand and stare at the ring on my finger. The large diamond flickers under the golden lights, and the barbed wire wrapped around my heart tightens. I look over my shoulder and off the balcony. Lennon is standing in a circle, talking to other men dressed in black suits and black ties. They all look the same. Except none of them aside from Lennon keep lifting their gaze up to where I'm standing on the balcony every five seconds. I catch Roe slowly walking toward the house, craning her neck side to side as if she's looking for someone. She pauses as she passes one of the small circular tables on the outskirts of the crowd. She grips the edge and wraps her arm around her middle as if she's going to be sick. I search for

Steven in the groups of guests closest to her, but I don't see him.

I gasp and frantically wipe at my cheeks. Sniffing, I quickly leave the balcony. I allow my feet to carry me without much thought to the speed I'm walking. I'm wearing six-inch stilettos, which aren't exactly the best for running. Nearly having broken my ankle ten times by the time I make it to the top of the grand staircase, I place my hand on the marble railing to steady myself. I lift the bottom of my dress and take one step before stopping dead in my tracks at the sight of the person waiting for me at the bottom.

I narrow my eyes, unsure if I'm truly seeing him or did I suddenly step into a dream?

Oxygen is greedily stolen from my lungs when I hear his voice for the first time in years.

"Beautiful house you have here." His voice is like poison. "I guess congratulations are in order, Mrs. Harding."

TWENTY-SIX

LAUREL

Bone structure like our father's. Eyes like our mother's.

Traitor to the ones who gave him life.

My brother stands at the bottom of the staircase looking up at me as if I haven't completely cut him out of my life for the past two years for the crimes he not only committed in the eyes of the law, but for the ones he committed against his family.

"Kellan." My voice sounds meek and far quieter than I intend it to. Panic spreads across my chest like a thousand pins being pricked across my skin.

I blink rapidly, wondering if I've stepped into some time portal taking me back to the last time I saw him outside of a courtroom.

He's wearing a dark gray suit, with his hands shoved inside his pockets. The gold watch dangling from his wrist clinks as he lifts his hand to scratch at the stubble lining his jaw. His hair is slicked back away from his aging forehead. He's only six years older than me, but he looks older than thirty-one. Prison must have aged him.

"What are you doing here?" I ask when I reach the bottom of the stairs.

My eyes dart across the foyer, reaching for anyone tangible —anyone I can use as a witness. We're alone. The doors to the courtyard are still propped wide open, but everyone seems to want to stay outside.

I don't know why he's here or even how. He's barely served out the first third of his sentence.

"I heard you got married, baby sister," he says coyly. A sneer plays on his mouth, lighting a spark in his gray eyes. "I believe I owe you a heartfelt congratulations."

"I don't want anything from you," I grind out through clenched teeth.

He pouts. "Oh, come on, Laurel. I wouldn't be a very good big brother if I didn't congratulate you on marrying into the richest family in Boston." He laughs mockingly. "I mean, let's face it, even our family never matched up to their status. You classed up."

Venom slithers up my throat, heat flushing my skin. I shoot him a glare, pinning him with daggers. "Shouldn't you be in prison?"

He laughs, taking a step back as he rubs his fingers on his chin. I can tell I've already gotten under his skin. Good.

His gaze falls back to me. "Didn't our uncle tell you?"

Fresh tears fill my eyes, spilling over. One by one they glide down my cheeks, falling and splashing onto the black and white checkered marble. I shake my head and inhale an unsteady breath.

"I was released early for good behavior." He grins. "Got out just yesterday in fact. Our criminal justice system sometimes rewards you when you least expect it. I guess I was simply one of the few lucky ones."

"Where..." The word gets caught in my throat. I swallow hard. "Where are you staying?"

"With Fred, of course." His once snide, delighted face transforms to one of disgust. Storm clouds fill his eyes. "You know, the only member of our family who hasn't turned their back on me."

"You did it to yourself," I spit back. "Roe and I didn't deserve what you did to us. You're a disgrace to the Branford name. What would Mom and Dad think if they saw you today, knowing what you've done?"

"You know..." He points his finger in my direction, stepping closer. He purses his lips and lowers his voice. "Funnily enough, that isn't much of a concern to either of you now, is it? Since neither of you are no longer Branfords."

"We'll always be Branfords. But you? You're nothing."

He nods, wiping his hand over his mouth. He looks around, leaning back to peer through the open French doors. "Speaking of, where is our sister? I assumed she would be here. You two were always attached at the hip."

My stomach lurches. For a moment, I wonder if he knows about her cancer diagnosis. But then I remember Roe telling me she didn't want Fred to know. Relief washes over me temporarily knowing Fred is the only way Kellan would know.

"I haven't seen her yet." I tell him the truth, but I also don't want her seeing him. Not only because I know Roe hates our brother as much as I do, but I don't know what seeing him would do to her physically. From the glimpse I saw of her before running down here, I don't think she's well.

The invisible string attached to Roe is tugging on my chest, urging me to go find her. But Kellan is blocking the way. He's standing impossibly close. He's all sharp lines, focused on what he came here to say or do, as if he's been planning this for months. Confronting me and exacting revenge.

"Where's that husband of yours?" he asks, still looking around as if he'll find him. "I wouldn't mind seeing Lennon again."

"Again?" I ask, jerking back. I didn't know Lennon and my brother knew each other.

"Oh." He smirks. "He didn't tell you?"

I look at him, wide eyed, terrified of what I'm about to hear. Lennon's kiss still lingers on my mouth, reminding me of the three words he said to me upstairs. Another tear spills when I close my eyes, his feather tattoo at the forefront of my mind.

Cautiously, I open my eyes. Admittedly, I'm shaking with fear. I hate that Kellan is eliciting this kind of reaction out of me, but he's not the same brother I knew growing up. He's changed, and I'm not exactly sure when it happened. It's been a slow, progressive change, one where every crime he committed was expertly executed with slick precision, remaining undetected. Until it wasn't.

He's devious and manipulative, pulling the strings until he gets what he wants.

"When our uncle told me you married Lennon, I couldn't help but sit in my cell wondering why the fuck my sister would agree to marry someone whose reputation precedes one such as his father's. He's the eldest son of the richest man in New England after all, and that man is James *fucking* Harding." He sneers, venom spewing from the tip of his tongue. "But then with a little more prying from Fred, he told me you didn't marry Lennon for love." He clicks his tongue against his teeth, shaking his head. "He told me Lennon *had* to marry you in order to inherit his father's company."

My bottom lip quivers as a sob escapes my chest. I press my hand against my heart, feeling it thrash under flesh and bone.

Kellan is standing closer to me now, ensuring I hear every single word.

His eyes form into two small slits as he tilts his head to the side. "Tell me, sister," he whispers. "Did you ever stop to think why James Harding put it in his will for his oldest son to marry a

Branford? Did you ever stop and wonder why he'd tried to get you to fuck one of his son's when you met them for dinner at Eclipse over a year ago?"

I swallow the lump in my throat and stare at my brother in disbelief. My heart is racing a mile a minute and my limbs have gone numb.

"That's right," he continues. "Fred tells me everything."

Fucking Frederick and his big fucking mouth. If I never felt betrayed by my uncle before, I certainly do now.

"Why?" I ask, choking out the word. "Why did he tell Lennon to marry a Branford?"

His shoes touch the toes of my heels. He looks down before lifting his hooded eyes, piercing me. My heart shatters when he tells me the truth. "James Harding was looking for retribution. James and I had an understanding for many years. I convinced him to sell me drugs and lend me money years ago, but I could never pay him back. When he realized I was never going to give him what I owed, he tried hitting me where he thought I would hurt the most."

"But that doesn't make sense."

"Of course it does, Laurel." He scoffs, stabbing his finger against his temple. "You're a lawyer. Use that fucking brain of yours. James Harding never did anything without making someone else pay. He planned out the whole dinner at Eclipse that night so that he could set you up for a news story branding you a slut if you slept with one of his sons. He was planning on using you as a bribe to get money from Fred. And when that didn't work, he crafted you into his will. He knew the only way he could get to you was in death. Lennon was set to marry a Branford sister to take our family legacy down from the inside. He figured he'd raised his son to be just like him. He wanted Lennon to take everything you own and everything you claim under our family name and destroy it."

"I don't believe you." I shake my head. I already know I'm lying to myself. I know Lennon didn't have anything to do with his father's scheme at getting my brother back for his debts. Deep in my bones, in every cell, I know Lennon does love me. Because loving him is as easy and as natural as breathing. Then I think back to our terms and conditions. Lennon easily accepted mine, laying out that I wanted to keep all of my assets and my job at my uncle's law firm. He agreed and signed without hesitation.

"I don't believe you," I repeat. "Lennon wouldn't do that."

"For a lawyer, you've always been a terrible fucking liar." He snarls. "He's going to destroy our family. You know that, right? That's all Hardings do. They bleed others dry until there's nothing left."

"No." I shake my head.

"You're nothing but a business transaction, Laurel. You're a piece of trash they'll think nothing more of once they're finished with you."

All my anger and frustration over the past several years boils over. My skin is hot, and my hands curl into tight fists at my sides. My vision turns to red, and all I can think about is back to when we were kids. Kellan taught me how to ride a bike. He beat up the group of bullies who used to follow me home from school every day, taunting and making fun of me. He used to sneak me into parties I was too young for, but he did it so I felt included.

But then all of it changed. He became a darker version of himself, stealing our parent's cars and money. He lied to them left and right. Eventually, his crimes escalated, and the more I saw his deeds go unpunished, the more my hate for him bloomed. And then when I discovered he'd wiped my entire trust fund clean, my hate transformed into something else entirely.

I bite the inside of my cheek, forcing myself to stand my ground and say what's been on my mind since the last time I spoke to my brother.

"Fuck you, Kellan." I curl my lip. "I really don't give a shit what did or didn't happen between you and James fucking Harding. The man was an asshole and deserves to rot in the grave he's been stuffed into for the rest of eternity. But don't act like you're some fucking saint." I raise my chin, suddenly getting a burst of courage and energy. "You stole from everyone. You stole from James. You stole from Mom, Dad, and Roe. And you stole from me!"

I'm yelling, my throat swelling with every word being pushed up and out of it. I press my finger against Kellan's stiff, puffed chest. The veins in his neck have popped, and his face turns beet red with anger. His gray eyes are like two circular pieces of steel, darkening and hardening with every word.

My insults and accusations are daggers being thrown in his direction after the door to my soul has been unlocked and swung open. Every dark thought and every resentment are finally being set free. "Do you want to know why I didn't say a word to you on the day of your sentencing?" I ask him, bitterly. "Why I wouldn't even look in your direction as they handcuffed you and escorted you out of the courtroom?"

I don't bother waiting for his answer.

"Because every word and breath I'd used to defend you up until that day had been a fucking waste. You think you're any different than James? You're the fucking same. You're a disgrace to this family. Honestly, it should have been you climbing that cliff instead of Mom and Dad. We'd all be better off."

The sting against my left cheek doesn't sink in right away. A gasp leaves my chest as my hand instinctively lifts to cover the side of my face from the amount of force used against it. I'm shaking as I look down at the floor. The stinging sensation starts in the middle, feathering out at the edges until it reaches the corner of my eye. Fresh tears fall to the marble floor followed by a drop of blood coming from the corner of my mouth.

"Kellan?"

I snap my head up and see Roe standing at the end of the hallway, leading to the other end of the house, away from the party.

"What are you doing here?" she asks breathily.

Between the stars in my eyes, I take in the way she looks. A black piece of silk is draped around her head elegantly, hiding her hairless scalp. Gaunt eyes and sunken cheeks. She's vastly different even from the last time I saw her.

I'm still holding onto my cheek when I feel a sea of black moving in front of me.

I turn to look at Kellan. I think he's going to still be standing in front of me, but instead, Lennon is between us.

With his hands clenched around Kellan's lapel, he shoves him backward until his back lands against the sandstone wall.

"Lennon!" I yell, but my voice can't be heard over the sound of their grunts of Kellan pushing against Lennon's arm pinning him to the wall.

"Touch my wife again," Lennon spits between clenched teeth. "I fucking dare you, asshole. Touch her again and you're dead. I will slit your throat and bury you next to my father's grave, I swear to God."

"She was my sister before she was your wife," Kellan spews back, lifting his chin. "Tell me, Lennon. How does it feel knowing the only reason your father made you marry her was because of me? Does it make your dick go limp every time you go to fuck her?"

"You fucking piece of shit." Lennon keeps his left arm pressed against Kellan's chest, and he lifts the other, quickly curling his hand into a fist. Without hesitation, and on a single breath, he rears his arm back and delivers a sharp, heavy blow to Kellan's nose. A loud pop followed by the sound of cracking bones make my stomach lurch.

My hands fly to my mouth, muffling my scream. Blood streams from Kellan's nose as he bends forward. Lennon lifts his hand again and punches him once more, not caring about the amount of blood he's spilling. His back is to me, but with the way his shoulders have stiffened and the force behind his punches, I know there must be fire in his eyes.

"Stop." I hear Roe's meek voice. She steps out from the hall-way, but steadies herself with her outstretched arm. There's nothing for her to grab onto when she takes another faltering uneasy step.

With panicked, widespread eyes, she looks up at me. And I'm completely gutted.

"Laurel?" Her chin quivers as a tear spills from her half-open eyes. They roll back as she takes another step, her heel never lifting from the floor. I run toward her, but I don't make it before her knees give out. She collapses, and though she tries to catch herself with her hands, the second she does, she immedi-ately falls to her side and onto her back.

"Lennon!" I scream. "Help me!"

I fall to my knees and bend over Roe. Her eyes are shut, and I'm too panicked to see if she's still breathing. My vision is blurry and my head pounds. Stars and dots of black fade in and out as I look down at Roe.

I yell over my shoulder again. "Lennon!"

Panicked, I wrap my hands around the back of her head and rest her in my lap. I gently place my bloodied hand on her cheek. "Roe," I cry. "Please, Roe. Stay with me."

"Here," Lennon says, fear laced in his deep voice. I gently lift her head as Lennon's hands slide beneath mine. I back away, crawling on the marble floor, giving Lennon space. When I'm a good distance away, I stay on my hands and knees, my shoulders racking with sobs.

"Monroe," I beg, willing her to wake up.

Lennon bends over her, placing his fingers to her neck. Then he leans down, bringing his ear to her mouth. He looks up, seeing Ray standing in the doorway.

"Call an ambulance."

Ray nods, scrambling as he pulls his phone from his pocket.

"She's breathing," Lennon tells me. His face is calm, but the panic in his eyes is evident, only solidified by the way his chest rapidly expands and contracts with every breath. "What happened?" he asks me, his eyebrows knitted tightly together.

I cover my mouth, muting my cries. My eyes dart back and forth between my sister and my husband.

Shaking, I lower my hand and finally tell Lennon the one secret remaining between us. The one he knew I was keeping. "She has cancer."

TWENTY-SEVEN

Lennon

Holding Roe's lifeless body in my arms immediately thrusted me back to seeing my mother in the hospital.

The paramedics were on her in no time and airlifted her back to Boston, so she could be near her oncologist. Laurel rode in the helicopter with her. Once I ensured they were on their way, I had Olivia cancel the party and ask everyone to go home. I didn't say goodbye to our guests, rushing to my own helicopter to catch up to Laurel and Roe at the hospital.

The rush of adrenaline hasn't worn off, and I think a small part of me hasn't allowed myself to address the trigger of what happened tonight. My focus is only on Laurel and Roe.

When my helicopter lands on top of my apartment building, I race down to the parking garage.

I climb into my black Bugatti and race out of the garage faster than I probably should, but all I can think about is getting to the hospital. I weave in and out of traffic, racing against the clock. I check my phone, but there's no message or missed call from Laurel. Having been in her situation, I wouldn't blame her.

I wipe my hand over my mouth but flinch when I see my

reflection in the rear-view mirror. Dried blood is caked across the back of my hand. I didn't even bother waiting to see where Kellan went after Roe collapsed. Last I saw of him was when he fell to the floor against the wall in a slump, holding his hands to his face. I know I fucked him up, but I don't give a shit. Fucker deserved it.

My tires screech against the pavement when I reach the hospital parking garage. I swing into the closest spot and run through the large automatic doors of the emergency room.

I stop at the front desk.

"Hi," I say to the nurse, breathless. "My name is Lennon Harding. My wife Laurel Harding was airlifted here with her sister, Monroe Caulder."

"Oh, yes," she says, her brown eyes softening. "Your wife told us you would be coming. They took your sister-in-law into the exam room, but your wife should be just down the hall." The nurse presses a button behind her desk. Followed by a loud high pitch buzzing sound, the door with a large red stripe painted across it clicks. I grab the handle and swing it open. My eyes scan the hall, frantically looking for Laurel, and when I see her standing at the end of the hallway with her face in her hands, memories slam into me, stealing the air from my lungs and forcing me to stop dead in my tracks. I've been here before. Every step is instinctual, as if I've taken this same path. Because I have. I must have been so intently focused on finding Laurel, I hadn't realized I'd done the same drive from my apartment building to the same hospital. I parked in the same garage and ran the same walkway leading to the large automatic doors. Muscle memory kicked in, rearing its ugly head.

This isn't exactly a situation I want to relive.

I blink, panic starting to set in. Slapping my hand to my chest, over my heart, I take a breath in. I swear, I see myself six years ago, standing in this same hallway talking to the doctor.

The one who handed me a clip board with a blank line, waiting for my signature.

But then I blink again, and the doctor and I disappear. All I see is Laurel. She's still standing with her back against the wall and her face buried in her hands. Her shoulders rack with sobs.

I run down the hall, calling her name. "Laurel!"

She gasps, snapping her head up to the sound of my voice. If my heart wasn't winning out, I swear my knees would give out. Laurel's face guts me. A broken heart, filled with fear, her faded red lip quivers. "Lennon?"

"I'm here," I tell her, immediately pulling her to me. I place my hand on the back of her head and hold her against my chest.

She curls in on herself, allowing me to hold her. I kiss the top of her head and run my hand down the length of her back.

I place both my hands on her mascara-streaked cheeks, willing her to look up at me.

When she does, my fractured soul splinters, the cracks widening. Seeing my wife broken tears me apart.

"Where is she?" I ask her.

"In there." She tries to tell me, hitching her thumb over her shoulder. Every word is choppy and caught at the end of a hiccupped breath. "When we got here, they immediately wheeled her into the room."

"Do you know how she is?"

"No," she says, tears spilling from her red eyes. "They haven't said anything. No one has come out. But the paramedic did tell me on the ride here that they called her oncologist. He's in there, too. I think."

"Okay." I nod, unsure of what to say. I take a breath and run my fingers through Laurel's windswept hair. "What's important is that they're with her. I'm sure the doctors will figure out what's happening."

"I hope so." She frowns, but I can see she isn't entirely

convinced. She's terrified. Her eyes are glossed over as if she's not exactly here in the hallway with me. She's in her own mind again, pulling herself back into her shell.

She shivers, wrapping her arms around herself to ward off the chill. I slide out of my suit jacket and drape it over her shoulders. As if on auto pilot, she slips her arms in, staring at the floor as she mutters, "Thank you."

"Come here." I wrap my hand around hers and walk her over to the opposite wall. We fall back against it and slide to the floor. Nurses down the hall and at the far station give us a sideways glance, but they don't say anything to us. I'm unsure why. Maybe they can see the fear and pain in Laurel's eyes. The emergency room is eerily quiet. It's odd, considering this is a hospital in the heart of downtown Boston.

I rest against the wall and bend my knees, not wanting them to stick out into the hallway. Laurel sits down beside me and rests her head on my shoulder. I wrap my arm around her and lay my cheek on the top of her head. I stare at the blank white wall, holding back my own emotion. I wait for Laurel to speak first. I know sometimes words aren't needed when you feel lost and helpless.

Minutes pass by in silence. My hand pulsates and aches, bruises already blooming under the dried blood.

"I'm sorry, Lennon," Laurel whispers beside me.

"Laurel." I say her name with as much energy as I can pull together, making sure she knows how sincere I am in this moment. "You don't have anything to apologize for."

She adjusts herself beside me enough to look up at me. Her tears have dried. For now. But the pain and fear are still lingering in her indigo eyes.

"How long have you known?" I ask her. I can't bring myself to say the word cancer. It's the same disease I watched drain the life out of my mother, and now Laurel has been forced to watch it do the same to her sister.

"A couple months." She inhales an unsteady breath. "She's been going through chemo treatments since before we got married."

I think back to all the times I saw the vacant, far off, distant look in Laurel's eye. It grew every day, transforming into something bigger than the day before. It was clear the burden of carrying Roe's secret was weighing on Laurel.

"But there's something else I need to tell you." She swallows, sitting up. She places her hand over mine. I look down at the emerald cut diamond. The stone shimmers, even under the dull hospital lights.

"What is it?" I whisper.

"You often asked why I suddenly changed my mind after turning you down when you first proposed."

I nod, closing my mouth and letting her answer the one question that's been on my mind since the day I found her in my office, sitting behind my desk, barefoot.

She looks back down at her hand. "After you proposed the first time, Roe came over to my apartment and told me about her cancer diagnosis. She told me she had the money for her first rounds of chemo treatments but wasn't sure she'd have enough for the surgery when the time came. I offered her my savings and all the money I had, but she refused. I couldn't sleep that night." She traces the back of my hand with her finger, and fresh tears spill, her voice straining as she continues. "Kellan used the trust fund my parents left for me when they died, and Roe had used hers when she and Steven bought their house after they got married. Our family money was running dry." She turns her head back up to look at me. "But then you messaged me that night, and I found a way to pay for Roe's surgery without losing my entire savings."

"By marrying me." I swallow.

"Yes." She frowns, her eyes softening. "I didn't plan on using your money for her surgery. Only my own. But this way I wouldn't lose everything by doing it. Roe didn't want that for me. I tried to get her to tell our uncle since he has money, but she quickly shot that down. She didn't want him to know or anyone else in case the media picked up on the story. She didn't want our family name to make headlines again, only this time they would be painting her as the victim. First her brother, now cancer. I understood, and if she wanted me to keep a secret, I wasn't going to deny her that. I would have taken this to my grave if that's what she wanted."

I nod and lay my head back against the wall. I can't explain it. I'm not upset at her for keeping Roe's cancer a secret. A bond between sisters is something I will never completely understand. But I do have brothers I would do anything for, and I would have done the same if I were in her position.

I'm not naïve in thinking Laurel married me simply because she'd always cared for me in some way. I was cruel to her in the beginning, leading with my cold, black heart. It was easier to lure the dark side of me out while keeping the scared and vulnerable side in.

But I'm in love with Laurel—I always have been—and seeing her this way, knowing she's going through the same pain with her sister that I was in with my mother, makes this black heart of mine shatter into a million tiny pieces. I want to take her pain away, but I know I can't. That's the thing about cancer. It doesn't give a shit about you. It takes and takes until there's nothing left in its wake.

"I'm sorry, Laurel," I say, rolling my head back down to her. I rest my thumb on her mascara-streaked cheek.

"What are you sorry for?" Her eyebrows tightly knit. "I'm the one who married you for money."

"So did I," I retort, a fact that tastes sour on my tongue.

"True."

"But I am still sorry."

"For agreeing to marry me for money?"

"No." I draw an invisible line down the side of her face. "I'm sorry your sister is sick, and you've spent the last few months having to carry that secret alone."

Her bottom lip quivers as tears spill over her red-lined lashes. It's written on her face, her love for me. But I told her I didn't want her telling me until she was ready. Until she felt like her soul was free. Although her secret is out now, it doesn't manipulate the facts. Her sister is dying, and there's nothing she can do. All I can do now is be there for her.

"Thank you." She sobs, but I catch her breath with a kiss.

I hook my fingers under her chin and lift her face to mine. I gently press my mouth to hers.

She cries against me, her mouth turning down against mine. Her lips part as she gasps for air, sobbing. I wrap my hand around her face, and she places hers over mine.

I want to wrap my entire body around hers—anything to comfort her and make her feel safe.

But I can't.

After our kiss, she pulls my hand away from her and stares down at the dried blood. She traces the bruises and still-open cuts.

"We should get this looked at," she says, swinging her eyes up to mine. "Now's the perfect time considering we're in a hospital."

I shrug, the corner of my mouth tilting to a smirk. Despite the cloud of darkness looming over us, I still see light.

"Mrs. Harding?"

Laurel and I both snap our heads to the other side of the

hall. A doctor with a white lab coat steps out of Monroe's room. He gently allows the door to shut behind him.

Laurel scrambles to her feet. She meets the doctor in the middle of the hall, and I'm quick to be by her side. I place my hand on the small of her back as she holds her hands in front of her, nervously wringing her fingers. Her knuckles fade to white before turning red again.

"Is my sister okay?"

The doctor nods, and Laurel's shoulders relax. She's still wringing her fingers, but she's not as tense.

"I'm Monroe's oncologist, Dr. White," he says, placing his hand to his chest. "I've been treating your sister ever since we discovered her cancer eight months ago."

"Eight months?" Laurel gasps. She quickly snaps her head in my direction before looking back at the doctor. "Eight months?" she repeats.

"Yes." Dr. White's eyes dart between us. "Monroe has been diagnosed since the end of last year."

Laurel slowly lifts her hand to cover her mouth. I wrap my hand around her waist, pulling her closer. "I'm sorry." She blinks. "I didn't know."

"We're all lucky you brought her in as fast as you did," he explains. "I feared since Monroe was going through this alone that she might have someone there for her in a situation such as this one."

Relief washes over me momentarily, thankful she wasn't unconscious long enough to end up on life support like my mother was.

"But she hasn't been alone," Laurel explains. "Her husband Steven has been with her every day, taking care of her."

Three lines crease the doctor's forehead as he continues looking between me and Laurel. He appears just as confused as we are.

"I'm sorry, Mrs. Harding, but your sister has never mentioned her husband, nor has he been to any of her appointments."

"I don't understand. Steven's been going to all her chemo treatments."

The doctor stares at us blankly, unsure what to say. "I'm sorry to tell you this, Mrs. Harding, but Monroe hasn't had a treatment in well over a month. Her scans were showing an aggressive progression of cancer cells moving to other parts of her body."

"But what about the surgery?" Laurel's face pales as her jaw drops. "Can't it be removed with surgery?"

"Unfortunately..." He shakes his head. "Surgery is no longer an option. The cells have multiplied in too many areas, and one of the tumors has latched itself onto a blood vessel making it inoperable. It would be impossible, at this point, to eliminate all the cancer cells. Monroe declined all chemotherapy or radiation treatments after we discussed her situation and the likelihood she would make it out the other side of chemo. The risk was worth more than the outcome. The cancer has weakened her immune system, which ultimately caused her to collapse the way she did."

Laurel sobs again, this time turning into me. She places her head on my chest, and I wrap my arms around her, squeezing her tightly.

"Again," the doctor says, "I'm so sorry. You're welcome to go in and see her. She's asleep, but we have her on an IV drip, and she's being closely monitored. We'll have her moved to the oncology floor here in a few hours."

The doctor disappears down the hall, stopping at the nurses' station.

My arms are still wrapped around Laurel's shaking body. I

kiss the top of her head and soothe her as much as I can, but it isn't until this moment do I realize I'm falling apart as well.

Holding Laurel is the only thing keeping me together. I'm thrust back into my nightmare, reliving the pain and grief I felt with my mother. Monroe isn't my sister, but she is family. Laurel is my family.

"Do you want to go in and see her?" I ask Laurel.

She pulls away, wiping at her swollen eyes. She nods and looks up, her eyes searching mine. "Yeah, I, um..." She looks down at her hands. They're tucked inside the long sleeves of my jacket. It's swallowing her, but it doesn't matter.

"Don't worry about it," I reassure her. "I'll have Ray bring some of your clothes."

Her round eyes soften. "Thank you."

"Of course." I kiss her on the lips. "I'll let you two have some time. I'll go see if I can track down a nurse to help me clean this up." I hold my hand up, turning it over.

"Good, you should." She lightly smiles, running her hand up the length of my arm. I start to walk away, but before my hand leaves hers, she tugs on my fingers. I look over my shoulder.

"Don't go too far," she says, a very weak, ghost of a smile tugging on her lips. "Please."

"I won't," I promise her. I wait until she turns on her heel and stands in front of the door. She looks at me with her hand pressed against the door, not quite pushing on it.

Sadness. Fear. Pain. Guilt. Every emotion I can possibly think of is written across her face as she looks at me one last time before pushing through the door.

I leave my wife, and groggily head toward the nurses' station. I rub my eyes with the heels of my hands, making sure to keep my head down, unwilling to look toward the room where I last saw my mother. An ache pulsates and thumps in my chest. I guess even when I'm awake, I can't escape my nightmare. Now Laurel's living in my nightmare, too.

TWENTY-EIGHT

LAUREL

My body hurts and my eyes feel like they're going to pop right out of their sockets, but I know the pain I feel right now is nothing to the pain I feel inside. Or the kind my sister is going through.

I leave Lennon in the emergency room hallway and quietly step into the room. I feel the absence of him immediately. It feels as if I've stepped out of a hot, sunny day and into a cold, blistering winter night. I wrap my arms around myself, allowing my fingers to graze over the silk black fabric of his suit jacket. The scent of him coming from it overpowers the sterile, unfeeling hospital smell.

Surprisingly, they didn't put Roe in a room with one of those curtain dividers, with the potential of another patient being only feet away from her. The room is quiet aside from the beeping of the machine monitoring her heart rate. My eyes dance around the room, taking in all the machines. An IV is stuck in the back of Monroe's hand, and a small, plastic clamp with a bright red light is pressed to the tip of her right index finger. She's no longer wearing the red gown she wore to the party or the black wrap around her head. Her hair isn't completely gone. Dark blonde strands feather across her forehead. Her hair is thin, and if I close my eyes, I can picture when it was full and layered with curls.

I stand beside her bed and reach over the railing, gently placing my hand over hers, feeling her warmth.

New tears spill over, and I suck in a breath. I'm so tired of crying. It feels like that's all I've been doing tonight. Just when I think I don't have any more left, another well fills inside me, overflowing.

"Laurel?" Roe turns her head against her pillow and cracks her eyes open. Her voice sounds weak, but I'm thankful for the bit of color that's returned to her face since I saw her lying on the floor unconscious.

"Shh." I gently squeeze her hand. "Everything is okay. I'm here."

The corners of her mouth turn down into a frown, and her chin quivers. She looks at me watery eyed, and my heart breaks. She sobs and shakes her head, blinking her tears away.

"I'm so sorry," she cries. "I'm sorry, I should have told you."

"No." I sniff. "You have nothing to be sorry about."

"Yes, I do." She nods slowly. "I should have told you. You deserved to know."

I shake my head and look down, rubbing my hand over hers. I can't imagine life without my sister. Ever since the day I was born on her second birthday, she's been my best friend. Almost like twins born two years apart.

"I'm not angry with you," I tell her. "Please don't think I am. I just wish you would have told me. I could have been there for you, and you wouldn't have had to do this all alone." I try not to let the guilt eat away at me. I think back to the guilt Lennon told me he feels every day for the decision he made to let his mother go. I don't want to let the feeling set in and overshadow being there for Roe.

I swallow hard, thinking back to what the doctor said in the hallway. "What happened with Steven?"

Pressing her mouth into a tight line, she turns her head and looks up at the ceiling. A nasal cannula is wrapped around her ears, feeding her oxygen. The sound of air blowing into her nose blends with the monitor beside her. Salty tears stream from the corners of her eyes as she blankly looks up at the ceiling.

"Steven left me months ago." She rolls her head back to face me. "After we found out about my diagnosis, he decided he couldn't handle it. I don't know if it was money or the gravity of seeing his wife go through the suffering of cancer treatments, but he'd decided he couldn't deal. I woke up one morning and he was just... gone."

She looks back up at the ceiling, the story of the past year playing out in her mind. "I couldn't wrap my mind around him leaving. I'd loved him since my second year of college. We bought a house together. And when I realized it wasn't the cancer that ruined my dreams of a future with him, that it was him leaving me, I decided to let go. I didn't want to be married to someone who didn't love me with the same capacity as he did the day he married me."

"Oh, Roe..." I trace my tongue across my lips, wrapping my head around what she's telling me. I hate the thought of her dealing with this alone.

She turns herself on her side and reaches across to wrap my hand in both of hers. She runs her thumb over the diamond on my left finger. The one for Lennon.

"When you told me you were marrying Lennon, I almost convinced you not to. I wanted to tell you I'd stopped treatments and I no longer needed the money. But then I saw the glint of excitement flicker in your eyes as you stared up at the sign above the bridal shop. It was then I knew this wasn't just a marriage of convenience for you or an arranged marriage for him. A part of your heart knew this was what you wanted. Your heart was in love with Lennon before it told your brain it was."

I cry, wiping the back of my hand across my nose. I sniff and bite down on my bottom lip.

"You do love him, right?"

I don't hesitate when I nod and look up at Roe. "I do."

"Good." She sighs, her eyes fluttering. "You deserve to be loved, Laurel."

"But you do, too," I tell her, my heart breaking at the thought of living in a world where she no longer exists or breathes.

"I've known what it feels like to be loved. Even before Steven. The beauty about love is that it takes many different forms, Laurel. I was first loved by Mom and Dad, and then you. I've known what true love feels like. Now you do, too."

"I've been blessed to have been loved by our parents and by you," I agree. "But I know what you mean. Loving Lennon is something that feels unexpected, but it isn't. I think you're right. My heart knew I loved him before I even knew it myself."

"Of course I'm right." She grins smugly, giving me a slice of her usual self.

A small spark of warmth lights in my chest.

"Do you know what happened to Kellan?" She hesitates, unsure if she wants to know the answer.

"I don't know." I shake my head. "I haven't paid much attention to anything outside of you, but I'm sure if the police didn't show up, Fred is most likely covering for him. Seems like he's always had Kellan's back no matter what."

"I didn't know Kellan had the chance to be released early." She frowns. "I hate what he did to our family, but it makes me sad knowing this is the way things turned out with him. I miss the old Kellan."

"I do, too."

"I don't know where he or Fred are, but if they try to come, I don't want to see them," she states firmly. "I don't want to live out the rest of my days spending time with family that only want to spend time with me because I'm dying. I don't want them to see me out of pity."

"I understand." I nod.

"I told the nurses that came in my room I didn't want to see them if they tried to show up." She inhales a deep breath. "Does that make me a bad person?"

"Are you kidding?" I ask, shocked she'd even suggest it. "No. They made their choices, and you have every right to pick and choose who you want in your life. Whether you were dying of cancer or not."

She nods and sniffs, squeezing her eyes shut as if she's willing her tears to disappear. She opens her eyes again.

"I want you to know something," she starts. "You're more than my sister, Laurel. You're my best friend. I think it's about time you start doing things because it's what you truly want for yourself instead of doing everything for everyone else."

We allow silence to fill the room. My eyes lift to the monitor above Roe's head, tracking her heartbeats.

The tight knot in my chest pulls even tighter, and it's difficult to breathe.

"Are you scared?" I ask her, looking her in the eye.

"I was, but I don't think I am anymore," she says in a stronger voice. "Because now I can let go knowing you'll live a full and happy life. I can let go knowing even though you'll be losing me, you won't be alone."

"I love you, Roe," I tell her, my phone buzzing in the pocket of Lennon's jacket. I slid it inside after Lennon offered it to me in the hallway.

"I love you, too," she says, her eyes darting to the buzzing sound. "Is that him?"

"Maybe." I shrug. "But that's not important right now. I'm here with you."

"Of course it's important. He's your husband, Laurel." She tilts her head to the side. "Seeing you happy makes me happy."

"Okay." I smile, pulling my phone free. I click on the screen and open Lennon's text.

"It's him," I tell her. "He said he found a nurse to fix up his hand."

"I saw what he did to Kellan before I passed out. I'm glad he was able to get it cleaned up."

I nod and text Lennon back.

> Me: I'm glad you were able to get it cleaned. I'm going to stay with Roe a bit longer if you want to go home.

> Lennon: Are you sure?

"You don't have to stay this whole time if you don't want to," Roe interrupts my texting.

"Stop." I drop my shoulders and look up. "I don't mind staying. I want to make sure you're okay."

"I'm fine," she says. "For now."

My heart sinks and plummets in my stomach knowing the deeper meaning behind her coy response.

She gives me a pointed look as her eyes survey me up and down. "You could use a little cleaning up yourself."

I look down, laughing. She's right. My skin is sticky with sweat, and dirt covers my dress. I run my fingers through my loose, tangled, windswept curls.

"I could," I agree.

Roe lifts her eyebrows, waiting for me to answer her.

"Fine." I groan, followed by a giggle. "I'll go home and

shower, but I'll wait until you get transferred to your own room."

"Sounds good." She nods once, but then she looks off to the side, her smile fading. Fresh tears line her eyes again when she turns her attention back on me. "Thank you, Laurel."

I give her a closed mouth smile before texting Lennon.

Me: I'm sure. I'm going to stay until they come in to transfer Roe to her own room.

Lennon: Okay, sweet nothings. I'll have Ray wait for you out in the waiting room whenever you're ready.

Me: Thank you xx

When I'm finished texting with Lennon, I drop my phone back into my pocket and pull up the doctor's stool in the far corner of the small room. I roll it until I reach the side of Roe's bed and sit down.

My eyes tire, growing heavier with every blink. Roe adjusts in her bed until she's comfortable. Her hollowed, tired eyes close as she tucks her hands under the side of her face. She's still wearing her wedding ring. A large, green emerald surrounded by dozens of tiny white diamonds. My heart breaks for her, knowing the one man she truly loved broke her already broken heart. I try not to think on it too long.

Anger for Steven blooms in my chest, but love for Lennon replaces it. I try to imagine if I were in Roe's shoes. The thought of my marriage to Lennon left in limbo because he decided to disappear leaves a gaping hole where my heart has made its home.

I wrap my hand around Roe's and lean over the bed, resting my head on our hands. Then I allow myself to fall asleep to the rhythmic sound of Roe's heartbeat through the machine.

"Ma'am?"

I snap my eyes open to find myself staring at a nurse. He moves beside me, dragging an oxygen tank behind him. I watch as he unplugs the tube to Roe's cannula from the wall and connects it to the tank.

"Monroe's room is ready for her up in the oncology room."

I look over at Roe. Her eyes are still closed, but she's breathing. The lights above Roe's bed are dim, and I wonder if one of the nurses came in while we were both sleeping and turned them down.

"Oh." I rub the sleep from my eyes. "I told her I would stay until she was taken up. I don't want to wake her."

"We'd like her to get as much rest as possible," the nurse says, rearranging tubes and wires. It's a tangled mess.

"Okay." I sigh, checking the time. I've only been asleep for an hour. "Will you let her know I was here until she was moved?"

"Of course." He agrees with a smile.

"Thank you."

Carefully and softly, I unravel my hands from Roe's and step out of her room. I squint when I step into the hallway. The bright lights of the emergency room stretch from one end of the hall to the other. I head toward the waiting room to find Ray. I tilt my head to the side, stretching the sore muscles in my neck.

When I push through the door, I find him waiting for me in the corner of the room. Dark green chairs line each of the three walls with more rows of chairs scattered in the middle. A children's table with toys is situated along the far wall. Surprisingly, the waiting room isn't busy.

Ray eyes me and stands, straightening the lapel of his black suit. He takes a step toward me, but I stop when I see Fred and Kellan walking toward me from the direction of the check in desk.

"Where is she?" Fred desperately asks. His facial expressions are tense and worried. I've lost all sympathy and respect for him. It's incredible how quickly you can look up to someone, and then one day, you don't even want to look at them at all.

"Why are you here?" I ask.

"What do you mean, why are we here?" he asks in disbelief.

"Well." I shoot Kellan a look. "Considering what happened back at the party, I didn't think you'd come all the way here."

"Enough." Fred groans. "We're not going to discuss what happened."

Excusing Kellan's behavior. Typical.

"How is Monroe?" Fred asks again.

"She's fine." I grind my molars, keeping my composure as best I can. "For now." I keep Ray in my peripheral, taking note of his continuous steps in my direction.

"We tried telling the nurse we were family, but they wouldn't let us back there to see her."

I wrap my arms around myself. "Yeah." I chew on the inside of my cheek. "Roe doesn't need or want to see either of you. It'll only make her feel worse than she already does."

"What the fuck?" Kellan takes a step forward, balling both

his hands into fists at his side. "Is this because of you? Did you fucking tell them to not let us see her?"

Ray takes a large step forward, readying himself for anything Kellan might pull.

"No, Roe told them she didn't want to see you before I even came into the room." I steel my eyes on him. His nose is broken and swollen. A large, white bandage is taped to the bridge. Deep red and purple bruises peek out from the white gauze. Kellan certainly won't forget what Lennon did to him anytime soon.

"I'm her uncle." Fred points to his chest, spit flying from between his lips. "I've always cared about Monroe. How dare you keep her condition a secret from me. I had a right to know."

"It was what she wanted," I argue. "She specifically asked me not to tell anyone. Even you, Fred."

"Roe is my sister." Kellen yells.

"Do you know what?" I scoff. "You two are fucking unbelievable. You only claim us as your family when it's convenient or when you see a way your relationship with us can benefit you." I pin Kellan with an icy glare. "Did you ever stop and think about me or her when you stole our money? What, now that Roe is *dying,* you suddenly care whether she's going to live? You're a fucking asshole, Kellan."

He takes a step forward, curling his upper lip. "You're lucky I'm not pressing charges against your husband for what he did to me."

I take another step forward. "And you're lucky to be out of prison at all."

"Kellan earned his early release," Fred interjects. "I think it's about time we all moved on."

I would say fresh tears spring to my eyes, but none come. Whether it's because I've run dry from how many tears I've already shed tonight, the exhaustion slamming into me, or it could be that I simply have no love for the two men standing in front of me, I feel absolutely nothing.

I think about the past several years of my life. I've gone from being a wallflower to graduating law school to becoming Mrs. Lennon Harding.

I look at my brother and uncle and feel hollow inside. They've done nothing but take advantage of the love I had for them. And now not only is the well of tears inside me completely dried up, my well of love is bone dry too.

"You're right." I nod, pressing my mouth into a tight line. I inhale a heavy breath through my nose and place my left hand in my right to finger the large diamond on my wedding ring. My chest spreads with a warmth I only get when I think about Lennon. "We do need to move on." I look up at Kellan then dart my eyes to Fred. "I quit."

"Excuse me?" he asks, confused.

"Yeah." I take in an unsteady breath, but I've never been so sure of anything in my life. "I'll draft up my resignation tomorrow and deliver it to your office on Monday."

Fred's jaw clenches under his full crimson cheeks. The dimple in his cheek deepens. It reminds me of my mother's. My heart aches wondering what she would think of her son and her brother now. Would she be proud of me for standing my ground? Would she be happy I'd found someone I love and who loves me in return?

"You're about to lose the only family you have," Fred warns. "You're going to regret this."

"No." I frown and shake my head. "No, I don't think I will. Besides, I already have a family. You just aren't a part of it."

I look at my brother and uncle one last time before passing Ray and heading to the exit door of the emergency room. I feel him follow behind me once I step out into the hot, sticky Boston summer air.

"Are you all right, Mrs. Harding?" Ray asks as I pass him.

"I'm okay," I choke out. I give him a nod, feeling Fred and Kellan's eyes staring at my back. "I'm ready to go home."

TWENTY-NINE

Lennon

I carefully remove the bandage wrapped around my hand and drop the bloodied gauze into the trash. Lifting my hand, I study the cleaned cuts and bruises, wincing as I flex my fingers.

The sound of my fist connecting with Kellan's face isn't a sound I've been able to forget easily. But when I think about his words in Laurel's ear, it was all worth it. The blood and pain shed were all worth it.

I haven't heard from Laurel since she texted me letting me know she was going to stay until they moved Roe into her own room. I don't know what the next step is or where we go from here but my heart breaks thinking of the future. The same heavy feeling falls on my chest and my shoulders, the way it did with my mother. It's like walking through a pitch-black room, searching for a light switch, but none exists.

"How is Laurel's sister?" Jude asks.

I look down at my phone resting on the edge of my bathroom sink.

"I haven't heard from Laurel since earlier, but last I heard, she's stable now. They're moving her up to the oncology floor.

From what the doctor made it sound like, she's probably going to be there a while."

"Man," Jude sighs on the other end of the line. "I feel terrible for Monroe and Laurel. Thinking about what they're going through reminds me of—"

"Don't," I cut in. My chest squeezes. "I'm sorry. I just..." I swallow. "I know where you're going, man, and we don't need to go over it again."

"I'm sorry, Lennon."

I don't answer him. The image of my mother in the same hospital bed as Monroe comes to mind, just like my nightmare.

"You have to stop blaming yourself."

I snap my head back to my phone, wondering if I must have accidently put him on a video call and he was able to read the expression I must have been giving for him to think I was thinking about our mother.

"Blaming myself for what?" I ask, shrugging off his comment. "Monroe didn't want anyone other than Laurel to know about her sickness. I don't blame myself for what happened tonight."

"I'm not talking about Monroe. I'm talking about Mom."

"I said I didn't want to talk about this."

"You did, and you say that as if it's going to stop me." He scoffs. "You're my brother, and I know you. You've blamed your-self for years for the decision you had to make."

"You're right," I fume, flaring my nostrils. "I do blame myself. She's dead because of me."

"No. She's dead because of the cancer, Lennon." He pauses, and I hear faint crying in the background. Must be my niece, Abbey. "Does Laurel know about your nightmares?"

"Yeah," I sigh. "I didn't have one until a few nights after our wedding, but I haven't had as many since. They come every now and then, but not nearly as often as before."

Abbey's cries grow louder. I hear Jude's footsteps and then his loud shushing fills the speaker. "Shh, it's okay, baby girl." He soothes her. She coos, immediately calming down when she hears her dad. "I wasn't a fan of you marrying Laurel for the sake of the company, but I can see your marriage is different. She's good for you, Len. Laurel is good for you."

Heat rises in my cheeks. I can't help but smile. "I know."

Abbey makes more fussing noises in the background. "I need to get Abbey back to sleep. Please keep me posted on how Roe is doing. And if you and Laurel need anything, Victoria and I are here for you."

"Thanks."

"No problem. Oh, and Len?"

"Yeah?"

"You really should stop blaming yourself. Mom wouldn't want you to. If she thought you couldn't have made the choice and been able to live with it, she wouldn't have trusted you to make that decision." He clears his throat. "You deserve to be happy, Len. It's what she would have wanted."

"Yeah," I sigh. It feels too heavy. All of it. "I'll keep you updated. Give Abbey a kiss for me."

"I will," Jude says before ending our call.

I stare at my phone for several minutes, letting the silence sink in. Jude is right, it's not what our mother would have wanted. All I need to focus on now is being there for Laurel.

Steam fills the bathroom as hot water flows out of the shower head. I step in and allow the water to slide down my back. It stings, but I welcome the relief it brings. I allow the day to unfold, crashing down on me like a tidal wave. It feels like it's never-ending. Only hours ago, I was back in my mother's house telling Laurel I love her. Now, I'm back at my apartment in Boston, staring at the bruises on my hand caused from hitting her brother.

I face the tiled wall and press my hands against it. I lower my head and stare at the floor. Water drips over my head. I close my eyes and think about Laurel, my heart swelling with love for her.

Seeing her in pain physically causes my own. She's a part of my soul. We're one, and until tonight, I didn't realize how she's not only a part of my soul, but she's also completely consumed it. She's claimed it as her own, and I have gladly fallen to both of my knees, begging her to take me.

My ribs expand with every breath, and my spine tingles when a hand slides across my side.

Two small arms slink under mine, wrapping around me. I feel Laurel press the side of her face to my back. I can't see her, but I feel her naked breasts press against my spine. I remove one of my hands from the wall and slide it across her arm wrapped around me.

I don't move, feeling her body contract against mine. Her breaths are labored, as if she's playing every single moment of tonight out.

I'm relieved she's finally home, but I know she hasn't stopped thinking about tonight.

"Fred and Kellan showed up to the hospital," she says over the sound of rushing water. Her lips move against my skin, sending shivers down my spine. "I told Fred I'm sending him my resignation letter on Monday. I quit the firm."

I drop my other hand and spin around. Laurel's arms unravel, falling at her sides. She stands under the stream of water. Her long dark hair clings to her face. Streaks of mascara still cover her cheeks. Dark sparkling eyeshadow that once covered the lids of her eyes has now faded and spread out past her eyebrows. Her bottom lip quivers as her shoulders slump with defeat. I know how much her job meant to her. How important being a lawyer is to her. She wrote it in her terms and conditions in fear I would ask her to leave or control her like her first husband.

I quickly place both my hands around her face.

"Oh, sweet nothings." I run my thumbs under her eyes, wiping the dried mascara clean. "I'm sorry."

"I..." She hiccups, nervously biting down on her bottom lip. "I know it was the right thing to do."

I don't speak. I let my hands roam her face, mentally taking note of every lash and every flicker in her eyes. She looks into mine, creating a dance between them. "Thank you for what you did tonight. I know I said it at the hospital, but I want to say it to you again. Now."

"You're my wife, Laurel," I tell her. "I would do anything for you."

Slowly, she lifts her hand, and with the tip of her index finger, she traces the letters under my feather tattoo. I follow her finger before looking back up. Her eyes meet mine.

"I love you, Lennon."

My heart plummets to my stomach. The sensation is unlike anything I've ever felt before. I feel weightless, like I'm somehow floating outside of my own body. No one has ever told me they loved me, and I've never done the same in return.

"I've always loved you," she says, pressing her palm against my ribs, covering the tattoo. "Ever since I saw you looking down at me in the backseat of your car, with your black heart, I loved you."

My chest feels like it's been ripped open, and Laurel has wrapped her fingers around my heart. I told her I didn't want her to say it until there were no longer any secrets between us. I didn't so much as care Laurel was keeping secrets. Everyone has them, including me. But if Laurel and I were going to be able to move past our contractual marriage, we needed to be able to face our feelings head on. Admitting your love for someone when all you've been raised to be is unfeeling, doesn't exactly come naturally. But somehow, Laurel made it as easy as breathing. Loving her is as easy as the oxygen pumping into my lungs.

I inhale a sharp breath before slamming her mouth against mine. She presses both her hands at my sides, digging her fingernails into my tattoo. She moans before I break our kiss long enough for me to answer her.

"You have no idea how long I've waited to hear you say those words." I kiss her again. "You own me, Laurel Eleanor Harding. Mind, body, and soul. You're not only mine, but I am yours." I grip the back of her neck, pulling her in for another kiss. I'm thirsty for more, never quite feeling satisfied with one kiss. "Utterly, completely, and wholly yours."

"I love you," she whispers against my mouth.

I wrap my arm around her and spin her until her back lands against the cool tile. My hand quickly trails up her bare leg, slipping between her warm thighs. I slide my fingers between her warm, wet folds, plunging three fingers inside her. She grips my shoulders and tilts her head back, gasping. I hook my fingers, pressing into the spot I know will quickly send her over the edge if I keep going.

"Tell me I'm yours," I say, my cock springing to life. My thumb finds her clit, pressing down.

She licks her lips as water streams down her face. Seeing her this way, reacting against my touch, spurs something inside me. Water streams down her face to her neck. I stick my tongue out and lick it before pulling away from her. She lowers her chin, staring into my eyes as I work my fingers in and out of her.

"You're mine." She growls.

"And you're mine," I agree. I quickly pull my fingers out of her. My patience has worn thin.

I shut the water off and wrap my arms around her waist.

She wraps her legs around me as I carry her out of the shower and toward our bedroom.

She's frantic as she drapes her arms around my neck, burying her face into the hollow of mine. She kisses and licks and bites. She's all over me, and when she sinks her teeth delicately into my collarbone, my cock twitches with need.

I drop her onto the bed and climb over her, greedy for more.

Her wet hair soaks into the sheets. It's dark in our bedroom aside from the lamp on my nightstand and the city lights behind me. Laurel's naked body is covered in highlights and shadows. Her arms are lifted above her head, and her breasts are on full display for me. She's damp with drops of water, so I lean down and lick them from her nipples. She arches her back as she fists my hair. She grips my strands and tugs on them, pulling me up to her. With a fiery stare, I look up at her, watching her writhe with need.

There's still a sadness in her eyes, considering the night she's had with her sister, but every kiss and every touch I offer are like a balm to her wounds. Wounds I can only see behind her indigo eyes.

I'm between her legs. She grinds her sweet pussy against me.

"Tell me something sweet," she requests, her sad eyes widening. She's begging to feel. Begging to know the world isn't as ugly as it appears. She wants me to remind her of all the love and of all the good that tends to get overshadowed.

My face is peeking below her still-damp breasts. I blow a gentle breath over her nipple before moving onto the other.

The corner of my mouth tilts into a smirk. "I fell in love with your eyes first."

Her mouth falls open as I give her my first sweet. She inhales a shaky, fevered breath, followed by a moan.

I lower myself even farther, bringing my mouth to her belly

button. I press my lips to her hip and flick my gaze up again. "The way your cheeks blushed red with embarrassment after telling me that removing the feather from your hair was sweet made me fall even harder."

Laurel bucks her hips. I love seeing her this way. Her feet slide up and down along the mattress as she tries to cling to anything that will keep her sane. She's begging for more, and I plan on giving it to her.

"Are you telling me every sweet from that night?" She gasps, struggling to catch her breath.

"Yes," I growl, crawling back up along her body. I plant a kiss on her hip bone again before making my way up her side, then along the full curve of her breast. I kiss her collarbone and then her neck. Bringing my face in line with hers, I bare my deepest darkest secret. "I've cataloged every sweet from every moment I've been with you."

"I doubt there's very many," she says, a smile playing on her lips.

"I have enough to tell you for the rest of our lives."

With my right hand, I reach down and grab her left. I hold it between us as I turn her hand over and press my lips to the diamond. I rub my thumb over its sharp edges before looking into Laurel's eyes. "This was my mother's ring."

Her eyes immediately soften, and for a moment, I worry I've scared her. I've never seen her face as shocked as it is now. Her eyes dart to her hand before she swings them back. "It was?" Her words get caught in her throat, full of emotion.

"Yes." I nod, swallowing. "She gave it to me after she found out about her cancer diagnosis. She said to give it to the one I couldn't live without. The one I would be able to tell all my sweets to, who would be able to do the same in return."

"I don't even know what to say." She's admiring the ring

with tears lining her eyes. "I loved it when you gave it to me, but knowing the meaning behind it..." Her voice wanes.

"It was meant to be yours," I tell her. "Always."

"I love you." She gasps, her eyes dancing between mine.

I pull my hips back and slide my cock along her folds. Her wetness coats my length as I let out a deep groan.

"And I love you." I reach down and plunge myself into her. This time I take it slow. "Feel every inch," I tell her. She lifts her legs and presses her bent knees into my sides. "I want you to feel every inch as I fill you. I want you to know I've always been yours."

"And me..." she moans. "Yours."

I slide myself out of her slowly before plunging back in. My cock swells, and heat expands across my body.

I watch Laurel's face as I move above her, and I allow her love to fill me up, making sure I return as much as I can to her.

The future is uncertain, and if I think on it too long, my stomach grows uneasy. But ever since I've known what it feels to lose the ones you love the most, I plan on savoring every moment and every sweet.

Because loving Laurel is more than I and my little black heart deserve.

And even if I despised my father to my very core, in the end, he's given me the greatest gift.

A life with Laurel and all her sweet nothings.

EPILOGUE

Laurel

Eight Months Later

The void I feel in my heart hasn't faded with time. At least not yet.

I've been told grief never fully disappears, instead only getting easier to manage in time. It's been six months since the cancer selfishly took Roe, and the pain hasn't felt any less visceral than the day she died.

I have my good days and bad. Some, I'm angry with the world. I scream into the void when I'm alone until the pain decides to crawl back into the shadows of my heart before resurfacing again. The grief comes in waves when I least expect it. Some days, when I'm stressed from work and I find myself in the kitchen making a batch of banana muffins, I think of Roe, and my heart breaks all over again.

But then there are days like today where I find myself standing in front of my new office space and the gold lettered sign bolted into the wall behind the front desk, and I feel my heart slowly starting to mend.

L. E. HARDING LAW FIRM

My heart swells with pride at the work I've been able to get done in such a short amount of time.

"Are you sure you shouldn't have put your full name on there?" Trey tilts his head to the side and scrunches his face. He waves his arm in front of the sign. "I mean, Laurel is such a beautiful name. I think you're doing yourself a disservice by just putting *L* and *E*."

I roll my eyes and laugh. It feels good to laugh. Each day, I've noticed one more laugh than the day before. Even Lennon has taken notice, pointing out another sweet whenever he hears it.

"I like it like this." I grin.

He shrugs and nudges my arm with his shoulder. "Maybe it'll grow on me."

"It better." I laugh again. "Or else you might be out of a job before you've even started it."

"I'll believe it when I see it." Trey purses his lips and crosses his arms over his chest, but his attitude quickly fades before he grins. "Remember, wherever you go, I go."

I give him one more smile before turning on my heel and heading down the hall to my new office. After I'd resigned from my uncle's law firm, Trey submitted his resignation as well. He told me wherever I went, he wanted to follow, and as the months have gone by, and especially after losing Roe, he's been a great friend to lean on.

I press my hand to my new office door and push through it. I spin around and immediately kick out of my heels and shrug off my black blazer. I hang it on the coat rack Olivia had given me as an office gift, and turn around.

A loud yelp jumps out my throat when I see my husband sitting behind my desk. His eyes light with amusement before he tips his head back in laughter. He's wearing a forest green tie today with his typical black on black ensemble. I love how he's venturing out of his usual black tie. *Baby steps.*

I place my hand against my chest when his laughter slows, his smile reaching those intense blue eyes of his.

"This never gets old, sweet nothings." He rocks back in my new office chair and lifts his leg, resting his ankle on his knee.

"Oh." I smirk, ignoring the way my heart still races at the sight of him. "It doesn't? I figured it would by now."

"Oh, no." He shakes his head. "I don't think I'll ever tire of watching you strip the second you step into your office." He lifts his arms out. "And now your new office is witness to it as well."

I cross my arms over my chest and give him a playful, pointed look. Lennon has been incredibly supportive of me these past few months. Considering his line of work, it was difficult for him not to involve himself too much in me creating and building my own firm separate from my uncle's. But Lennon helped without hesitation when asked and was there when I needed him. My heart swells knowing how lucky I am to call him mine.

"I must say, though." He pouts, standing from my chair to walk around the desk and meet me where I'm standing. "I can't say I'm not disappointed that your office is no longer three floors below mine. Makes it slightly more difficult to catch my wife off guard when she's undressing herself in her office." He slides his hands along my waist, pulling me to him.

"It's only two blocks over from your building."

"Too far."

I stand on my toes and kiss him on the lips. He tastes like peppermint. "Hmm," I moan. "Is that why you came down here? To air your grievances? I think that might be a conflict of interest, seeing as I'm your wife."

"No." He kisses me back, tracing his finger along my bottom lip. "That's not the only reason I came down here."

He reaches behind him and picks up a sheet of paper from my desk. When he hands it to me, I take it from between his fingers and read the text.

It doesn't take me long to realize what it is.

"It's the clause in my father's will that states we only need to be married a year before we're off the hook."

"What?" My heart sinks, and nausea wobbles in my stomach. "But, I thought..."

I look at Lennon, hoping he's only bringing this up as a joke. I don't think he ever intended for us to be married the minimum amount of time required by his father, but old insecurities threaten to rise in me. Sometimes I still lay next to Lennon at night, pinching myself to make sure I'm not dreaming. Did I really marry him? Is he truly my husband? But then I eye the ring on my finger and know it's true.

I take a step back, but Lennon's hands grip my sides, unwilling to let me walk away.

"You don't want to be married to me anymore?" I ask him. I'm not entirely sure I'm prepared for his answer. I can't hold back the old feelings threatening to resurface.

"Are you crazy? Who said anything about not wanting to be married anymore?" He jerks his head back, concern knitting between his eyebrows.

"No one, but..."

He lifts my gaze by hooking his fingers under my chin. "No but." He tilts his head to the side. "Do you not know how much I love you?"

"Well..." I look off to the side before lifting my arms up and around his neck. "I do, it's just..." I play with the ends of his dark hair, and my heart skips a beat.

"Are you telling me you doubt my love for you, Mrs. Harding?" The corner of his mouth tilts into a smirk.

"No." I shake my head. "I know our marriage was never transactional. Ever."

"It isn't." He lifts his thumb to my bottom lip before looking into my eyes. "I brought it here so we could celebrate and to tell you we made it. Even without my father's requirement, the year was never even a question."

"It wasn't for me, either," I tell him, never feeling more confident.

Lennon has broken me *and* he's healed me. But he's also made me feel more alive and loved than I've ever felt before.

"Well, then," my husband says, lifting my hand and pressing his warm lips to the feather tattooed on the inside of my wrist. "Happy anniversary, sweet nothings."

GO to www.brittanytaylorbooks.com to read more of Laurel and Lennon with an exclusive bonus epilogue!

ACKNOWLEDGMENTS

Every time I write a book, each experience is different, and I end up writing it back here in the acknowledgements. While I would like to say I wouldn't do that this time, it would be a lie.

So, in the name of transparency, I will. I've been trying to get better at that.

Writing this book came at a tough point in my life. I always think the world has a stigma around mental health and depression. Not only in the fact that those who suffer from it are reluctant to talk about it, but the idea that depression must only happen to those who are unhappy. Depression only happens when you lose a job or are suffering from heartbreak or struggling financially. Or even when someone you love passes. But sometimes depression can sneak up on you when you feel like your life is full and happy. It did for me. So many pivotal and unforeseen moments happened in my life this past year that dragged me into a depression. It wasn't swift and it wasn't fast. I didn't wake up one day and realize I was in the thick of it. It was a slow, progressive, all-consuming emotion. It took what it wanted, little by little, each day. But despite the pain it was causing me, I woke up every day and planted my feet on the ground. I pushed through, knowing this feeling wouldn't last forever. I trudged through it like one would through mud. I put one foot in front of the other and fought like hell to get to the other side. Writing Lennon and Laurel's story was a part of that path. I channeled my grief and depression into their story. And for the first time, I finished ahead of deadline and this book became one of the smoothest writing experiences I've ever had. (Woohoo!) I'd like to think it was the depression crumbling away but it could have been Lennon's easy love for Laurel. His OBSESSION with her.

Either way, this book is a piece of my soul and without those who had a hand in getting it to a point where I'm writing the acknowledgements for it, it wouldn't be here.

Thanks to the love of my life, my husband. Without you, I wouldn't have this life of mine. I wouldn't get to do what I enjoy most. Thank you for cheering me on as always. For always pushing me to be a better version of myself. And for tackling the business side of this business. Numbers aren't my thing. I'm glad they're yours.

To my family. Dani, Lisa, Ian, and Jasmin. Thank you for riding this out with me and for your encouragement. I love all of you.

To my second mom, Sylvia. So much of this book has pieces of you in it. I poured my fears and hopes into it. Life is scary and unpredictable but you tackle every fear head on. Thank you for raising me at a time when I needed you. You taught me so much of what and who I am today. Your strength and love is inspiring. I love you so much.

Thanks to my assistant, April. For checking in with me every day and holding me accountable. For being the first pair of eyes to ever land on every book I write. For being my biggest hype girl.

To my beta readers, April, Amy and Ana. My three A's. Thank you for pushing me out of my comfort zone when it comes to my stories and for your feedback. I value you more than you'll ever know.

My agent, Nikki. Without you, this book simply wouldn't be. I'm grateful for our video chats and for your advice. Your encouragement is second to none. Thank you for taking my books to the next level and allowing them to reach more places in the world.

My editor, Vicki. For all your notes along with your edits. They made me smile, they made me cry. They made my heart swell one hundred times. Thank you, love!

My Book Lovers. For your continued unwavering support and for simply being here. Thank you!

And to you, the reader. Thank you for giving this book a chance and for any other one of mine you might read. Your support means the world to me.

And finally, to those who feel like you're still trudging through mud. One day it will clear, and each step will get easier. Until then, just keep walking. I'm right there beside you.

ABOUT BRITTANY

Brittany Taylor grew up all over the world including places such as California, England, and Texas. Her love of reading started at a young age. Finally deciding to fulfill her lifelong dream, she took the plunge into the writing world and published her first book when she was twenty-eight. Today she resides in Maine with her husband, two sons, two cats and one dog.

www.brittanytaylorbooks.com

You can join Brittany's reader group

Brittany's Book Lovers

Or follow her in these places

Facebook Instagram TikTok Goodreads Amazon BookBub